"WE'RE LINKED FOR THE REST OF OUR LIVES."

Hannah sagged back on the velvet-covered bench, her gaze turning to the nearly dark window.

Dread filled Benjamin. My God, the girl was regretting marrying him, even after so short a time, not even a full day! He fought down a feeling of utter vulnerability. He should never have allowed his heart to soften, his thoughts to stray, imagining the possibility that she might grow fond of him. Foolish idea. "As you say."

"Are you always so in control?"

Being in control was not at all how Benjamin felt around this woman. *His bride.* He hesitated for a moment, wondering if he should take her hand, so small in its lacy white glove.

"What do you expect from me, Hannah?"

He had never used her given name until now, and it filled him with a stange sense of intimacy and warmth. He sensed she felt it, too, for her entire posture softened.

"I . . . I don't know," she said, abashed.

"The circumstances are not ideal. I concede that. But it's clearly in our mutual interests to make the best of the situation."

"Stated very logically." She turned her gaze once more to the window. Several minutes ticked by. He watched the English countryside disappear, mile after mile, taking them toward London and their new life together. In less than an hour, they would pull into Charring Cross Station and, shortly after that, arrive home. He was bringing home a bride. He had every right to expect what naturally followed from their union. Every right to take her to his bed . . .

Dear Romance Readers,

In July of 1999, we launched the Ballad line with four new series, and each month we present both new and continuing stories set everywhere from medieval England to the American West—the kind of passionate, romantic stories you love best, written by the most gifted authors. At the back of each book, we tell you when you can find subsequent books in the series that have captured your heart.

First up this month is **Just North of Bliss,** the second book in the fabulous new *Meet Me at the Fair* series by Alice Duncan. An ambitious photographer thinks he has no interest in a certain Southern belle except for her pretty face—until he learns that love knows no boundaries. Next, Sandra Madden introduces Elizabethan-era siblings *Of Royal Birth* with **A Princess Born.** Everything changes when you discover that you're a princess . . . except the man you love.

Also this month, author Tracy Cozzens presents another fabulous new series called *American Heiresses*. **Flight of Fancy,** the first of five books about the wealthy Carrington sisters, takes readers from New York to Paris to London—and straight into the heart of passion. Finally, ever-talented Sylvia McDaniel begins a provocative new series called *The Cuvier Widows* with **Sunlight on Josephine Street,** in which the wife of a philanderer discovers that she's not her deceased husband's only widow—and she's suddenly prepared for a second chance at love.

From Bourbon Street to Elizabethan England, these are stories we know you'll love!

Kate Duffy
Editorial Director

AMERICAN HEIRESSES

FLIGHT OF FANCY

TRACY COZZENS

ZEBRA BOOKS
KENSINGTON PUBLISHING CORP.

http://www.kensingtonbooks.com

ZEBRA BOOKS are published by

Kensington Publishing Corp.
850 Third Avenue
New York, NY 10022

All Kensington titles, imprints and distributed lines are available at special quantity discounts for bulk purchases for sales promotion, premiums, fund-raising, educational or institutional use.

Special book excerpts or customized printings can also be created to fit specific needs. For details, write or phone the office of the Kensington Special Sales Manager: Kensington Publishing Corp., 850 Third Avenue, New York, NY 10022. Attn. Special Sales Department. Phone: 1-800-221-2647.

First Printing: May 2002
10   9   8   7   6   5   4   3   2   1

Printed in the United States of America

*For my mother, who always supports
my own flights of fancy.*

CHAPTER 1

New York City, 1889

"You're staring at Lily's bosom."

Thirteen-year-old Meryl watched Joe Hammond react to her bold statement. The sixteen-year-old had been lurking in the shadows of the balcony, gazing down at the first-floor landing where Meryl's older sister, Lily, was modeling a ball gown for her mother. His jaw had hung slack, as if Lily were a sugarcoated marzipan.

But Meryl had snapped him out of his trance.

"Shhh!" Joe grabbed Meryl's arm and yanked her back in the shadows. "Be quiet! I was not staring at her—her—*Her,*" he concluded lamely.

"Her bosom, you mean? Then, why is your face turning red?"

"It is not." He reached up to rub his cheek. With his fair complexion, it was a lost cause.

"You won't be able to scrub it off, Joe." Meryl grinned pertly, reveling in the older boy's mortification. Joe was far too full of himself, going on about how he would someday be running Atlantic-Southern Railroads, a company owned jointly by their families. She had caught him out this time. It felt good to be the one doing the teasing, for once.

His eyes narrowed. "You, Meryl Carrington, are a brat. It comes from being the youngest, I suppose." He gave a world-weary sigh.

As if he was so much older! Meryl lifted her chin and smiled coolly. "I merely remarked on what I saw, which was you, staring at Lily's bosom."

"Stop *saying* that." Joe looked as though he wanted to melt into the floor, no doubt worried that Meryl's voice would carry to the women below. He needn't have worried. Mama and Lily were too engrossed in discussing her gown, which Lily was modeling in front of the gilded looking glass against one wall.

"If you weren't a girl, I'd punch you," Joe said.

"You boys are fascinated by bosoms," Meryl observed. "I can't imagine why."

"Why should you? You're just a little girl." His gaze skidded up and down her body. "You certainly don't have any."

Meryl was quite aware she didn't measure up yet, that she still wore a girl's knee-length dress and pigtails. But her chest *had* started to grow, not that she would share the information with Joe. "I'm not worried. Someday I'm going to be just as beautiful as Lily."

Joe snorted. "In a pig's eye."

Meryl ignored his jibe. "Not that beauty matters,

of course. What's important is what's between the ears. Hannah says so."

"That's because she's Hannah," he said. "Everyone says she's an odd duck."

"She is not." Hannah, Meryl and Lily's oldest sister, had opinions about everything, including the unimportance of the female figure. Meryl hadn't quite convinced herself that Hannah was right. Looks certainly seemed to matter where Lily was concerned.

Where young men like Joe were concerned.

His blue eyes sparkled in the dim light cast by the electric wall sconce. Briefly she imagined Joe looking at her as he had looked at Lily a moment ago, and a strange, warm sensation filled her.

Then he snorted, and the feeling vanished. "You shouldn't be thinking about bosoms. It isn't ladylike."

"Who said I'm a lady?" Meryl countered. "I'm going to grow up and run Father's business; that's what I'm going to do. You don't need a bosom to do that."

Joe burst out laughing. "I should live so long." Reaching over, he tugged one of her blond braids. "Why don't you run on back to the nursery and behave yourself?"

Meryl badly wanted to sock him, but was afraid to draw too much attention to their confrontation, considering what they had been discussing. If Mama knew, she would die of humiliation. And if she knew the thoughts that had begun to occupy Meryl's head . . .

Meryl sighed. She couldn't help it. She looked at everything differently these days. Clothes, her body. Boys. Even her feelings for her childhood tormentor had changed into something else, something a little frightening.

"Joe, is that you?" Mother's voice echoed up the foyer. "Did you find the book you were looking for?"

Joe stepped out of the shadows and toward the head of the grand staircase, which was lit from above by a two-tiered electrified chandelier. "Yes, ma'am. Thank you for letting me use your library." He held up a book about the Wild West and started down toward her mother.

Meryl followed behind, stewing. Just because Joe Hammond was a man, he could do whatever he wanted. The thought caught her up short, and she paused halfway down the wide stairs, beside a stained-glass window. She had never thought of Joe as a man before. What a silly idea. Shaking the thought away, Meryl marched down the stairs behind him.

"This gown is lovely," Lily said, doing a pirouette. The narrow, bustled skirt of the ice blue gown wrapped alluringly around her legs for a split second before swinging the other way, catching the eye attractively. "Honestly, Mother, I don't need a new formal gown. No one's seen this one, since I've yet to come out into society."

Mother had chosen to delay Lily's debut after the fiasco surrounding Hannah's earlier that year, when very few of the eligibles of New York society attended. Hannah continued to insist she didn't care, but Meryl wondered if she was only trying to convince herself of that.

"Besides, a new ball gown will cost a fortune!" Lily continued.

"Nonsense," Mother said, waving away Lily's protest. She tugged at the velvet caught high on the bustle in the back. "Bustles are going out of style, Lily, according to Lady Godey's."

"Surely Monsieur Worth would be willing to make alterations—"

"Monsieur Worth would never alter another's design, a New York seamstress's at that. It's clearly last year's fashion, and you mustn't be seen in it, not even in front of Monsieur Worth. Certainly not in Paris or London, and not by a titled nobleman who would know the difference." She glanced over her shoulder at Meryl and Joe. "Have either of you seen Hannah? Was she in the library?"

"No, ma'am," Joe said. "I haven't seen her."

Briefly his eyes met Meryl's, and she knew he was recalling their discussion on the balcony. His gaze shifted to Lily, who stood tall and regal like a princess. Despite her mother's claims that the dress was outdated, Lily looked picture perfect, her glossy black hair in a chignon contrasting dramatically with her ivory skin. "Hello, Joe," she said, smiling at him.

"H'llo," Joe muttered, as if embarrassed to be talking to her. He backed away from Lily as if she were poison—or as if he found it hard to tear his eyes from her. He backed all the way through the foyer to the front door. Reaching behind him, he found the doorknob and turned it, letting himself out.

"Stupid boy," Meryl muttered as the door closed.

Her mother gave an exasperated sigh. "Hannah has to be around here somewhere. I told her we were going to spend the afternoon reviewing our wardrobes. She hasn't tried on a single item yet, and we're going to be leaving for Paris in a week!

I don't know how many undergarments she needs, or which color gloves to order—Meryl, make yourself useful and find your sister."

Mother looked so harried, strands of salt-and-pepper hair had sprung loose from her chignon, a highly unusual sight. Meryl was glad to help track down her wayward sister. She headed down the central hallway and through the conservatory, then out a door leading to the garden. She had an idea where Hannah might be.

"Paris," Hannah grumbled to herself for the thousandth time. "Why should I have to go to Paris, just to be measured for clothes? I can't think of a more tedious activity."

Kneeling on the roof of the carriage house, Hannah Carrington tucked a loose strand of brown hair behind her ear and reached for another feather. Nearby, half a dozen charcoal-colored pigeons perched on the roof wall, watching her with interest, looking for food. She didn't have any food for them. She just wanted their feathers once they were done with them.

She stuffed the feather into a small satchel, one that matched a tea dress she never wore, so she had taken it for this new purpose. Rising to her feet, she licked her forefinger and held it aloft to test the wind direction. Lifting a feather, she dropped it over the two-foot-tall roof wall and studied how it twirled and twisted away, borne by invisible currents in an ocean of air.

By itself, the feather danced whichever way the wind took it. Obviously, it took more than feathers to fly a direction of one's choice.

A pigeon alighted on the roof wall. For the hundredth time, Hannah studied how it accomplished such a seemingly easy feat. As far as she could tell, the bird checked its speed by moving its tail and wing surfaces against the direction of its flight.

Air. Flight had everything to do with air. Because of upward air currents, a bird could take off from level earth with its wings outstretched and motionless. The problem was replicating such wings for people.

It had to be possible, somehow. How marvelous it would be to have wings, to stretch them wide and fly upward toward the sun and stars, to look down and see the world spread out below one's feet like a living map.

Bending down, Hannah retrieved a piece of paper which she had already folded into roughly the shape of a bird, a triangular shape with a pointy beak and outstretched wings. For her next experiment in flight, she bent each wing into a curve, to see what effect this change might have on her bird's lift.

She had practically memorized Otto Lilienthal's recently published work on gliding flight. Lilienthal stated quite clearly that a curved wing was essential, as it offered far more resistance than a flat surface. Hannah wanted to see this principle in action for herself.

Pulling her arm back, she launched her bird— one of a dozen she had already sent flying off the roof. A gust of wind sprang up, carrying this bird farther than the others. Hannah grinned and clapped her hands, hardly noticing or caring when the wind also snatched her straw hat off her head. Hannah reached for it, but the wind sucked it over the edge of the roof into space. Its yellow ribbons and lavender flowers fluttered as a breeze tossed it into the air.

Hannah looked over the edge, following the progress of her hat as it headed for the hedgerow on the side of the yard. For some confounding reason, her hat had flown farther than any of her paper birds, which now littered the lawn below. How frustrating! What could the reason possibly be?

"There you are! Mother will be furious with you for letting your new spring hat fly around like that."

Caught. Hannah sighed and looked down at Meryl, standing with her hands on her hips like a mother substitute. "Must you be quite so loud, Meryl?"

"Why?" Meryl lowered her voice. "Are you hiding something?"

Sighing, Hannah crossed to the ladder attached to the side of the carriage house and carefully made her way down. "The progress of science isn't a secret, Meryl," she patiently explained over her shoulder. "But it does take time and careful study, the full devotion of a person's mind. Distractions—like fashion and trips to Paris—should be avoided at all costs."

"Stop doing that," Meryl said as soon as Hannah's feet touched the ground.

"Doing what?"

"Sounding like my teacher."

"Well, all right. I suppose I was lecturing," Hannah said as they both stooped to gather the paper birds from the lawn. "Thank you for helping me gather my birds."

Meryl held one up in the air. "Why are you

playing with toy birds? I thought you liked rocks. Crystal this and agate that. And before that you were keen on ancient ruins, Pompeii and stuff." She peered at Hannah, who ducked her face to avoid her little sister's too-inquisitive gaze.

"You wouldn't understand," she said, knowing it was a sad excuse for her shifting interests. One might even call them short-lived obsessions. She wasn't proud that she lost interest in her projects, either. It made her feel unsettled, directionless. All of science fascinated her, but she had yet to discover the one true scientific calling that was right for her—the one she could devote herself to body and mind. The area where she could truly contribute.

No doubt she would if left to her own devices. She rose to her feet, her hands filled with paper birds, and passed them to Meryl. Catching sight of a muddy smudge on her skirt hem, she batted at it, but it refused to vanish. "I honestly don't see why I need a new wardrobe, when this one suffices."

"You need to show off your bubbies, like Lily's dress does, so you can catch a nobleman and make Mrs. Astor green with jealousy."

Hannah jerked upright and stared at her impertinent little sister, focusing on a single shocking word. "Did you just say bubbies? Where did you learn such a word?"

Meryl shrugged, then knelt to retrieve another bird. "Around."

"Around where?"

"Joe and the boys. I heard them talking in the yard, when they were playing croquet. They didn't know I was there." She grinned. "Boys are so silly, don't you think?"

"And they're not whom you should be imitating, Meryl." Hannah reached for her hat on top of the boxwood hedge, then discovered it was caught on a branch.

Behind her, Meryl scolded, "Now you sound like Mother. Can't you ever sound like yourself?" Hannah heard her crunching over the gravel path back toward the house.

Frustrated, Hannah yanked, tearing a hole in the hat's crown. She sighed at the destruction, then fell into step beside Meryl. "Maybe I'd sound more like myself if I knew who that was." Truth was, she didn't fit in. Though her large family was loving, none of them understood her fascination with the unexplained mysteries of the world. At the Stafford School for Young Ladies, she had at least gained a measure of satisfaction excelling at her studies in the few academic subjects provided. Now that she had grown up, she dreamed of going to the university, where men and women enjoyed deep, intellectual discussions about any topic which struck their fancy. And people listened to them!

But Mother had other plans for her, namely marriage. Since Hannah was the eldest, Mother felt it only proper that she be the first to take that walk down the aisle, or risk being deemed an old maid. With five daughters in the family, Hannah couldn't dillydally for long.

And she wouldn't let her family down, of course. She only wished she could feel as enthusiastic at the prospect of marriage as she did for her research.

"Why do men care so much about women's looks?"

Hannah shrugged. "Good question. It seems a woman's mind has no value compared to certain other . . . attributes." Just one of the many reasons she found the idea of marriage so distasteful. The men her age who were looking for wives easily dismissed her as either not lovely enough or too intelligent. And her humiliating entrée into polite society earlier in the year had done nothing to change her opinion of courting.

"What good are bosoms, anyway?" Meryl said.

Hannah arched her eyebrow. Meryl certainly had developed an interest in what men thought—and how women appeared to them. It wouldn't be that many years before Mama was seeking a husband for her, as well. Hannah wondered if she would be married by then.

"They're not of much use at all, except for nursing babies, of course."

"Do you think I'll grow to resemble Lily? Except with light hair, of course. Or . . ." Her eyes slid sideways to Hannah's relatively flat chest.

"Or will you be small like me? That's what you're wondering. Trust me, it's no disappointment to me not to be shaped like Lily. She can have all the male attention." They crossed the veranda, and Hannah swung the conservatory door inward. "I have more important things to do than worry about pleasing men."

Her statement was ill-timed, for Hannah found herself face-to-face with her distraught mother. She slipped her damaged hat behind her back. "Hullo, Mother."

Her mother's cheeks were flushed pink. "Hannah Alexandreena Carrington, I don't want to hear such talk out of you. It's bad enough you disappear when I need your attention on your wardrobe. Then you talk nonsense about not pleasing men!"

She shook her head and sucked in a breath. "It is *vital* to please men, darling." She scooped up Hannah's free hand and patted it. "The right men, at any rate, not these ill-bred New York boys. We're going to get you an earl or a baron. *Then* they'll talk."

Her eyes fell to Hannah's other hand, where she was desperately trying to hide her hat behind her skirt. "Is that your hat?" Mother reached for it and held it aloft. Sunlight poured through the conservatory window and straight through the hole. "This hat was brand new. What a sorry state it's in!" Her eyes narrowed suspiciously. She scanned Hannah's skirt, then grasped her shoulder and turned her around. "What's that stain on your skirt? Where *have* you been?"

"On the carriage house roof," Meryl supplied. Hannah groaned inwardly.

"Oh, my. Whatever for?" Mother heaved a sigh. "Never mind. I don't want to know. Now come to the parlor and *try* to take an interest. Lily has already inventoried her wardrobe, so that when we visit Worth's—"

"Mother, my clothes are fine."

Her mother stopped in her tracks, her thin frame making her appear twice as tall as usual. She spun to face her wayward daughter. "You're nineteen and you aren't getting any younger, Hannah. You know how hard it's been for us, ever since *that woman* threw her considerable weight around to shut us out."

That woman had become Mother's moniker for Mrs. Astor, reigning dowager of New York society, wife of the wealthy William Blackhouse Astor, Jr., a woman who had ruled New York high society for decades, dictating mores and behaviors through-out the upper crust.

When Mrs. Astor bestowed her favor upon a young lady and her mother, she was "in"—invited to the best soirées, wooed by the sons of old money, deemed suitable for the bluest blood. But when Mrs. Astor withheld that favor, the daughters might as well resign themselves to forever looking in from the outside. Shunned. Just like Hannah.

Except Mother had a plan. Iron-willed, she was determined to marry her daughters well, and she planned to use their wealth to do it, new as those dollars might be. Moreover, she wanted to rub Mrs. Astor's nose in their marital successes. To do that, she was bound and determined to marry her two eldest off to titled noblemen—this year. The other three could wait their turn for their chance at join-ing the ranks of European—preferably British—nobility. Their husbands would be men with blood bluer than any Mrs. Astor could hope to entertain.

Hannah sympathized with her mother's feelings. It couldn't be an easy task to marry off five daugh-ters. Worse, *that woman* had snubbed her, called their family nouveau riche and bourgeois, and cast aspersions on their mother's Italian heritage. Natu-rally that hurt.

But Hannah was hard put to get seriously bent out of shape over missing a few stuffy parties on the road to the dreaded altar. She felt more sorry for her sister Lily, just turned eighteen and denied a proper coming out. As long as Hannah could remember, Lily especially had been groomed to make a wonderful match. And she should—lithe as a swan, as poised as a princess, her gracious manners reflecting her good heart. Simply put,

Lily was gorgeous, but without the self-conscious affectations of so many debutantes her age.

Beside Lily, Hannah might have felt seriously inadequate if physical beauty mattered to her. She had much more important things on her mind, like figuring out how birds changed direction midflight . . . .

"Oh, Hannah, you are coming to Paris with us, aren't you?" As they entered the parlor, Lily hurried forward and grasped Hannah's hands, heedless of the yards of velvet and satin that made up her formal skirt. "It won't be the same if you aren't there."

Hannah stared at her sister, taking in her narrow waist, gently flared hips, and generous décolletage pressing against the scalloped neckline of her gown. Meryl was right—even a monk would be affected by Lily's womanly figure. Despite herself, Hannah glanced down her simple shirtwaist at her own pancake-flat chest. Somewhere in there were her own "bubbies." She sighed. "You look lovely, Lily. You don't need me in Paris. You'll take the city by storm, and London, too."

"Nonsense. Of course I need you! You're my big sister! Please say you'll come." She gave Hannah a swift, tight hug, then whispered in her ear, "You're so sensible. We'll sorely need common sense, Hannah. Mother wants a whole new wardrobe for each of us, though this gown is perfectly fine."

"Of course she's coming to Paris," their mother said, at the same time glancing through a copy of *Harper's Bazaar* featuring the latest Paris fashions.

"She'll never attract a nobleman's eye if she isn't wearing a Worth wardrobe. Aristocrats notice such things, and I won't have them saying we Americans don't know how to properly dress our daughters."

"But, Mother," Lily exclaimed. "We're supposed to keep our dresses in storage for at least a year, so as not to appear too stylish—"

"Balderdash! Only here in New York. Frankly, I find that practice ridiculous. Why spend so much on the latest fashions if one is afraid to wear them in public when they're fashionable? I'll tell you why. *That woman* dictated that practice, just to prove she could—and to make beautiful young women like you terrified of offending her."

She turned to Hannah. "Once we equip you with a stylish wardrobe, you can finally have a proper coming out in London, and *that woman* will have nothing to say about it!"

Another coming out? Dread formed like an icy pit in Hannah's stomach. To face another crowd of strangers, the other debutantes who gossiped about her behind her back, young men who danced with her merely to ascertain the extent of her dowry . . . . *Not again.*

Rather than reveal her terror, Hannah attempted simple reasoning. "Truly, Mother, I can think of nothing less exciting than buying a bunch of new clothes. What are clothes, after all, except protection from the elements? And my serge skirt works fine for that."

Her remarks earned a worrisome look from her mother, who peered at her as if she had grown two heads. "Where *did* you come from, girl? If I hadn't been there when you were born, I would

swear there'd been a mix-up. All the advantages
of your station, and you refuse to enjoy them!"

"That's because I—"

Hannah's intended remark about what was truly
important—discovering the secrets of life—was cut
off by the arrival of her father striding through
the parlor door. Hannah smiled. Her father always
looked so well turned out in his three-piece suit
and top hat. His neatly barbered mustache held
only a hint of gray. He passed his cane to Edgar,
the butler, who had appeared on cue, then handed
him his hat and gloves and shrugged out of his coat.
Before Edgar took the coat away, Father removed a
folded newspaper from an inner pocket.

Hannah caught a glimpse of a photo on the
cover, printed larger than normal. It showed a large
steel tower. A scientific weather tower, perhaps?
She had been reading about such things. Knowing
about the weather was a critical element in
unlocking the secrets of flight.

"What's this?" She grabbed the paper before
her father had a chance to deposit it on the marble-
topped hall table. Immediately she saw that the
tower was much larger than she had first thought.
It dwarfed buildings in the background. Made of
steel girders and beams, the tower swooped upward
from a four-point base to arrow toward the sky.

She scanned the caption. "This tower here. This
is in Paris?" She glanced at her father, who no
doubt had already read the story. He kept abreast
of everything and seemed to know about every
important event in the city and the world. Hannah
often wished she could accompany him to his
men's club to take part in the conversations held

there over brandy and cigars, but of course that was out of the question.

"It just opened to the public today," he said. "A monstrosity, or so I hear. Built for the World's Fair."

"World's Fair . . ." Where scientists from all over the globe converged to demonstrate their latest achievements. Excitement built within Hannah as she realized the importance a simple matter of timing would play in her life. How could she be so lucky?

Her father continued, "That tower was designed by a fellow named Eiffel. Some of the Frenchies want to lynch him for it; they think the tower is such an eyesore, like a skeleton." He lowered his voice a notch. "Or a hole-riddled suppository."

"Richard!" Mother scolded, but she pressed her fingers to her mouth to hide her own smile.

"It's so tall," Hannah said. "It says here it rises almost a thousand feet into the air. Imagine that! It's the highest structure in the world. It must feel like walking in the clouds to be up that high. People are going up in it?"

"As of today. Scientists, dignitaries and the like."

"Scientists? Truly?" Scanning the article, Hannah spotted Thomas Edison's name among the visitors. A world where science was valued—how exciting!

Father asked, "What makes you so interested in the Eiffel Tower, Hannah, my dear?"

"I'm afraid I'd faint if I went up that high," Lily said, peering over Hannah's shoulder. "Afraid I'd fall off. There are no walls!"

"Who needs walls? Think of the weather up there. What an opportunity to study the atmosphere!" Hannah knew then she wouldn't object to visiting Paris, but not for her mother's reasons. Clutching the paper to her chest, she spun to face her. "I can't wait to go to Paris. When do we leave?"

CHAPTER 2

Paris, France

From all over the world, millions of people had converged on Paris for the Exposition Universelle. Every street, every shop, displayed posters and sold wares celebrating this greatest of world's fairs.

The spirit of the show pervaded the town and took possession of an entire quarter, centered on the wide boulevards and gardens of the Champs de Mars, where prominent men shared progress in science, economic theories, and groundbreaking art. Anthropological exhibitions, including pre-Columbian artifacts, were being shown in Europe for the first time. At the Galeries des Machines, Hannah's countryman Thomas Edison was demonstrating his new phonograph machine, which actually recorded music.

To France, the fair celebrated the centennial

of the French Revolution and the strength and prominence of the French Empire throughout the world. To Hannah, it celebrated knowledge, the best that mankind was capable of. It was utterly thrilling. And she was spending it shut away in a dress shop.

Certainly, Worth's was the most elite dress shop in the world. But Hannah knew that beneath the gilt and glamour, it would do nothing more than provide her with clothes to wear, clothes to impress others with her family's wealth, clothes to catch her a suitable husband.

Carriages lined the street outside 7 rue de la Paix, their drivers waiting patiently for the women inside, who were also waiting. In back rooms, hundreds of employees stitched gowns for dozens of the elite's daughters. In the wide, high-ceilinged salons, ambitious mothers and their fashionable daughters glided up and down the stairs, relaxed in alcoves sipping café au lait, and waited in anticipation of an audience with Monsieur Grandhomme, the Great Man himself.

"Will he see us personally?" Lily asked their mother, her tone low so as not to attract the attention of the other waiting women. Heaven forbid the Carringtons be seen as too anxious, too desperate. Lily knew as well as Hannah their mother's raw spot for such accusations.

Their mother patted Lily's hand. "He must. We wrote for this appointment, traveled all the way across the Atlantic."

From what Hannah could tell, that was nothing unique. Most of the young ladies present seemed to have American accents. A few were English. Even fewer were French. Worth himself was English, though he had lived in Paris for decades. Only a few of these customers would actually be seen by Monsieur Worth. The rest would have Worth-designed gowns, but be measured and fitted by his assistants. Still, they would be sporting a wardrobe on the cutting edge of fashion. No one need know they had not been granted Worth's personal attention.

A rustle in the group of women standing closest to the door drew Hannah's attention. Instantly the tension turned up a notch as all eyes followed the sound of effusive greetings. When the women stepped back, Hannah caught her first glimpse of Charles Worth. He strolled like a king through his palace, his diminutive frame garbed not in a business suit, but in a bohemian's artsy combination of jacket, button-down shirt, and bright yellow cravat, a color Hannah had never seen on a man before. She guessed he was in his sixties. His gray mustache matched the gray of his thinning hair.

Hannah didn't care whether Monsieur Worth himself dressed her. She hoped not to be embarrassed during the process. Mostly she wished their appointment would pass quickly, so they would have time to visit the World's Fair.

He stopped beside one of the women near the door, who Hannah knew was an English countess. "Why do you wear those ugly gloves?" he immediately asked her. "Never let me see you in gloves of that color again." With a guilty look, the lady slipped off her gloves and shoved them in her pocket as Worth swept past her.

He paused in the center of the room, leaned back on one leg, and scanned the gathering. His eyes drifted around the collected women, his gaze alighting here and there. Behind him, an assistant placed a gold-wrought chair behind him. After a moment, he turned and sat down.

Everyone in the room was silent, straining to hear the pearls of wisdom which were sure to drop from his lips. He gestured with a single finger. A second assistant, a buxom woman holding a notebook in her hand, called up Mrs. Taylor and her daughter. As hesitant as if approaching royalty, the two women walked slowly toward Monsieur Worth.

He looked first at the daughter, a young blonde about Hannah's age. The girl looked alternately terrified and thrilled to be receiving his undivided attention, which he gave mostly to her figure, now clad in a very lovely day gown.

"Miss Taylor, you should cease wearing green. It is not the color for you."

The girl blushed furiously and lowered her eyes.

"You do show promise," Worth continued. "Those Nordic looks would complement the colors I am experimenting with. I shall show you the colors you were born to wear." He nodded curtly, sending the debutante into an apoplexy of excitement she could barely contain. She bounced on her feet and grasped her mother's arm. His assistant continued to scribble in her notebook.

Worth's gaze turned to the girl's mother. "You, too, seek a fitting?"

The woman bowed as if in the presence of a king. "Yes, monsieur, if it would please you."

"I see no . . . essence to clothe here. My assistants can meet your needs, I am quite sure."

He turned away, ignoring the distressed look on the woman's face—and the fact she was the wife of a millionaire banker back in the States.

"Oh, my goodness, he's looking over here," Lily whispered, her hand squeezing Hannah's so hard she feared it would snap off.

Instantly reading his interest, the assistant gestured for them to come forward, explaining to Worth who they were as the three of them crossed the carpet in a tight knot. Nevertheless, Hannah's mother took it upon herself to make introductions, a defiance of protocol which Hannah admired.

"Monsieur Worth, I am Mrs. Olympia Carrington of New York, and these are my daughters. Hannah is the eldest, and this is Lily."

"I see. To me you are female figures, seeking clothing which will bring out the essence of your souls, which will show your best face to the world. Am I not right? And that gown would be better suited to a scullery maid than a social dowager."

"I don't care what you think of my clothes," Mrs. Carrington said, keeping her temper and her poise. "I care that you see fit to clothe my daughters so that they may make the best impression during the coming Season."

Worth's eyes shone just a little brighter, and Hannah guessed he wasn't too put off by her mother's lack of obsequiousness. "Very well. Which daughter is first?"

"Lily—" Hannah volunteered.

"Hannah, my eldest," her mother said, overriding Hannah.

Hannah stood as stiff as a board while the small man perused her, *judged* her. How she hated this! She felt his eyes on her bustline, then on her waist. "Your gloves are not pulled up evenly, and I see a stain on the left one. Your hat is askew, and your posture entirely too tense." Hannah knew she had failed to intrigue him even before he pronounced judgement. "Since you clearly do not enjoy wearing clothing, I can dredge up little enthusiasm for dressing you. Your other daughter . . ."

His gaze alighted on Lily, and his eyes brightened considerably. He leaned forward in his chair, his aspect taking on one of intense interest. Hannah knew her sister wasn't even breathing and hoped she didn't pass out. How any girl could get so excited about clothing was beyond her, but Lily loved this, she knew. She loved fashion, and fabrics, and looking her best. Everyone else seemed to love that of her, too. Her role in life seemed secure, and her place in the world a given. She had been born for this. Hannah knew she hadn't been, but born for what, she had no idea.

"My, my. What a lovely visage has appeared before me," Worth mused. "Thick tresses of ebony silk, such a slim neck. And your hands—slender fingers well cared for. Lovely, simply lovely. So many debutantes every year, all young buds upon the face of spring. But very few an orchid such as this. Dressing you shall be an honor, Miss Carrington."

Lily gasped, but softly, not obviously and déclassé as the Taylor girl had done. How Hannah admired that about her sister! Her poise came so naturally to her.

"Thank you, Monsieur Worth," she said, her voice a clear bell in the transfixed room.

"We shall start immediately. Today. I shall make a gown worthy of you, and dozens more, each highlighting your considerable and varied assets."

"No, you shall not," their mother said.

"Mother!" Lily looked as though she wanted to

cry. Hannah couldn't blame her. Lily had been dreaming of being fitted by Worth himself ever since their mother had started talking of this trip.

"My eldest must be fitted personally by you as well, if you are to dress Lily. I won't have you slighting one of my daughters for the other."

Hannah groaned inwardly. While she appreciated her mother defending her, she was now the center of the room's attention and speculation. Monsieur Worth frowned, and bright patches of color flared in his cheeks. He opened his mouth to respond, and Hannah braced herself for their immediate dismissal.

Then his gaze flicked back over Lily, and his posture softened. "Very well. So be it." With that, he rose and left the room.

Hannah leaned her head against the back of the gilt armchair and closed her eyes. The voices of her mother, Monsieur Worth, and, to a lesser extent, Lily, continued.

"I seek to emphasize the upper torso, in balance with the hips. Perhaps, for Miss Lily, a lesser bustle. I am, as you must know, the creator of the bustle, and it has served us all well. But I feel its value is lessening as a fashion statement. If all women had figures such as your Lily's . . . A true canvas to inspire the creative muse! You will be my vessel to display a new style to society, a new day."

"Oh, Mother, I love this one. Hannah, look at this fabric. It's so soft and smooth. So sheer! It looks like sunshine!"

Hannah cracked her eyes enough to see Lily holding a swath of fabric up to the room's window, which backed on a private courtyard. Presumably this way Monsieur Worth could take advantage of natural light while avoiding the eyes of curious passersby.

"Hannah?" Lily prompted.

"It's lovely," Hannah acknowledged with a small smile. And it was. But it was the twenty-ninth fabric she had been asked to admire this morning. When would it ever end?

"Ah, yes," Worth said. "Sheened silk from Lyons. It arrived just last week. I see this for the underskirt of the gown."

"The tea gown?" Mother asked.

"Heavens, no. Much too dressy. The evening gown. Perhaps with an overlay of . . ." Hannah watched as Worth approached a cart filled with bolts of fabric in every shade of gold imaginable. "The damask, yes." He pulled out a bolt and unrolled several yards onto the ground. "See how it lies?"

"It flows like a river," Lily said, her face alight.

Worth returned her smile across the yellow swath. "Yes, my dear. You will be a vision in gold. A goddess of the sun. We must think of the proper mask costume for you, as well. Hmm . . . Perhaps a Greek goddess. Or a princess royale. I will have to meditate upon it for a few days to find the exact fit to bring out your essence."

Hannah felt as if her own essence was dissipating by the minute. She and Lily had both had their measurements taken by one of the female assistants. After redressing, they had been taken to Monsieur Worth's inner sanctum for an exclusive dress-design session. He had taken Lily first. Hannah had been sitting on the side of the room for the past two hours, awaiting her turn. The day was advancing, and all she could think about was the Eiffel Tower and the crowds of people visiting it, experiencing it, going aloft into the sky.

Beside her chair rested her satchel, unstylish but large enough to hold a very important item. She had brought it along because she had had the ridiculous notion they would be quickly done at the dressmaker's, at least with this introductory visit. That was how Worth typically worked. Afterward, with time to spare, she would have talked her mother and Lily into going with her to see the Eiffel Tower.

Instead, she had ended up in an interminable session of dressmaking indulgence. She sighed. She needed only a few hours. Maybe even a single hour, depending on how fast the taxi could get her to the Champs de Mars gardens and the World's Fair. If she could get away for just an hour . . . .

An assistant passed Hannah's chair, carrying yet another bolt of gold fabric. Sitting up straight, Hannah called out to her. "Ma'am, how long—is this usually how long Monsieur Worth takes?"

"Ma'amselle, *excusez-moi?*" The woman frowned. "*Il est un artiste.* He takes the time he needs."

"*Oui,* but—do you think he'll fit me out today? I'd love to have this done with."

The frown grew deeper. "*Non,* ma'amselle. He is fitting Ma'amselle Lily today, tomorrow, all the week long. He has asked me to arrange his schedule thus."

Oh, my. "And me?"

"Oh! He will take care of you as well, do not

fear." The woman patted her shoulder, then continued on to where Lily and her mother waited.

A few long minutes later, while Worth was deep in musings over the right design for a day gown, Hannah's mother moved near her chair. "Mother," Hannah said.

"Yes, Hannah," her mother replied, without looking at her. Her gaze was fixed on Worth, who was holding yet another fabric sample up to Lily's face. Mother's cheeks were bright, and she looked hardly older than Lily herself. Unquestionably, today was a great victory for her. Today, her very own daughter had captured the imagination of the Great Man himself. Word would get out, and the Carrington family social cachet would increase accordingly. Why, Lily and Hannah would be invited to parties and events simply so others could see what they were wearing. Odd, how being nothing but a body wearing clothes—essentially fabric and stitches—could change a woman's life.

"Mother, I would like to go out for a bit. For a walk."

"No," her mother burst out, startling Hannah—until she realized her mother wasn't addressing her. "Not the lavender, I think. It seems so . . . pale."

Worth nodded. "Yes, but when used thusly . . ." He combined it with a creamy wool.

Mother nodded. "I see . . . It is lovely like that."

Hannah rose to her feet. "A walk, Mother? If you don't mind."

This time her mother said nothing, merely gazed at Worth doing his magic on Lily.

Hannah tried a third time. "Mother, I'm going

to leap from the Pont Neuf into the Seine and drown."

"Very *well*, Hannah." She shot Hannah an irritated glance, then lifted her voice and strode forward again. "Monsieur Worth, have you thought about accessories for that fabric? What sort of gloves would possibly match? I've never seen gloves that color."

Hannah shrugged. Grasping her satchel, she fled from Monsieur Worth's exclusive dress shop.

Hannah had never seen so many people in one place, not even in Times Square during the annual Independence Day parade. Carriages clogged the streets surrounding the Champs de Mars. Men, women, and children filled the walkways, strolling among the more than sixty thousand exhibits.

Above it all rose the tower. Hannah stood on the wide path and gazed at the elegant four-footed base. Her gaze drifted upward, past the first and second walkways to the pinnacle, nearly one thousand feet in the sky. Clouds drifted behind the tower, then briefly shrouded the top.

Hannah studied the sky. The sun had been playing hide-and-seek with the clouds all morning, but with luck they would clear by the time she made the ascent. Certainly she would be foolish to wait too long. Picking up her pace, she hurried through the crowd.

The carriage had dropped her as close as traffic permitted to the World's Fair entrance, where she had paid a franc for a ticket. Inside she found herself in the midst of the international displays. An entire town of pavilions and palaces stretched

from the Champs de Mars to the Trocadero, repre-
senting all of France's territories from the Far East
to Africa. The noises, sights, and smells of dozens
of cultures vied for Hannah's attention. In a lively
bazaar, Algerians demonstrated blanket weaving,
while across the way Tahitians performed a sultry
native dance that caused Hannah to blush.

She hurried on, wishing she had more time to
explore but vowing to return. As she passed the
Senegal exhibit, her gaze locked with that of a
young woman about her age, who cradled a baby
at her shoulder. Her jet-black skin and exotic face
contrasted sharply with the pale, well-dressed Parisians gaping at her.

Hannah paused, glancing at the collection of
huts behind the woman. She wondered what the
woman must be thinking, having traveled so far
from her home to be put on display along with
her own family and seven other families. Hannah
knew the intent was to aid in understanding human
life in all its aspects, a scientific view she well understood. Yet seeing the natives living their lives for
her edification left her uneasy. Could their villages
here at the fair truly show Parisians how these people lived in their native lands? Beyond that question, should people be staring at them as if they
were animals in a zoo?

She decided then and there that she would never
pursue the popular new science of anthropology.

Leaving the international villages, Hannah
headed for the north leg of the Eiffel Tower. Hundreds of people clustered, waiting to take the elevator to the top. Elevators on the east and west legs
traveled only as high as the first level, not nearly

high enough for her and, she realized, most other visitors.

After riding the elevator, she would still face a long climb up the stairs to reach the top.

Hardier souls took the stairs from the ground, but Hannah knew climbing sixteen hundred steps would probably take her as long as waiting her turn. She took her position at the back of the line and prayed the elevator would move quickly.

When she had imagined coming here, she had pictured herself dashing to the top of the tower and accomplishing her goal, then returning to Worth's before her mother or Lily had the chance to miss her. She had had no idea the crowds would be so large. She had only envisioned herself and the tower. How foolish of her! She would be lucky to be on the tower within the hour.

She tapped her foot impatiently and tightened her grip on the ivory handles of her satchel. A breeze threatened to pull her hat from her head, so she set her satchel down and retied the pastel green bow under her chin.

Long, rolling bell tones sounded from nearby churches, and her stomach growled in accompaniment, demanding lunch. She hoped her mother and sister weren't missing her too badly.

Benjamin Ramsey, Seventh Earl of Sheffield, gripped his case and dashed out of his carriage. He glanced up at the gray and threatening sky. In a short time, the clouds would surely open, pummeling Paris with a spring downfall.

And he would be in the middle of it. Already wind whipped his overcoat and threatened to snag his bowler from his head. He clamped it down with his free hand and charged as fast as possible through the meandering crowd. How could people move so slowly? Didn't they have someplace to be, something important to do?

He was running out of time, and any delay, even a small one, felt like a piece of his life being ripped away. He had less than two weeks before presenting his findings before the London Society for Scientific Advancement. And precious little fresh information to present. It was difficult enough to convince the old-guard scientists in London that his theory of a layered atmosphere, composed of various gases, was correct. His reputation hinged on it.

Using balloons, he had conducted hundreds of experiments to measure the atmosphere. Yet since he had sent the instruments up unmanned, the other Society members scoffed at his discovery of a blanket of cold above the earth. He certainly had no intention of ascending again, even to prove them wrong. As an alternative, he was determined to prove his instruments were accurate. He would record barometric and temperature changes on the tower during a storm, figures that could be compared with data gathered from the meteorological laboratory at the tower's top.

Assuming he could gain the French scientists' cooperation in this small matter. At every turn, the competitive French had blocked his work. He grimaced. True, the first manned balloon flight had taken off from this spot a century before. But that hardly meant the French owned the heavens!

He owed it to Peter to beat them at their own game. When Peter had first proposed studying weather, even Benjamin had laughed. Weather—how mundane!

Then, during a private dinner at his London men's club, Peter had posed a simple question. "What is the one topic of conversation which even strangers can discuss? What is the one field of science which affects everyone every day, no matter where they live?"

"Taxes?" Benjamin had suggested over his brandy.

"No, weather! Farmers worry about there being enough rain for their crops. Fishermen worry about hurricanes. Even well-bred ladies are concerned about getting too much sun and dressing for the elements."

Peter had leaned forward, his elbows on the mahogany table between them, the gaslight accentuating the shine in his gray eyes. "I know you're studying flight, but even if men do succeed in building a flying machine, what good is it if we can't understand the weather we would be flying in? If we understood the weather—why it rains when it does, how tornadoes work—think of the advantages! I've gathered every instrument made. They measure humidity, barometric pressure, wind velocity. But I haven't been able to make proper use of them. That's where you come in." Peter told him how much he admired his methodical study of ballooning, which he had presented the previous season to the Society.

"We can do it, Benjamin. You and I. I have the instruments, and you have the balloons to carry those instruments aloft. It's a tremendous opportunity for mankind to progress in his control of the world around him. And we'll be at the forefront."

Yes, they would be, if the Scientific Society would recognize the value of his contribution to the field. If the French would cooperate. If Peter hadn't died.

With an effort, Benjamin shoved away the painful memories. He looked upward, straining to see the top of the tower amid the encroaching clouds. France's Eiffel Tower was a perfect gift to the study of weather systems. No man-made structure had ever stretched so far into the heavens. If only Peter himself could have been the one to explore its potential.

He slowed his pace, pausing at the back of the crowd that waited to take the elevator to the second level. He bounced impatiently on his toes, straining to look over the crowd and assess how fast the line was moving. The elevator took several dozen passengers at a time, but carried them only to the second level.

"Blast this," Benjamin swore, drawing the outraged glare of a buttoned-up woman standing beside him. Ignoring her, he left the line and circled around to the front.

"Pardon me. Excuse me." The deep voice, accented in cultured English, reached Hannah before its owner did. She turned around just as a tall man bumped into her, almost knocking her off her feet. She stepped back, catching her balance, then turned to say a few tart words to the stranger.

Her words jammed in her throat as she found herself staring at a black-wool-clad shoulder higher than her head. The man had already turned his back to her. If she spoke up now, she would create a scene. Since he towered over the crowd, he obviously considered her far too easy to ignore.

He placed himself squarely in front of the elevator conductor. "Please, I must take the next car. The weather may not hold, and my work is critical," he said in perfect French.

"Monsieur, you must wait your turn."

"You don't understand." The man's lips turned up, but Hannah wouldn't define his expression as a smile, more like barely leashed aggravation. "I am a member of the Scientific Society. I have a permit."

He pulled a paper from his inside coat pocket and thrust it at the conductor. With a frown, the conductor began to unfold it.

Behind him, the elevator arrived, and the operator inside pulled a handle to open the doors. A small crowd of people exited, and Hannah impatiently counted along with the conductor as he allowed a set number of passengers inside, enough to fill the seats on both levels of the immense car. She should make it aboard this trip. Sure enough, she was allowed to board the steel box and took a seat in the front row of the bottom level. Excitement surged in her chest. Soon she would be on top of the world!

A seat beside hers on the end remained empty when the mesh doors began to close. Before the doors met, the rude man shoved his heavy case between the doors, then followed it into the elevator car. He took the empty seat as the doors snapped shut. The car jerked, starting its ascent.

Through the mesh, Hannah saw the conductor look up from the paper and cry out, *"Arrêt!"*

The elevator operator either hadn't heard the conductor or pretended he hadn't. He shrugged, and the elevator continued rising. "I will stand during this trip," he said mildly.

The Englishman nodded to the operator, but said not a word of thanks. Hannah decided she detested the man. Despite occupying separate seats, they were packed in so close his shoulder brushed against hers with each sway of the car. Her blood heated, fueled by embarrassment and indignation.

"You're occupying the operator's seat," she said in English, her gaze flicking sideways to catch his reaction to her sally.

It didn't alter even a fraction. He replied coolly, "That is not a concern of yours, miss."

"If I had to stand up during the trip because of your rudeness, it certainly would be."

"You are comfortably seated; therefore you have no complaint against me."

"I reserve the right to rail against rudeness in all its forms."

"I concede your right, as long as you refrain from subjecting me to your self-righteous and naïve opinions. I have no interest in the opinion of a pushy American chit."

Hannah stiffened. She opened her mouth to reply, but a young boy let out a squeal, drawing her attention to the view. "Look, Mama, you can see my school!"

"Oui, mon cher, we are far above the city," his mother replied. *"C'est belle, non?"*

It *was* very beautiful. Hannah determined to put the rude Englishman at her side out of her mind and enjoy the amazing sight now visible through the latticework of the tower. Every second they climbed higher and higher, the elevator putting more distance between them and the ground below. What a wonder this machine was, this tower! Her stomach lurched, and she heard the gears grind. For a brief, shocking moment she imagined the cables snapping, sending them plummeting to their deaths. She shook off that appalling thought. The world's wisest men, engineers and scientists, had created this tower. Of course she trusted them.

Unable to contain her curiosity, Hannah asked the operator how the elevator was able to lift them at an angle. He explained that the huge cabin was being pulled up the sloping runners by a hydraulic-powered cable. "It was built by an American company named Otis," he said.

"American? Really." Filled with national pride, Hannah shot a look at the Englishman. Unfortunately, he seemed oblivious, staring into space.

Finally, the elevator stopped at the second level, and the doors folded back. The only way to the top level was a spiral staircase. The rude Englishman dashed off before the rest of the passengers even stood. He rushed toward the stairwell as if he were racing the clock. Hannah also felt the press of time, but definitely didn't want to be the one slowing that man's progress. He would probably knock her down the stairs in his haste.

When Hannah stepped out of the elevator, she caught a glimpse of the man rounding the first curl in the stairway. She could only hope she had seen the last of him.

Blast the man for putting a stain on what should have been a perfectly lovely and memorable adventure. He was nothing to her, and she was less than

nothing to him, obviously. Pushy American chit—
the nerve! She had heard how pompous
Englishmen could be and only prayed he was the
worst of his ilk, or she and Lily would have a terrible
experience in London during the Season. So cold
and arrogant—how did Englishwomen tolerate
them?

She prayed noblemen were of a better, more
mannerly class, since her mother was so determined to wed her to one.

Distracted, she reached the top faster than she
expected. She stepped out onto the third level high
above the city. Crossing to the railing, she took
several minutes to acclimate herself, to absorb what
she was seeing, to accept that she was finally as
high as a bird could fly.

For a long moment, she forgot to breathe at the
panorama of Paris spread below her. Despite the
overcast sky and the mist in the air, she could still
see quite a long way, longer than she had ever seen
before, all the way to Notre Dame Cathedral and
beyond.

"That is the mayor and his wife," a man next to
her said to his companion. Following their gaze
to the ground below, Hannah spotted the couple
surrounded by a crowd. The mayor stood on a
stage giving a speech, his wife beside him. They
looked the size of ants. The man beside her
brought them into focus with a little telescope.
Hannah wished she had one.

A drop of moisture landed on her cheek, and
she swiped it away with her glove. The sky looked
more threatening by the moment. She shouldn't
linger, much as she longed to soak in the sights.
She had a job to do.

She wandered along the walkway looking for an inconspicuous place to conduct her experiment. Bypassing a knot of people, she ran into a wall.

No, not a wall—the ill-mannered Englishman.

CHAPTER 3

The scent of wet wool filled Hannah's nostrils, she was pressed so close against the man. She leaped away from him, nearly tripping over his wooden case, which lay open on the ground. Inside rested a collection of exotic-looking instruments.

"Excuse me," she murmured, embarrassed to the core.

He merely gazed down at her, a frown causing a crease to appear between his dark brows, which further shadowed his deep-set eyes. Hannah quickly turned her attention to his equipment. He stood at the rail holding a megaphone-shaped object into the wind. It was attached by a cord to the machine in the case.

The entire setup looked remarkably like scientific instrumentation.

"You're a scientist!" she blurted out.

He gazed down at her, and Hannah found herself

caught in the power of his gaze, unable to look away. Eyes dark as coal, and just as remote. Not quite cold, not exactly lifeless. But certainly untouchable. What struck her most, however, was a barely veiled intensity, a power of the spirit she had never seen before. Clearly this man knew what he was about. Unlike her.

The corner of his mouth quirked up briefly, then straightened so fast, she thought she had imagined it. "You," he said blandly, as if he could think of nothing less interesting than running into her again.

"Yes, it's me."

"The nosy American girl," he said placidly. His eyes actually seemed to twinkle, and suddenly he appeared much more approachable. To her dismay, Hannah's face began to heat.

He didn't seem to notice. He returned to his work, holding the megaphone over the railing. Both frustrated and relieved he wasn't looking at her, Hannah spoke to his back. "Since you've already deemed me nosy, I lose nothing by asking you what you're studying. And, I should point out, you lose nothing by telling me."

"Is that so?" Slowly, he lowered his megaphone device and turned around to face her. The power of his full attention caused Hannah to freeze, all her senses on alert. The realization struck her like a bolt of lightning. He was not only physically imposing, but terribly attractive. A strongly chiseled jaw and dark brows accentuated those captivating eyes. Her stomach turned to mush, and she fought to remind herself that she was above such female nonsense. She had a *mind*.

"I–I'm interested in science," she plodded on

lamely, wanting him to believe her but doubting he would.

"How charming." That twinkle sparked in his eyes again. "You collect leaves and shells, no doubt. Maybe you can even identify a few constellations."

"I'm not a hobbyist. That is, I don't plan to be. And I resent . . ."

She lost her train of thought as he stepped close to her, so close she felt the heat of his body. She refused to move back even an inch. He glanced over her shoulder as if looking for someone.

"Does your husband find the discipline as fascinating as you do?"

"He's—I'm not married."

He leaned toward her in an alarmingly familiar way. "Then, you have a chaperone? Or, if not . . ."

Uncomfortable with his probing, Hannah gestured to his open case on the ground. "Are you studying the weather? I see you have a siphon barometer. And that's a condensation hygrometer, isn't it?"

His demeanor altered in an instant. He stiffened, and a cloud seemed to cover his eyes. "How do I know you aren't working for the French Society? Bloody bastards have been less than cooperative— pardon my French."

No one had ever spoken to her in such a way. It wasn't merely the curse that stunned her, but the fact he was talking to her as one adult to another. Her lack of a chaperone was no doubt the reason. "I'm not with any society," she said.

"Hah. Right. I wouldn't put it past them to send a pretty girl to check up on my progress. Be off with you."

Pretty girl? A warm shiver swept through her at

the unexpected compliment. No one, not even a schoolboy, had ever called her pretty, much less a man in his masculine prime such as this one.

"I'm not whoever you think I am, sir. But you have proven indisputably that you are, indeed, the rudest man I have ever met." Hannah adopted her most imperious mien and strutted away from him toward the nearest corner. She had the abysmally deflating feeling, however, that he was smirking at her bravado.

She rounded the corner, but had barely begun to enjoy the new view displayed beneath her when she noticed a uniformed gendarme talking with a family of five and gesturing at the sky. The small man seemed quite animated. The wind had picked up, whistling through the tower's steel girders. She could barely hear him warning the family about a coming storm and recommending that they return to the first level. As if to punctuate his words, another raindrop slapped her forehead.

Yesterday had been beautiful. Why had the fickle weather turned foul today of all days?

The family headed inside, and the gendarme moved along the railing toward the next group of tourists. In another moment, he would be talking to her. Her time was almost up.

She turned on her heel and walked as quickly as seemliness allowed back around the corner, ignoring the rude Englishman, who was engrossed in his work and had already forgotten all about her. She walked twenty feet past him, then paused at the railing. Crouching down, she opened her satchel. The parts of her largest, most elaborate model bird rested inside. As quickly and furtively as possible, she assembled it right inside the satchel.

When put together, it extended fifteen inches from nose to tail, with an equally long wingspan. She had painstakingly glued real bird feathers to a wing-shaped framework, hoping to replicate the weight and shape of a bird's wings. She had worked for hours on it, applying all her knowledge of flight dynamics.

How long would her bird glide before coming to rest? One mile? Two? Since there was a very real chance she would lose track of it, she had tucked a note in its belly asking anyone who found it to contact her at the home of Mrs. Digby, the society matron who was hosting her family during their Paris stay.

Mrs. Digby would have no idea what the call was about. None of them would. She had confided her plans only to Lily, but hadn't told her when or how she would sail her bird. And she had sworn her younger sister to secrecy. Lily had thought it all rather silly, but had agreed not to tell Mother.

Hannah began to lift the bird from the bag.

An argument between two men drew her interest, and she paused. The gendarme had apparently asked the Englishman to leave the tower, but he was resisting, ranting on about a permit of some kind. Maybe the policeman would arrest him for disorderly behavior. Even better, he was keeping the gendarme occupied. Turning away, she freed her bird from the satchel. Wasting no time, she cocked her arm and threw the bird as hard as she could over the railing.

The wind picked it up, caressed it in midair for a long, wonderful moment, then dropped it gracefully in a curve back toward the tower. Fascinated, Hannah watched as it completed the circle and headed outward again, seemingly floating in the air for the longest time. A success! She had created wings that glided in the air, just like a real bird's wings! She had no idea if it would work full-scale, or if so, how one might attach a man to such a contraption. But it was a start; it was definitely a start.

"My God, what in heaven's name *is* that thing?"

The Englishman's deep voice snagged her attention. She realized he and the gendarme were now standing next to her, also watching her bird.

The man with the telescope had run over to join them. "I've been watching it with my scope," he panted. "Where did it come from?" He lifted his telescope to train it on her bird once more, and Hannah wished she had thought to bring one.

"*C'est magnifica,*" the gendarme said, his voice hushed with awe. "It flies as if alive."

Pride swelled within Hannah. Let the rude Brit stew on that, she thought. It took her a moment to realize the Englishman was equally taken with her creation. "That thing is yours? It flies with surprising precision. How did you make it?"

Tingles shot up and down her spine at his compliment and interest. She lifted her gaze from her bird long enough to glance at him. As their gazes locked, she found herself looking at him for much longer than she had intended. A strong gust struck her, and she felt as if the wind had been knocked out of her, but couldn't explain why, for she remained standing.

In the next instant, the storm broke. Huge, pummeling drops blew sideways, slapping her face and soaking her dress. She barely noticed, for the man with the telescope cried, "Look! It's turning!"

Hannah saw a streak of white, now hundreds of feet below them. It flew much closer to the tower than she had anticipated, then was swept away at an angle by another gust. The bird's nose lifted for a fraction of a second, as if straining for release from gravity, then pointed down, plunging hard and fast toward the earth.

It disappeared in a cluster of people listening to the mayor's speech. Hannah sighed. At least she would be able to retrieve the bird and try again. If it wasn't for these strong winds—

A barely discernible scream sounded from far below. The man with the telescope leaned so far over the railing, Hannah worried he would tumble off. "She is hit! *Mon Dieu!* You have struck her!"

"Who? I've struck who?" Hannah asked, panic rising in her throat. She had never meant to hurt anyone.

"The mayor's wife! *Oh, Mon Dieu, c'est terrible.*" He passed the telescope to the gendarme, who focused on the scene so far below. Hannah could barely breathe, terrified of what he might be seeing.

The gendarme lowered the instrument and looked sharply at Hannah. "That bird was yours?"

Hannah's neck felt so stiff she barely managed a single nod.

"You have no permit for experiments on the tower?"

She shook her head.

He pulled a whistle from around his neck and blew into it. Though muffled by wind and rain, the sound pierced through her. "Please remain here. I am placing you under arrest."

CHAPTER 4

Hannah had never been more miserable. The gendarmes had treated her well, even as they had escorted her down from the tower to a waiting paddy wagon. No one had said a harsh word to her, or mistreated her, during the ride in the threadbare, musty-smelling wagon through town to the police station. Once there, an officer had asked her name and address, and in that moment Hannah saw the end of all her mother's dreams for her and her sisters.

So she had lied. "Alice Brown" was the name she had given them, adding that she had no family in Paris but was visiting from Wisconsin. They had looked at her oddly, no doubt wondering what a young lady was doing wandering the streets of Paris on her own. She had tried to act innocent—though the weight of her lie suffocated her. She hadn't meant to hurt anyone, yet she had. How could she have predicted her bird would fly into a crowd instead of out into the countryside as she had envisioned? Why hadn't she realized her bird might hurt someone?

Regrets aside, nothing changed the fact she had conducted an experiment without a permit, something she shouldn't have done. For all her excellent grades in school, she obviously lacked common sense and knowledge of the world. For that, she had no one to blame but herself.

Now she sat in a chilly jail cell awaiting arraignment before a judge on the morrow, worrying about her mother and sister worrying. They must be frantic by now. Not only hadn't she returned from her walk, but she was in jail! When they found out, they would be appalled. Mortified. The family would never live this down. Despite Lily's enviable wardrobe, what quality home would ever invite the sister of a criminal to visit?

Hannah groaned and buried her face in her hands. She had never felt more alone. Tears pressed against her eyelids, but she forced them back. She had to solve her problem, but couldn't determine how. No amount of thinking would take back her rash actions. No amount of pondering would bring an easy solution. She felt like a rat trapped in an endless maze with no exit.

Wind whistled through the stones of her cell's outer walls. The rain caused a steady drip of water to run down one corner, forming a puddle on the floor. The only furniture provided was a bunk with a stained and smelly mattress, a blanket, and a chamber pot in the far corner—with no screen for privacy. Thank goodness she was alone in this cell block, as far as she could tell.

A loud slam accompanied by male voices startled her. She glanced up in time to see a man being escorted past her cell to the next one. He glanced toward her, and their eyes locked.

Him! She sat up on her bunk, every sense on alert.

She heard his voice demanding in impatient French that the guards make certain that some fellow named Winthrop was alerted of his arrest. The metal door rattled on its hinges, then closed with a bang. The clicking lock reminded her of her own incarceration, and she shuddered.

Soon the English gentleman had been left alone in the cell next door. He immediately started to pace. She heard his even footfalls on the hard stone floor, then his cell door rattling.

"You can't shake it open," she said dryly. The rattling stopped. Knowing he might not appreciate her question, she decided to ask it anyway. "What are *you* doing here?"

She couldn't see him, but she heard his movements stop. "I should think that's quite clear. I'm enjoying the state's fine amenities."

"But you had a permit. Your experiments weren't hurting anyone."

She pictured his wry expression, that robust male countenance made warm by the sparkle in his eyes. "Be careful, miss. You're using logic. That doesn't always work in the modern world." She heard a heavy sigh, then the creak of his bunk, and pictured him sitting down. "My permit had expired. As I have no funds with me to pay the fine, I am cooling my heels here."

Hannah glanced around. Their cell block was small, only three cells on each side. She had been put in an end cell, and he was right next door. She could see into the cells across the way, but he remained out of her line of sight, which was definitely for the best. Warily, she glanced toward the chamber pot in the corner, which she would surely have to use before the day was out. "But why did they place you in a women's cell block?"

He chuckled, but the sound carried no humor. "This isn't the section for women. If you go down a few levels, you'll find all manner of female riffraff from the Paris streets jammed together into cells not much larger than these. These cells are for those of a better class, which apparently you've been deemed a member of—either because of your American citizenship or your obviously well-tailored clothing. They expect to process us rather quickly come morning, as both of us should be bailed out by our relatives or friends, unlike the poor sots who spend weeks behind bars before a proper court hearing."

"These are the good cells? That's appalling!"

"The truth is not always lovely, despite what your governess told you."

Her governess certainly had never discussed *this* appalling situation. Yet this man also appeared to be an aristocrat. So why was he such an expert on jails? "How do you know so much about this place?" she asked suspiciously.

He didn't answer, and Hannah wondered how often he ended up here. Who was Winthrop? A friend or colleague, most likely, or perhaps a butler.

She rose and crossed to the bars, straining to catch a glimpse of him, but it was impossible. She recalled his expensive wool coat and gentleman's derby, however. Adopting a wry tone, she asked, "Do you get arrested often?"

"Impertinent chit," he shot back, but he didn't seem angry with her so much as amused. "What exactly were you trying to accomplish up on the tower?"

"That should be quite clear," she said loftily, echoing his own earlier words.

"You wanted to see a pretty wooden bird fly through the air?"

Irritated, she gave up trying to be coy. "It was an experiment in aerodynamics. I was assessing Otto Lilienthal's recently published theories on flight dynamics. According to his book, *Birdflight as the Basis of Aviation,* birdflight is the key to human flight."

Silence from next door, then the carefully worded question, "And this interests you?"

She bit her lip. That question didn't deserve an answer.

"Let me picture this," he said as if deep in thought. "In between attending soirées and balls and courting eligible young gentlemen, you're building an aeroplane in your dressing room."

Hannah found herself smiling. "I wish. But I wouldn't know where to start."

"The problem with so-called aeroplanes is the lack of a powerful enough engine. That's an engineering problem, not a problem pure research can solve."

"What about using a steam engine?"

"Men keep trying steam engines, but they're impractical," he said calmly. Hannah liked his change in tone. For the first time since meeting him, she felt he was honestly talking from the heart—or at least the head. "A steam engine large enough to lift a person would have to carry so much water it couldn't get off the ground. But the real problem is how the pilot can control his craft once he's aloft. No one has found a way to do that."

Hannah's heart beat with excitement despite her circumstances. In such a strange place, she had found a kindred spirit. "That's just what Lilienthal said! You've obviously done research yourself. Are you attempting to solve the problem of flight?"

"No. I prefer terra firma, thank you very much. I'm not a tinkerer or engineer. That's the sort of fellow who will build a flying machine, when it happens."

"But you're a scientist."

"I dabble."

"Oh." Hannah sensed the conversation dying, something she didn't want to happen. Talking with him, despite his aggravatingly arrogant manner, was much better than thinking about the mess she had made of her life. "If you only dabble, then why do you know so much about the problems of flight?"

"Balloons, miss. Hot-air and hydrogen-filled balloons."

"You study them?"

"I use them. It's the only flight that works, certainly much better than putting on wings and leaping off a roof, only to land in a barnyard dung heap—or bashing in a lady's head."

His rebuke stung, and Hannah debated continuing the discussion. Still, she had never discussed this topic with anyone, and to have a conversation with a real live scientist—even a "dabbler"—exhilarated her. "But balloons can't be directed. They go only where the wind goes. That's rather limiting."

"That's not my concern. They meet my needs."

"How?"

"You *are* nosy, aren't you? Balloons allow me to send instruments into the atmosphere to take readings, something your wooden birds could never do."

Hannah leaned back against the wall, thinking about his words. Perhaps he was right. Perhaps she should be thinking of how to use balloons to explore the heavens, instead of her birds.

She smiled to herself. The man had definitely managed to take her mind off her dire situation. "You're remarkably composed, sir. You've almost made me forget where we're having this conversation."

"Perhaps it keeps my mind off of other matters," he said, echoing her own sentiment. "Besides, my associate Winthrop will find a decent solicitor and drop by this evening to present bail. I'll pay the fine, and that will be that."

Hannah sighed. That explained his composure. He had contacts. Besides, he was a man, a man with power, obviously. Unlike her.

When he spoke again, his voice was surprisingly soft. "Surely you've asked the jailers to contact someone for you?"

Hannah couldn't bring herself to answer; it was all so embarrassing and complicated by her lies.

"Miss?"

"You needn't concern yourself with me."

"Your colonial independence is showing. How fascinating. Let me see . . . You're obviously young.

No doting husband, as we've established. And you're hardly dressed like a street urchin, with that neat green dress and matching hat and gloves."

"You can describe my clothing?" He had noticed her, just as she remembered every detail of his imposing countenance. Again her skin flushed. He had been as struck by her as she had by him.

He deflated that thought when he elaborated. "I am a scientist, miss, trained to notice details. And you *are* American."

Instantly she felt defensive. "What does that matter?"

"I find it difficult to picture you traveling across the Atlantic under your own steam, so to speak. You must be visiting Europe with someone, most likely an older female chaperone."

Hannah glared in his direction, which unfortunately he couldn't see. She didn't like being so transparent. "Now you're the nosy one. I've asked only about your work, not your private life." It struck her then—he could be married. Did his wife care about science, too?

"Don't take it personally, miss—"

"Carring—Brown, I mean. Brown."

He chuckled. "You lied about your name. How amusing."

Wonderful. She amused him. "My name is Carrington," she said in resignation. She saw no reason to lie yet again, at least to this man, and telling the truth this time made her feel marginally better. "Hannah Carrington."

"Miss Carrington. I assure you my interest isn't personal in the least. It's strictly of a deductive nature. You present an interesting puzzle that begs to be solved."

"I am not a puzzle. I am a lady, a lady who isn't supposed to end up in a place like this!"

"Ah, another clue, one of reputation. While it would never look good for a pretty unmarried lass to end up in the clink, even overnight, little true damage has been done to your wholesome reputation, I'm sure. Your whereabouts are accounted for. You might say you have the best chaperones the city can provide. Certainly no one can claim your honor has been sullied."

"Please be quiet. I'm developing a nagging headache."

Benjamin Ramsey listened to the rustling of skirts from the cell next door. Miss Carrington was no doubt settling down, tired of talking with him, though he doubted her pat excuse of a headache.

She had lied about her identity. That intrigued him almost as much as the contrast of finding a well-dressed young woman attempting to conduct a scientific experiment off the Eiffel Tower. Who was she? Why had she come to Paris? Hannah Carrington . . . He didn't know her, but he felt he should know the name. At least her family name, Carrington.

Realization struck him, and he swore under his breath. He had heard of an American family named Carrington, railroad kings and financiers, a leading family in New York. A family wealthy enough to travel abroad. If she belonged to *that* family, it might make her concerns for her reputation understandable, even justified. No scrutiny was as sharp as that turned on those of wealth and privilege, as he well knew. Yet, as guardians of hearth and home, the fairer sex of his class was held to much higher standards than the men.

"I believe I have a possible explanation," he said slowly, into the silence. He hoped she hadn't fallen asleep, for he longed to know if his assumption would prove out. "Are you—can you possibly be—one of the lady buccaneers who have invaded Europe? The young women from America seeking to buy a title in exchange for a hefty dowry?" The young women who had attempted to ingratiate themselves with him time and again, and whom he had ignored as insipid pests? "Or am I making too big of a leap in logic?"

"Buccaneers!" she cried out. Apparently she wasn't asleep. "I am *not* a pirate. That's ridiculous."

She had as much as admitted he was right. He found himself smiling, larger than he had in a long time.

"You make light of it, but you're a man," she railed on. "How could you begin to understand the importance of reputation to me and my sisters? If a young man of my class ended up in here, it would be deemed a youthful indiscretion. But I'm a lady! My reputation is my calling card, my family's ticket to society. My family will never live down this shame. And I'm supposed to help pave the way for my younger sisters."

"How many sisters?"

She sounded quite miserable when she replied. "Four."

He whistled. "A lot of work, marrying off a gaggle of girls that large, I imagine."

"And I'm not making it any easier." Her words were almost a whisper, but that didn't begin to disguise the pain in her admission. "This will destroy their chances as well as my own."

"Chances at what?"

"Suitable marriages, what else? I'm not upset so much for myself, truly. I have no real desire to find a husband. But my poor mother—how Mrs. Astor will gloat! Poor Lily, she's so excited to be coming out. She would have taken London by storm."

Hannah settled back, amazed at her own talkativeness. How odd that she was opening up to this virtual stranger, when she rarely shared her most heartfelt feelings with her family. Perhaps the answer lay in the question. She had no relationship with this stranger and no reason to cultivate an image as a dutiful daughter or vibrant socialite. She had no emotional ties to him whatsoever. So she was allowing her vulnerability to show.

For his part, Benjamin sensed just how difficult her admission came. This young woman seemed to take pride in doing things her way and found it hard to meet expectations placed on her by her family. He well understood that feeling. Since his father's death, he had found the expectations of his own traditional role a burden, not a gift. Or rather, himself a poor fit.

He lay back on his bunk, letting silence descend between them as the storm raged on outside. Rain pummeled the narrow window at the top of his cell, and water dripped steadily from the ceiling in one corner. Damp, dank, and chill. A perfect representation of how low he had sunk. He had allowed the chit next door to think this was all a lark to him. He had seen no reason to reveal his vulnerabilities, especially to a stranger and a woman. He prayed Winthrop would come through with the bail. If not, he could be spending a while in here.

Winthrop would show. He had to. Eventually.

The question was when. It would be like Winthrop to delay arriving, finding humor in his situation. What a wonderful story he would become at the club. He sighed and rolled over to face the damp wall. The further question was how he would pay Winthrop back. He already owed his colleague a thousand pounds he could ill afford.

How embarrassing. A Ramsey stooping to borrowing, then being in arrears. His father and grandfather would roll over in their graves if they weren't already at fault for allowing the family estate to erode so badly.

Winthrop, however, continued to thrive. Ramsey suspected the money he spent was mostly his wife's. Winthrop often gloated that he had snagged a hefty bank account when he married a homely widow the year before.

Finding an heiress to marry . . . Benjamin had resisted that course as long as possible. God knew he needed the money. He had sold his country manor years ago, and his city house ran on a shoestring from what was left of his inheritance.

But his work had taken precedence over social events where he might meet eligible young women. Besides, he hated wasting time engaging in chitchat over tea when he could be working.

What on earth would he do with a wife? Besides the obvious nighttime pleasures to be had, of course, assuming the female was at least decent to look at. If not, he would rather continue to visit Madame Hornbecker's, thank you very much.

Most wives ran their households, but his spinster sister Georgina performed that function for him. Her declining health had caused things to be overlooked recently, however, such as the payment on this ridiculous permit.

He imagined looking across the breakfast table and seeing a strange woman sitting there every morning for the rest of his life. If she came with money, she would be a cultured, pampered thing who had been bred for her role, who spoke of clothing and parties and friends—a language he barely understood. She would expect him to be a doting husband. She would be needy; she would grow demanding, no doubt, as all women did. She would want attention he was disinclined to give her.

My God, what would he even say to such a woman? Perhaps if they had a child, they would have something in common worth discussing in regard to its education, if not the rearing of it. Children were as foreign to him as a wife would be.

For a brief instant, the image of the girl in the next cell sitting across his breakfast table filled his mind. She did not possess the round-faced, small-mouthed classic beauty that was all the rage. Quite the opposite. Yet she was relatively easy on the eye. Her longish nose accompanied a longish face, which put together provided an aesthetically pleasing balance. Pretty, yes. But most attractive were her pert manner and surprising, often amusing, comments. An interest in science, of all things. How charming. Not that he believed for a moment she even understood the discipline.

Her spring green, ornately trimmed dress screamed money. As little as he knew about clothes, he had noticed hers. He was surprised to realize the chit had made a strong impression on him.

She wasn't at all what he imagined an American heiress to be like. Clever, if confused. She had looked so proud of her accomplishment when that bird had soared off the tower. Odd, that she had done such a thing.

Perhaps . . . .

The idea that occurred to him could only come under extreme circumstances, he quickly acknowledged. Of course, what else could one consider being broke and jailed while abroad, except an extreme circumstance? He had exhausted his options, sunk most of his capital into his experiments and his sister's doctor bills with little to show for it. The next to go would be his London house. God knew what would happen to his sister and him then.

Unless . . . .

She did have a certain . . . pleasantness about her. She would be clever enough to do his books and manage his household, no doubt of that. If she had been bred to be an aristocratic wife, she could handle the social obligations he had badly neglected. She could manage dinner parties and soirées with her hands tied behind her back—and a great deal of flair.

He pictured the Society's president and officers relaxing around his always-lonely dinner table, this time bearing the platters of a fine repast. They would discuss pure science as they did at the club, but the conversation would also move along political lines. They would finally understand his vision. They would enthusiastically support his atmospheric experiments and accept his findings without question.

As for Miss Carrington, she needed this more

than he did. He had to remember that, so he didn't feel even more like a beggar than he already did.

He swung his legs over his bunk and braced his hands on the edges. "Miss Carrington, I have a proposition to make to you."

"Hmm?" She sounded sleepy. Well, she would surely grow alert by the time he finished.

"Miss Carrington," he said, speaking coolly and carefully. "In reviewing your circumstances, I have come to the conclusion that you are right to be worried. I apologize for my light treatment of your situation earlier. In fact, I believe I can offer a solution which will satisfy the threat to your reputation as well as offer an explanation for your absence to your family."

"What?" She sounded more alert now. "What are you going on about? How can you possibly—"

"The solution is so obvious, it's amazing it took me this long to reach it. I have been considering the acquisition of a wife for some time, but until now have delayed for . . . various reasons."

"A wife?"

"Yes, Miss Carrington. I believe we should marry, with all due haste."

Hannah felt as if the wind had been knocked out of her. Was this man pulling her leg, or was he truly deranged? "I—I don't even know you. My God, I don't even know your name! What reason would I possibly have for marrying you?"

"I can offer you the one thing which will save your reputation."

"You can turn back the clock?"

"No, a title. Benjamin Ramsey, Seventh Earl of Sheffield, at your service, Miss Carrington."

Hannah perked up. "You're a lord?" Despite herself, she immediately realized the truth of what he had said. She would be a social success, just like that. She imagined showing off this man—tall, broad-shouldered, imposing—to her sister and mother, and introducing him to them.

"Not just a lord, miss. An earl. There are only a few hundred of us in all of England, and most of us already have wives. I assure you, I am considered something of a catch to buccaneers such as you."

"I am *not* a buccaneer!"

He chuckled. "As you wish, Miss Carrington."

Hannah frowned. "I admit that title of yours would greatly appeal to my mother, but it means little to me."

"I find that rather refreshing, actually."

Hannah sighed, her thoughts racing ahead, puzzling through the ramifications. "It's true, if we were to marry, this awful adventure would have no impact on my sisters' reputations, at least not a lasting one," she admitted. "Oh, there might be talk over the speed with which we wed, and we'd have to concoct a story about what we were doing this night—" A deep blush suffused her face, not helped by an odd noise she heard from his cell. "I wouldn't want it to seem we *had* to marry," she said quickly, playing the what-if game. And that was all it was, a game. She couldn't seriously consider this shocking proposal.

Then again, it would solve so many problems, not the least of which was taking her out of the looming social Season which she dreaded. "They would have to think we were deeply in love," she said suddenly, surprising even herself. Her mother and sister must never know she was less than deliriously happy.

"As much as I am capable of acting, that can be arranged," he said dryly. "But I warn you: Englishmen aren't known for their demonstrative emotions, and I am no exception to that rule."

"I understand that. What I don't quite understand is how you would benefit by marrying me."

Silence again, the longest yet. A minute ticked by, then another. "That should be obvious," he said flatly.

Money. Of course. The man wanted her money. A chill colder than the stone walls surrounding her crept through her blood and up her spine. She felt as if she were selling her soul to the devil, a lifetime of servitude with a virtual stranger to save her reputation.

Why should she feel so terrible about such an arrangement? She had always known her generous dowry was her most attractive feature to a man. Besides, was marrying her for money any worse than her marrying him for a title?

She closed her eyes and swallowed her pride. Just as he said, she was a buccaneer.

"Yes," she said on a breath. She uttered the word so faintly, she was certain he would miss it, and she would have a chance to take it back.

"Very well," he said, as if ordering liver paté. His tone brightened. "Ah, we've settled our business just in time. Winthrop is here to bail us out."

CHAPTER 5

Hannah trailed behind Benjamin and Winthrop, down the steps from the courthouse to the sidewalk. She lifted the hem of her skirt to avoid the wet pavement, but knew she looked a state no matter what measures she took. Her hair hung half out of its once-neat chignon, and her dress was wrinkled and clammy from the earlier soaking she had received.

The rain hadn't let up. If anything, the storm had intensified. Hannah found it surprising that Benjamin had wanted to be out in such foul weather. His love for science eclipsed even hers.

She was so glad to be out of jail, she skipped a step, then caught herself and prayed her future husband and his friend hadn't seen.

They hadn't. The two men were deep in a discussion of Benjamin's experiment, with Benjamin describing his failed attempt at an instrument test.

Harold Winthrop was a plump, blond man about Benjamin's age, with none of the shadows that seemed to hover over the earl. He had been most generous in paying the bail for both Hannah and Benjamin.

Hannah wished she could like Harold Winthrop. Especially since he was a friend of her intended. But the man apparently took nothing seriously. He seemed to think of their predicament as a lark. Benjamin hadn't told Winthrop that being jailed was the reason she was marrying him, but Hannah knew the man suspected as much. He seemed to find the news of Benjamin's sudden engagement enormously amusing.

He glanced back at her, then smiled at Benjamin. "You, engaged! Most exciting, truly. And so many times you claimed to have no use for a wife." He shot an assessing look at Hannah. "Pardon, miss, no offense."

"Apparently I found a use," Benjamin said dryly, without even looking at her. Mortified, Hannah almost wished she were back in the jail rather than be referred to as a useful implement.

"Am I to be invited to the blessed event?" Winthrop asked, his expression entirely too jovial. "I'd enjoy being a witness. One must, after all, see such a thing to believe it."

"We plan a small ceremony. Very small."

"Family only," Hannah broke in.

"We must be going," Benjamin continued. "It's late, and this stop wasn't exactly in our plans." Grasping Hannah's arm, Benjamin began steering her away.

"Ah. Well, my best wishes, then. At least allow me to buy you a drink to toast your . . . find. What's another quid or two on top of your debt?" He smiled.

Benjamin shook his head, smiling tightly. "I couldn't allow you to, Winthrop."

Hannah wondered how much more needling the stoic man beside her would put up with. Perhaps he had brought it on himself by borrowing money from this man, but she didn't like Winthrop's tone or his false joviality. She wondered if Benjamin really considered him a friend. For her part, she didn't trust him, despite the favor he had done Benjamin.

Adding grist to her feelings, Winthrop called out with glee, "Now that you have a source of ready cash coming, I look forward to seeing your debt repaid."

His blatant demand for his money mortified Hannah, and no doubt Benjamin. She didn't know her fiancé well, but she had already ascertained that he was a proud man. He merely nodded, his thin lips turned up slightly—not quite a smile, and not revealing any emotion other than politeness. Directing her to the curb, he hailed a passing cab.

The carriage pulled up, the paired horses' snorts forming small clouds in the rainy evening.

They climbed in. Benjamin slammed the door closed and tapped on the ceiling with his cane, then paused and glanced at her.

"We must go straight to my family," Hannah said, sensing his question. "They must be worrying themselves sick." She supplied Mrs. Digby's address.

"As you wish. Driver!" Benjamin communicated their destination, and the carriage jerked to a start.

He settled back in the seat. Hannah realized this

was the first time she had sat next to her future husband, in the same small space, alone. The dark carriage heightened her other senses. She breathed a tantalizing hint of his scent—a male musk that couldn't entirely have come from a bottle. Even more disconcerting, she could feel the heat of him, less than a foot away on the small bench seat. In truth, she knew next to nothing about him and precious little about the life that awaited her. Closing her eyes, she tried to pretend he wasn't there, that she was alone, blissfully alone.

She almost succeeded in her self-deception, until he spoke. "I apologize for Winthrop."

"I suppose he's allowed to say what he wants, since he bailed us out."

"That is one debt I will be happy to repay, as soon as possible."

Again that blatant reminder of how useful her dowry would be. It made her feel stiff and cold, like a useless but valuable doll. *You're going to use him, too,* she reminded herself fiercely. *You'll take your equal measure in turn.*

She wished she had been born with a more ambitious nature. Many of her peers would consider it great fortune to be marrying an earl, no matter the circumstances bringing him into their lives. They would relish the presentation at court, serving as hostesses to high society, wearing the title of countess like a crown. To Hannah, it felt like an unnecessary weight on her shoulders, dragging her into a world she knew nothing about and where she didn't belong.

Silence descended between them. Hannah thought again of the debt Benjamin owed Winthrop and of his grand plans for scientific research.

There was no doubt he badly needed her money. Were there other debts, perhaps gambling debts? Would he waste her dowry as he apparently had his family fortune?

He seemed awfully willing to break the law to get what he wanted. Did he engage in any other criminal occupations? Worse, was his temperament always so unflappable, or did he possibly have a mean streak his gentlemanly manner hid most of the time?

He seemed to love science, but was that all he loved? He could be a dissolute man, a drunkard or abusive, yet she was putting her life in his hands. She had agreed to his solution to their mutual problems so quickly, she hadn't considered the ramifications.

Another frightening question prodded her, and she couldn't help turning it over and studying all sides of it, like poking her tongue at a sore tooth. Did the man beside her have a mistress? Did she want him to? If not, would he expect her to fulfill her marital duties right away? She had a fairly good notion of what those duties entailed, as much as she could glean from natural science texts and the murmured comments of other women. Yet the reality seemed so dark and mysterious, so unspeakably intimate. Her stomach tightened a notch. She wasn't ready for that. Not anytime soon. She had never even held this man's hand. Would he be angry if she denied him a husband's lawful right?

Maybe she had made a terrible mistake agreeing to this marriage. But it was too late now. A lady would never go back on her word. Besides, she had no other way of rescuing her reputation, even if it meant a life of misery married to a stranger.

Perhaps when she knew him better, she would find it easier to imagine intimacy with him. If she had some genuine feeling for him, and he for her. If he liked her, at least a little, as a person ... Certainly not as a woman, she would never expect that. She knew she was no beauty to make a man's heart beat fast and his dreams center on her. But to be a friend ... Perhaps that wasn't outside the realm of possibility.

She must think positively. She must also accept that she had made her choice, and the only intelligent course was to make the best of it.

"Hannah is always making light of things at inappropriate times. Naturally I didn't take her seriously!"

Lily Carrington watched from the sofa as her mother made yet another round of the room, stopping before the fireplace only long enough to swivel on her feet and pace back again.

"Mother, what are you saying?"

Olympia Carrington paused, then turned away, as if ashamed to tell her daughter.

"Mother?" Lily prodded. "If you know anything, anything at all that might help us locate her—"

Her mother burst out, "Right before she left Worth's, she mumbled something silly, something about jumping off a bridge. But I didn't think she meant it!"

Lily gasped. "Oh, no. She couldn't possibly have done ... that." She shuddered, imagining her older sister—devastated, crushed with disappointment—walking onto one of the city's many bridges, climbing over the railing, and hurling herself into the river. "No," she repeated, aghast. "She had to be joking!"

"That's what I thought, but then, where is she?"

Where, indeed? Hours had passed, and there had been no sign of Hannah. Night had fallen long ago, and still she hadn't returned. She had vanished. Lily and her mother finally left Worth's, begging them to send word immediately if she appeared there.

Lily knew their mother hadn't thought twice about letting Hannah take a short stroll on her own. All of them took walks in their neighborhood in New York City. M. Worth's shop was in a good neighborhood. Carriages with reliable servants had lined the street. And Hannah knew not to go too far.

Their mother now thought she had shown poor judgement letting her daughter out at all and was imagining Hannah meeting some nefarious end.

In turn, Lily blamed herself. The more she considered the possibility of Hannah doing harm to herself, the more feasible it seemed. "It can't be. It's just too dreadful to contemplate. Not that I would blame her for feeling that way, after Monsieur Worth cut her so rudely." She sighed and rubbed her arms. "And I didn't defend her! I was too caught up in his admiration to even think how she was feeling! Naturally she would be devastated. Oh, I'm a horrible sister. I should have insisted she be fitted first. Mother, if she isn't . . . Oh, I can't say it! . . . I'll give her all of my new gowns. I'd rather have my sister back!"

Mrs. Digby entered the room, wringing her hands. "The footmen have returned. They saw neither hide nor hair of your daughter, Mrs. Carrington." She paced around the carpet, her large form moving surprisingly quickly, like a galleon parting the sea. "This is dreadful, simply dreadful! You never know who is roaming the streets. There was that Jack the Ripper character in London just last season, and—"

"Mrs. Digby!" Olympia scolded.

Mrs. Digby fluttered her hands before her flushed face. "Oh . . . oh, my . . . such images in my mind! Surely you have heard some word by now?"

Tears pressed behind Lily's eyes, and she had to fight not to let them fall. "No word at all."

"We will have to contact the authorities," Mother said.

Mrs. Digby paled. "Then everyone will know!"

"I see no other course of action. Do you have a better suggestion?"

Lily admired her mother's poise, when deep inside she must be even more worried than Lily.

Instead of answering, Mrs. Digby continued to wring her hands, looking past Mrs. Carrington to the window. "None of my girls have ever gone out without a proper chaperone. I can't believe this is happening to me. How will I ever explain this? No aristocratic mother will ever trust me with her daughter again!"

Lily stiffened. How could Mrs. Digby think of her own reputation when her sister was probably wandering Paris's streets lost, injured, or something even more horrible? She felt her temper growing perilously short. "Shouldn't our concern more properly be over my sister's welfare at this juncture?" she bit out.

Mrs. Digby opened her mouth, and Lily braced for the coming rebuke for her impertinence.

The interruption of Mrs. Dibgy's housekeeper saved her. "Mrs. Digby, Mrs. Digby! I have news. Wonderful news." She slid to a halt just inside the doorway and pulled herself back into her proper servants' demeanor, elbows bent and hands clasped. "Miss Carrington has arrived!"

"Oh, thank the Lord," Mother said, sinking next to Lily on the sofa. Lily clasped her mother's hands, weak with relief.

"But that's not all," the maid said. Her voice lowered to a stage whisper. "She brought a gentleman!"

Hannah paused just outside the parlor, attempting to gather her thoughts—and her courage. This was it. She would have to go through with it once she told her mother and sister about her sudden engagement. Not that she would ever seriously consider backing out, no matter how cold her feet grew, how tense her nerves stretched.

Behind her hovered Benjamin Ramsey, silent and forbidding. "Remember our agreement," she said to him under her breath.

"I wouldn't dare forget," he replied wryly. Hannah wondered how seriously he was taking this, wondered whether her family would see right through this farce.

"Wait here." She left him and entered the parlor. Instantly she was surrounded by her mother, sister, and Mrs. Digby. Her family hugged her, and Mrs. Digby talked on and on about how she could have met some hideous end on the street. "Where have you been, gel? We were worried to death!"

"I'm fine, perfectly fine." Hannah pasted a big, happy grin on her face for the benefit of the three women before her.

"Your dress—it's in a terrible state!" Mrs. Digby said. "What have you been up to? This sort of behavior isn't proper for a young miss, surely you know that. I know you Americans have different standards, but—"

"She looks beautiful," her mother said, giving her another hug. She placed her at arm's length and called out to the housekeeper, "Please, some tea for Hannah. And dinner. She must be famished."

At the thought of food, Hannah's stomach suddenly felt terribly empty. The gruel and hard bread in the jail had been less than appetizing. "I wouldn't mind something to eat."

"Hannah, I'm so sorry! I didn't know you were upset." Lily grasped her hand and led her to the sofa. "I'm such a blind idiot sometimes! Can you ever forgive me?"

Hannah was truly mystified. "Upset?"

"About the fitting. You know . . ."

"Oh, no. I'm not upset at all. I only wanted some fresh air, really."

"Then—"

Lily's question was interrupted by the arrival of the tea service. While a maid poured the tea and set out biscuits, her mother sat on her other side. "Mrs. Digby is right. This adventure of yours might have serious repercussions on your reputation, depending on who may have seen you. And depending on what you were up to. You said you were going for a walk, and you've come home with a man? Where is he? Please tell me what happened, in detail."

Hannah gulped down some tea to put off the moment, but all pairs of eyes were glued to her expectantly. She prayed the story she and Benjamin had concocted in the carriage would ring true. She had imagined most of it, and he had stoically agreed to go along. More important than the details was her ability to portray a young woman in love. She had to make them think she had truly lost her heart to the stranger who even now waited outside the parlor door.

"There's just so much to tell," she chirped excitedly. "It's been the most—amazing—day. I was walking, just as I said I was going to, when—well, there was this gentleman, and he ran into me. Not literally, but almost. And he looked at me, and I looked at him, and—and—" The words jammed in her throat and refused to leave. Panic started to well up from deep inside her. She couldn't say it! She couldn't.

"Hannah! Are you serious?" Lily squealed. "You fell in love at first sight?"

Bless her romantically inclined sister for saying the words! "Yes, yes, that's right! Just like that. We completely lost track of time." Hannah giggled, hoping she sounded like a woman giddily in love. Her laugh drew strange looks from her mother and sister both.

"Hannah, are you feeling all right?" her mother asked, pressing her hand to her forehead.

"Why wouldn't I be? I met this man, you see, and—"

"You already told us that," Lily pointed out.

"She never giggles," she said, looking at their mother.

"I'm fine!" Hannah insisted. "I'm wonderful. Being in love makes you feel that way, Lily, as you'll find out someday."

"What happened after you ran into this gentleman?" her mother asked, brow furrowed in suspicion. "Why were you so late returning home?"

"Because we lost track of time, as I said. And we had a bite to eat. Then we walked in the park. Then the rain started, and we took his carriage for a ride, and then I said yes."

"Yes?" Her mother's eyes had grown as round as two saucers. "What, precisely, did you say yes to?"

"When he asked me, of course. I said yes. It seemed the prudent thing to do." She skated perilously close to the truth. "I mean, because we're so in love. He's a scientist, you see. Perfect for me. Just perfect." As if she would know a perfect man for herself if she really met one. She sighed and sank back into the cushions.

"Are you saying he proposed to you?" her mother pressed.

"Yes. In the park. He took my hand, looked deeply into my eyes, and asked me."

"But—you just said that you were in the carriage when you said yes," Lily pointed out. "This is getting confusing."

"I proposed in the park. She accepted in the carriage." The deep male voice silenced all the female voices. Benjamin strode into the room. He faced Mrs. Carrington and bowed properly from the waist. "Lord Sheffield, at your service."

CHAPTER 6

Amazed, Hannah watched Benjamin introduce himself to her family. He seemed completely unflustered, as relaxed as if he were in his gentlemen's club. Nor did he seem at all concerned about her family believing their story.

There was something innately attractive about his complete control, Hannah realized. The moment he had stepped into the room, he became its center. His considerable height and bearing coupled with his confident manner left no doubt he was master of his world. Hannah hadn't thought of him in such glowing terms before—because she had seen the reality, she fiercely reminded herself. A man in debt. A man in jail.

Lily leaned close to her and whispered, "There's a definite spark in your eyes when you look at him. You can't tear your eyes from him! He *is* dynamic."

"Lily, don't be—" She stopped herself from saying silly. If starry-eyed Lily wanted to see an attraction that wasn't there, it was all to the good.

"He's such a brooding English gentleman," Lily said appreciatively. "So serious and intelligent. I can definitely see you're suited."

Hannah said nothing, merely kept a smile plastered on her mouth.

"Excuse me, sir, I find this all just a little sudden," her mother said, putting a damper on the atmosphere. "What gives you the idea you can claim my daughter's hand after a single afternoon's acquaintance?"

"True love, naturally," Benjamin said. Was it only Hannah's perception, or was there a sarcastic edge to his voice? Mortified, she suddenly wanted to die right there. Surely a ruined reputation could be no worse than this farce of an arranged marriage.

"Did you say you're a lord?" Mrs. Digby interrupted, her face lighting up. "Named Sheffield?"

He nodded.

"I *know* you! Or rather, I know of you. You're Benjamin Ramsey, aren't you? Oh, my. Oh, my. Excuse us." Pulling Mrs. Carrington to the side, she whispered excitedly, loud enough for most of the room to hear. "He's a *catch*, I tell you. Hannah is so lucky! I promise you, she couldn't have done better had she come out in London for a full Season!"

"What are you saying, Mrs. Digby?" her mother asked.

"Don't you know who that is? That's the Earl of Sheffield himself!"

"An—an earl?" The transformation on her mother's face was almost laughable. Hannah knew she was imagining the look on Mrs. Astor's face when that woman discovered Hannah had married a nobleman. She looked back at Benjamin in awe. "Excuse me, Lord Sheffield. Mrs. Digby seems to think you hold a—a title of some sort?"

"Yes, I'm an earl, a peer of the English crown. The title's been in our family for centuries."

"Oh. Oh! Well, very well. Please, take a seat."

Flipping up his coat tails, he positioned himself on the sofa across from Hannah.

"You say you want to marry Hannah?" Her mother sat adjacent to him on a settee. "Mrs. Digby, could you have the maid pour Mr.—I mean *Lord* Sheffield—some tea? And perhaps some biscuits? Oh, piffle, what am I thinking? It's past time for tea. Would you like a brandy, Lord Sheffield?"

"A brandy would hit the spot, thank you."

"Right away," Mrs. Digby said. "This is so exciting!" She gestured to a maid to pour him a drink, then, having nothing better to do with her hands, clasped them in her lap as if to keep them in check.

After he received his drink and had taken a sip, Benjamin set the glass down on a side table. He leaned forward and faced Hannah's mother. "Mrs. Carrington, I am here to ask your permission to marry your daughter Hannah. I am quite swept away by her charms." He punctuated his outlandish lie with a wide smile.

Hannah had never seen him smile, not like this. It transformed his face. Suddenly, he had turned from a dour scientist to a devastatingly handsome gentleman. Every woman in the room felt the effect, Hannah could see. Their gazes were riveted to him, and beside her, Lily had stopped breathing. Hannah was also frozen in place, mesmerized by his magnetism. How dare he have such an effect on women? She hadn't bargained for that! But she couldn't deny that she felt it, too.

Suddenly she felt like a trapped animal, tussling against her own reaction to him. She didn't want to react to him, didn't want to feel vulnerable to him, in case he ever directed that potent charm on her.

Her mother pressed her hand to her mouth, as if to contain a girlish squeal. Once she composed herself, she removed the hand and smiled back. "I'm so thrilled for Hannah. For both of you. She is quite a catch, you know. Lovely, and from an excellent family, if I do say so myself. You won't be sorry to take her as your wife."

"I would marry her were she as poor as a church mouse," he said calmly, his gaze sliding across to meet hers. He was far, far too good at lying. Only Hannah could see the spark of secret laughter in his eyes. She had the urge to slap that mocking grin off his face. She decided then and there she would never trust a word out of his deceiving mouth.

"And how soon do you—" her mother began.

"Immediately. We plan to marry immediately, don't we, Hannah?" He glanced at her, and she nodded dumbly. "It suits us both."

"Why? Why so soon?" her mother asked. "I can't possibly be expected to plan a proper wedding in less than six months. It's simply unheard of."

"No, I cannot wait that long," he said firmly. "We will marry within the week. How does Saturday suit?" He looked from Mrs. Carrington to Hannah.

Hannah continued to stare silently at him, until he raised his eyebrows at her. She had nearly missed her cue. "Yes, Saturday is perfect." She leaned forward. "Please, Mother, I can't wait a minute longer. I know it's short notice, but I so want to start my married life. I don't want a large wedding anyway. I only want the family there."

"But your father and sisters can't possibly travel from New York in so short a time!"

Hannah was well aware of that, and it hurt her deeply that her wedding day—what should be a young lady's most memorable day—could not be shared with them. But she had to keep up her end of the bargain. "I know, but they'll have Lily's to attend . . ." she said softly. Tears burned in her eyes, threatening to overtake her.

Thank goodness Benjamin leaped in before she completely lost her composure. "I must withdraw to my home in London," he said firmly, "with all due haste. There are schedules in place, inflexible timeframes for my work. I am sorry, but I cannot wait past Saturday to wed Hannah."

Hannah knew an ultimatum when she heard one, the implied threat that if he couldn't have her by Saturday, he wouldn't have her at all. Hannah knew it to be a false threat. After all, the man needed her as much as she needed him. She was a walking bank account to him, and what man would turn that down?

Whether her mother heard the warning in his statement, she couldn't tell. She merely shrugged, accepting the earl's verdict. "Very well, if you must return that soon . . . Mrs. Digby, perhaps you can recommend a nice chapel for the service? We'll tell Monsieur Worth to put a rush on a gown for you, Hannah. I'll pay a surcharge if need be. We'll have you properly outfitted, don't you worry about that."

Hannah didn't have the heart to tell her that what she wore on her wedding day was the least of her concerns.

Hannah hugged her mother close, suddenly terrified of letting go. She had started the morning as her daughter, part of the Carrington household. In a matter of minutes, she had transformed into the Countess of Sheffield of England. She had become part of someone else's family more than her own.

She could barely recall the actual wedding, which Mrs. Digby had insisted be conducted in her parlor. A visiting pastor had performed the ceremony.

Indeed, as far as her family was concerned, this was a day of great celebration for the Carringtons, her mother's dreams for her daughters coming true. Hannah was deeply thankful—whether to God or Benjamin, she didn't know—that no one suspected the truth. Her husband had done his duty without fault. He had magnanimously smiled at her when she entered the room in her gown. He had recited his vows, placed a ring on her finger, and even brushed his lips on hers for a heartbeat, his touch so potent it shook her to her toes and threatened to make her believe the lie. He even said a few words about being a lucky man.

Only she could see through his ruse. His luck came in the form of dollars soon to be converted to pounds and deposited in his London bank account.

After the ceremony came refreshments and photographs of the newlyweds. The moment the photographer had exploded his last flashbulb, Hannah had darted upstairs. She had quickly changed out of the far-too-expensive Worth wedding gown her mother had commissioned on short notice. She now wore the red serge traveling suit she had donned for the Atlantic crossing which had brought her to Paris and this fateful day.

"You must write often, dear," her mother said upon releasing her from her embrace. "Lily and I will be visiting you very shortly for the height of the Season. The Countess of Sheffield—how thrilling!" She patted at the dampness that seemed determined to sparkle on her cheeks, mocking Hannah with a sentimentality that didn't belong. "I only wish more people had been able to attend, to see you in your gown. Wasn't she simply the loveliest thing?" she asked Benjamin.

"As fresh and lovely as the first day of spring," he said with a smile. Hannah resisted the urge to smirk at his performance.

"It will be so nice for you to have family among the nobility," Mrs. Digby said from behind her. "What an entrée into society that will provide! You will become part of the Four Hundred as soon as Mrs. Astor gets wind of this." The Four Hundred represented the cream of New York society, a number determined by how many guests fit comfortably in the Astors' ballroom.

"It was a beautiful ceremony, Hannah," Lily said, her face glowing from overly romantic and completely untrue notions. "He obviously adores you. And you looked just like a fairy-tale princess!"

Hannah accepted another hug from her sister,

whose ingenuous happiness made her sick with guilt. Though she and Lily were as different as night and day, she had never lied to her sister. Not about something so important. For years, they had been co-conspirators, usually with Lily covering up for Hannah's adventures. How she longed to tell her the truth! But she lacked the courage.

Indeed, this marriage was a coward's way out.

Her stomach had wound so tightly, pain lanced through her. She needed to end the goodbyes. She retreated to stand beside her new husband, who again bowed over her mother's hand. "It's been a pleasure, ma'am. You have my address—our address in London."

"Oh, yes."

Hannah could almost hear him mentally adding, *So you'll be sending the dowry forthwith.* In that instant, she hated her new husband, with a deep, abiding, wholly unreasonable passion.

"We must be off, darling," she said brightly, "or we'll miss the train."

"Very well. Goodbye, Mrs. Carrington, Miss Carrington. Mrs. Digby." Perfect gentleman that he was, Benjamin said his proper farewells, then helped her into the carriage. He joined her, and in another moment, the carriage jerked to a start.

Out of the corner of her eye, Hannah watched her new husband's reaction. For the first time since the scene in the parlor when she had announced her sudden engagement, they were alone.

He sagged back on the seat. He lowered his top hat, crossed his arms over his chest, and closed his eyes. He remained like that until they reached the station.

* * *

Benjamin didn't know what to think. He felt a strong desire to stare at his new wife. His unruly thoughts were pulling him in carnal directions even now, despite the fact he hardly knew the girl.

It seemed his body didn't care. For some reason, she had grown on him, igniting a fierce desire to possess her. The urge was wholly uncommon and entirely out of place. He compensated by focusing on the copy of the *London Times* which he had purchased in the Dover station.

Still, he couldn't help stealing glances at his bride, while she stared out the window at the passing English countryside. From her frown, he gathered she wasn't pleased with the rainy, overcast, dreary landscape. As twilight faded, her face became reflected more sharply in the train's window—a comely silhouette, strong and intelligent. Certainly he would not have proposed to the girl, no matter her wealth, if he didn't find her somewhat appealing to gaze upon—or take to his bed.

She glanced over and caught him staring. He nodded slightly, then returned his attention to his much safer and more predictable newspaper.

"You're content to read?" she asked, her sudden query startling him.

He studied her, noted the distress in her gaze and the challenge in her voice. "I enjoy keeping informed," he responded.

She threw up her hands. "That's it?"

"What's what?"

"You have nothing to say, no reaction to all that's happened?"

He sighed, wondering what fault she would find

with him. He was well used to females finding fault. "I believe it went well. Your family seemed delighted by our nuptials. They welcomed me most graciously." He looked back at his paper, hoping that would end the confrontation.

He was wrong. "Yes, they welcomed the Earl of Sheffield into the bosom of the family with open arms," she said, irritation edging her voice.

Giving up, he folded his newspaper and parked it on his lap, his hands crossed upon it. "I take it you're not pleased, but I confess I am unable to fathom why. Did I not fulfill my end of our agreement? Did my performance not serve?"

She stared at him for a long, painful heartbeat. Benjamin braced himself for a litany of complaints.

Her expression softened. "Were you ever, even for one moment, thinking about something other than my dowry?"

Benjamin had the distinct feeling she was asking something else entirely, but he couldn't decipher what. Women were such strange, illogical creatures! "You do not know my mind, miss—"

"*Mrs.* We were married, 'til death do us part." She sagged back on the velvet-covered bench, her gaze turning to the nearly dark window. "Linked for the rest of our lives."

Dread filled Benjamin. My God, the girl was regretting marrying him, even after so short a time, not even a full day! He fought down a feeling of utter vulnerability. He should never have allowed his heart to soften, his thoughts to stray, imagining the possibility that she might grow fond of him. Foolish idea. He crossed his arms, kept his body stiff. "As you say."

"Doesn't the sheer weight of what we've done affect you at all?"

He turned away. "This new married state will take getting used to, for both of us. We'd be foolish to think otherwise."

"Yes, but you're certainly calm about it. So unflappable. Are you always so in control?"

Being in control was not at all how he felt around this woman. *His bride.* He hesitated for a moment, wondering if he should take her hand, so small in its lacy white glove. He started to reach for it, then pulled his hand back. The distance between them was too great to comfortably reach her.

"What do you expect from me, Hannah?"

He had never used her given name until now, and it filled him with a strange sense of intimacy and warmth. He sensed she felt it, too, for her entire posture softened.

"I . . . I don't know," she said, abashed.

"These circumstances are not ideal. I concede that. But clearly it's in our mutual interests to make the best of the situation."

"Stated very logically." She turned her gaze once more to the window. Several minutes ticked by. He watched the English countryside disappear, mile after mile, taking them toward London and their new life together. In less than an hour, they would pull into Charring Cross Station and, shortly after that, arrive home. He was bringing home a bride. He had every right to expect what naturally followed from their union. Every right to take her to his bed.

His gaze flicked over her slender form, contemplating the figure beneath the ruffles and corsets. When she had appeared in her elegant wedding dress, his smile had not been feigned. She was lovely, as reedlike and graceful as a goddess. He had decided right then he had made the right decision, but to his dismay, her answering smile had seemed forced. Nothing she had done or said had given him any reason to think she found him appealing as a man. When he had kissed her, in contrast to the surprising pleasure he had felt, she had shivered with distaste at the familiarity. He was nothing to her but a means to an end, a title, a shield for her shame.

He, on the other hand, had begun to feel smitten like a schoolboy. He found it difficult not to stare rudely at her, even after she had changed into her cardinal traveling suit. As the miles rolled past beneath their private Pullman car, he imagined heady things, carnal activities which their private car would make possible. Closing the drapes on the narrow door, sliding beside her on the bench, unbuttoning each of the pearl buttons on her blouse until she lay revealed to his touch, small pants of excitement swelling her cleavage as he dropped his lips to taste her . . . .

Benjamin forced his attention back to the *Times*, trying to comprehend the stories and keep his mind—and body—in check. He had no idea whether this young lady wanted or expected such attentions from him. She was intelligent, well read. Certainly her mother had seemed down-to-earth, assuming her husband's role in discussing money which most women would find tasteless. Together, Mrs. Carrington and he had arranged transfer of Hannah's dowry—a shockingly large amount. Surely such a stalwart, no-nonsense woman had talked to Hannah about a wife's duty in the bedroom.

Duty. The word turned his stomach. He hated thinking of something potentially so pleasurable for them both as a duty.

The silence strung out between them while the minutes passed, taking them closer to nightfall—and bed. He had to know, before another second went by. Quietly sucking in a breath, he posed a question designed to keep from embarrassing her, yet reveal her expectations. "Hannah."

Arching her swanlike neck, she met his gaze.

Now or never. "Will you be wanting children anytime soon?"

She shrugged, as if she hadn't given it a second thought and wasn't inclined to now. "It would be best if I first became used to the idea of being a wife." She turned back to the window.

Sitting stiff and silent, Benjamin tried to absorb her easy dismissal with a grace he didn't feel. He would never have expected her rejection to hurt so deeply.

Her message was perfectly clear. She had no interest in marital relations. He was enough of a gentleman not to force the issue and had adequate pride not to demand something she was unwilling to provide. This, then, was where it would stand.

"Understood," he said, concentrating on making his reply sound neutral of any feeling. "I would appreciate it if you would let me know if circumstances change."

She nodded, seemingly distracted by the passing train lights in the night.

CHAPTER 7

Children? Hannah chewed her lip, stunned beyond speech. How could she possibly think about children at a time like this? She had said her vows only this morning! Certainly, he was an earl and would want to carry on the family line. But to talk about starting a family when they had only just become a couple!

Furtively she twisted and tugged at her wedding band, pulling it partly off only to shove it back on. She could hardly picture herself as a wife, much less a mother.

The man had no understanding of what a monumental change marriage was for her. *He* was going home, to his own house, to be surrounded by all that was familiar. She was in a foreign country, moving in with people she had never seen before, to be tended by servants whose names and personalities she knew nothing of.

When their train pulled into Charring Cross, Benjamin's carriage was there to meet them. Hannah stayed beside the porter, who pushed a cart filled with their bags, while Benjamin's hurried pace threatened to leave them both behind.

When he arrived at the side of his own carriage, his driver jumped down to greet him.

"Milord, good to have ye back, right enou'."

The driver bowed from the waist no less than three times, clutching a top hat with a dented crown. His worn attire matched the run-down carriage hitched to a team of horses clearly past their prime, the harnesses cracked, the rigging rusted. The door bore a once-elaborate crest, the paint now faded and chipped.

"Your presence was sore missed, milord," Chauncy continued in his thick cockney brogue. "Mighty sore. Lady Georgina got herself in a right huff, if you don't mind my saying. Scared the missus into letting her stay put. It was decided you should handle the *sit-eeashun* when you returned."

"Is that so?" Benjamin patted Chauncy's shoulder. "You needn't concern yourself. It's a woman's job to handle the household. My wife—that's her area of expertise," he said with great assurance, then cast a smile in Hannah's direction.

Expertise? She hadn't even met the servants yet, or figured out who this Lady Georgina was!

The driver turned his attention to her. His eyes grew wide, and he smiled gamely, then bobbed in her direction. "M'lady."

"Hannah, this is Chauncy Pocket. He's been with our family for decades. His wife is the family housekeeper."

Chauncy adjusted his jacket hem. "The missus

told me to get this right." He cleared his throat and spoke stiffly. "Welcome to England, my lady Countess. We are here to serve you."

"That's a marvelous speech. Thank you so much." Her praise made the little man blush. He rushed to open the carriage door and help her up.

As she waited for Benjamin to join her, Hannah mulled over the title the driver had used to address her. *Countess.* How poorly the word fit her! She had always pictured a countess as a confident woman draped in an ermine robe dispensing orders to her vassals, not a girl barely one year out of the schoolroom.

Benjamin leaped easily into the carriage and settled his tall frame on the worn bench across from her. The carriage began negotiating the busy London streets. Soon she would be meeting a houseful of servants, all of whom would expect her to be able to manage Benjamin's domestic affairs. True, she had been reared for the task. But in practical fact, her astonishingly capable mother had spent more time lecturing her and her sisters than allowing them to try their hands themselves. As a result, Hannah had precious little experience managing anything, much less conflicts between people. How difficult was this Lady Georgina?

"I sent a telegram yesterday from Paris informing the household of our wedding," Benjamin said.

"Including Lady Georgina?" she asked.

"Yes, of course."

"And . . ." He missed her hint to explain, so she asked right out, "Who *is* Lady Georgina?"

"Did I not say? Quite sorry. Georgina is my sister."

"You have a sister?" The hope only a lonely,

homesick woman could feel blossomed in her chest. "Is she younger than you?"

"Yes, by a few years."

That had to mean Georgina was not far from her own age. Maybe, if she wasn't too difficult after all, they could be friends. She hoped so. No one could replace the comfortable, loving company of her mother and sisters, of course. But having a new sister to talk with, to confide in, could certainly help fill the void.

"I admit having you here is a blessing," Benjamin said, startling her. His eyes sparkled in the dim carriage, and Hannah suddenly remembered this was her wedding night.

Any romantic notion his comment spurred vanished when he continued, "Georgina finds managing the household a difficult task. With the Season under way, she's exhausted herself trying to respond to the various invitations and obligations. It doesn't do me or my work well to be perceived as a hermit, yet I like to make the most profitable use of time spent socializing, spending only the necessary hours at the task."

That was how he looked on parties, as a dreaded chore? While she didn't care for stuffy gatherings, the company of friends could be delightful. Perhaps things were different in England.

"You may not realize it, but women possess a secret power," he continued.

She arched an eyebrow. "To answer invitations?"

"To influence men," he said grimly. Hannah got the distinct impression he wouldn't allow *her* to be influencing *him.* "One whisper from a woman in her husband's ear about the eccentric, unfriendly Lord Sheffield, and my support vanishes."

"I take it this has happened to you before?"

"Aye, but with you managing my affairs, I have faith it shan't happen again."

So that was her role, Hannah thought, mulling it over. Social secretary. Certainly, if she applied herself, she could learn to recommend which affairs Benjamin would be wise to attend and which he could pass by. How hard could that be?

The carriage turned from the main thoroughfare onto a quiet residential street lined with grand houses. Gaslights burned before each home's walkway, revealing little in the misty night.

The carriage pulled up before a mansion, neither the largest nor smallest on the street. Hannah gathered only a few impressions as she followed Benjamin to the door—dark stone, few windows lighted, and a tree branch stretching so low over the path she had to duck. She tripped on a loose cobblestone and clutched Benjamin's arm. He steadied her, then led her up the steps and opened the door.

That was when Hannah began to understand just how desperately Benjamin needed her money.

Like a grand lady in her twilight years, the house had clearly seen better days. The once lovely home showed signs of serious neglect, from the obvious—threadbare carpets and worn furniture—to the subtle—a chandelier coated with dust and a slightly musty tang in the air. Money hadn't paid for new furnishings or the help to keep the house maintained.

The truth stared her in the face. Benjamin had been without adequate funds for years. Odd that he had waited for happenstance to thrust an heiress in his arms instead of pursuing one, as so many impoverished lords did. Hannah didn't know quite what to make of that.

She began removing her hat and coat, and Chauncy rushed forward to take them from her. Apparently he doubled as the household butler. He quickly assembled the servants in the parlor—all four of them—and made the introductions. His wife, whom even Chauncy called Mrs. Pocket, served as the housekeeper. Redheaded Maggie, who looked perhaps thirteen, served as the only maid for both the upstairs and downstairs. And Frick, the handyman, cared for the horses *and* the garden, with the help of the Pockets' eight-year-old son, now abed.

"That's it?" she whispered to Benjamin. "Your full staff?" Her own family home in New York employed no less than fifty servants.

"Well, yes," he said, looking a little discomfited. Hannah's heart lightened considerably. Suddenly, the prospect of managing the household seemed like a walk in the park. How difficult could it possibly be? And in her free time, she could study science to her heart's content, perhaps even calling on Benjamin for help. Perhaps even helping him with his experiments.

With a new lightness, she took his arm, a show of intimacy that startled a smile from her new husband. "Your home is lovely. I believe I shall be quite happy here."

He covered her hand with his own and gazed down at her. Her skin prickled with sharp awareness of him as a man. Did he now plan to take her upstairs?

He did, but not for the reason she expected.
"Come. There's someone special I want you to
meet." She followed him up the winding staircase
to the second level, then down the hall to the first
of two sets of double doors.

He rapped gently on a finely carved mahogany
panel. "Georgina, it's me."

"Come in."

Slowly he opened the door, ushering Hannah to
follow. She did, and found herself in a dim room
that smelled of camphor and mothballs. A candle
guttered in the breeze from the doorway, threatening to cast the room's lone occupant in darkness.
The woman in the bed was dwarfed by the huge
bed, her slender form almost lost amidst the
feather mattress and comforter. Hannah found it
hard to believe she was younger than Benjamin,
who was just past thirty. Her complexion appeared
sallow, and dark rings accentuated her deep-set
brown eyes. Benjamin had neglected to mention
his sister was an invalid. Hannah was quickly learning that Benjamin forgot to clue her in on a lot
of things.

He pulled her to stand beside him. "Georgina,
meet Hannah, my bride."

Georgina narrowed her eyes at Hannah. "So,
she's American." It wasn't a compliment.

"I certainly am, yes," Hannah responded defi-
antly.

"Well," Georgina said, toying with a delicate lace
handkerchief. "She may not understand this,
seeing as she comes from a country with precious
little history. But she must be made to understand,
Benjamin, about this home. About our family
name. This house has been in the Ramsey family

for hundreds of years and must be properly cared for, with a loving hand."

Hannah's gaze met Benjamin's, and she knew they were both onto Georgina's lie. The house couldn't be more than fifty years old. And it certainly *hadn't* been cared for, in Hannah's opinion.

"You're thinking of the country estate, Georgy," Benjamin said mildly. He commented to Hannah, "Father lost the traditional family seat when Georgy and I were children."

Georgina waved her handkerchief. "The point is, how is this girl suited to care for our only remaining home, Benjamin? How can she possibly be prepared? This is no schoolgirls' exercise."

Hannah bowed her head, hoping to make peace with Georgina, if not have the irascible woman as a friend. "I'll do my best, ma'am."

"My lady."

"Excuse me?"

"My title is lady."

"Georgina," Benjamin cut in. "Surely you don't expect my bride—the countess—to address you as a servant would! It's not seemly. I say you call each other by your Christian names. Hannah, Georgina." He nodded to each of them in turn.

"I would like that," Hannah responded, gamely giving her sister-in-law a friendly smile. "After all, you're now my sister."

Georgina continued to direct her comments to her brother. "If you insist, Benjamin," she said, a huge sigh issuing from her. She began toying with her handkerchief again, twisting it around her fingers. "You know I can deny you nothing."

"Excellent!" Benjamin clasped his hands and rubbed them together. "Now to dinner. I'm fam-

ished. Will you be joining us?" He seemed to think
he had achieved a great victory, Hannah thought
ruefully. And his sister hadn't even spoken directly
to his new bride!

Georgina pursed her lips, appearing as petulant
as a child. "Usually you take supper up here, with
me."

"Yes, well, I think it's more practical now to use
the dining room. I'll help you down." He headed
for the side of her bed.

"No," Georgina demanded. "Truly, leave me.
I'm not hungry anyway."

Benjamin sighed, and Hannah had the impression he was quite used to putting up with his sister's
volcanic moods. "Very well. Hannah?" He headed
for the door and opened it. Hannah left the room
first, thinking he would follow. Instead, he closed
the door behind her, shutting her out.

The heavy door didn't completely latch, and
Hannah heard Georgina's voice, much more force-
ful than when she had been in the room. "You
wrote that she was pretty. She's as angular as a
poorly bred horse!"

"Your opinion of her looks is immaterial, Georgina," Benjamin replied stiffly. Hannah realized
she was eavesdropping, but the two were discussing
her behind her back, which was equally rude. She
remained there, listening. This was the second time
Benjamin had referred to her as pretty, and she
reveled in it.

"I admit she is young. *That's* quite apparent,"
Georgina continued. "But she's so thin! Are you
sure she's even healthy?"

Benjamin's tone turned placating. "Georgina,
listen. Hannah is well read, accomplished for a

girl her age. She'll be able to lift the burden of managing this place from your shoulders. I'm quite lucky she agreed to be my bride. I could have spent years searching for a wife and not done nearly as well. I wish, Georgy, you would be happy for me, at least a little.''

Happy? Was he happy for himself? Did he truly feel that way about her, or was he merely trying to convince his sister?

A moment later, Benjamin opened the door and slipped out, this time latching it behind him.

He turned to face her, and Hannah knew by his guilty look that he was well aware she had heard the conversation.

"You shouldn't have lied to your sister about me," she said coolly.

"I didn't lie," he said. "I did, perhaps, commit sins of omission, which is more than I can say for how we dealt with your family."

She stiffened. "Is that a rebuke?"

"Take it any way you wish."

"I would find it easier to take things if I was informed of the situation beforehand. You didn't tell me your sister was an invalid."

"That is up for debate," he said cryptically.

"What is her condition?"

"It is none of your concern."

"I live here! She's now my sister, too. What are her symptoms?"

He smirked. "So, not only are you a scientist, you're a doctor, too?"

She glared at him until his expression sobered, his voice softened. "A weakened constitution brought about by a heavy emotional blow. That is all you need to know."

Heavy emotional blow? What did that mean? Hannah longed to ask, but held her tongue.

"More relevant at this juncture is the fact the suite Georgina is now occupying, and which she apparently refuses to vacate, is intended for the countess. Since our mother's death, my sister, Georgina, has been using it." He sighed and rubbed a hand over his face. "Of course, I'll insist she move to another chamber so that you may have it."

The suggestion appalled Hannah. "You want to expel her from her room? I can't let you do that. I wouldn't want to put anyone out, much less your sister if she's been ill."

"She can be ill in another room, Hannah."

His cold words shocked Hannah. What kind of man had she married? "How crass! How could you be so heartless?"

His expression darkened. "Think what you will of me. You are not the first. But you are damned naïve."

"I'm not naïve. I know exactly what's going on."

"You do?" He took a step closer, which brought him almost against her, trapping her between his strong body and the wall.

"Yes," she said, her voice quavering. "This house is huge. I'm sure there are other rooms as lovely."

He gazed down at her, his dark eyes reflecting twin flames from the wall sconces. His face had taken on a strange cast, more emotional than Hannah had ever seen. But what emotion? Anger? Frustration? She felt his touch on her arms before she saw his hands move. His fingers grazed her sleeves, traveling from her forearms, past her suddenly sensitive inner elbows, up to her shoulders. One of his fingers traced the edge of her blouse, making her skin tingle. She felt herself swaying toward him, longing for something she couldn't name, something more . . . .

His voice sounded so deep, so intimate, her stomach flipped. "So, you truly want it that way, Countess?"

"I—" Hannah fought for a reply. What had they been discussing? What way? His mere presence, his undivided attention, scattered her thoughts, and she failed to focus on anything logical, anything beyond his surprisingly attractive presence. The man was weaving a spell around her, and it both terrified and exhilarated her.

Desperate to shake the spell and reclaim her reason, she stepped sideways, away from him. Instantly he dropped his hands. He pulled back, again returning to his stoic self as if nothing had occurred between them. "Mrs. Pocket can find you a guest room, then," he said, as if it were of little import after all. "It's been a very long day, and I'm going to bed. I suggest you do the same."

Guest. She wasn't a guest; she was his wife, the mistress of this house.

Like a bucket of cold water, the import of the room arrangements struck her. She reached out to stay him, but he was already beyond her reach, heading through Georgina's room to a connecting door within. Connecting to the next-door suite, no doubt. *His* suite.

Oh, what a little fool she could be! Naturally he would expect her to want the room next to his. They were man and wife! He must now think she was turning a cold shoulder to him, that she did not want to consummate their marriage. The thought distressed her more than she would have imagined possible.

She didn't feel comfortable with the thought of such intimacy this first night. Of course not. She hardly knew him. Yet she did not want her marriage to be a complete and utter failure. True, it had started off under terrible conditions. But she had just made the situation between them worse.

CHAPTER 8

Hannah awoke disoriented, in a darkened room. Not her own bed . . . Mrs. Digby's? No. Her eyelids shot open. She lay in a guest bed in the green room, one of many unused rooms in her new husband's home. Her husband . . . what a strange concept. Her stranger, more like it.

Where was he? Was he cooling his heels in the breakfast room, waiting for her to rise? Was he still abed, alone in his huge suite? Was he thinking about her at all?

Climbing out of bed, she tugged the bellpull, but Maggie failed to appear. Hannah didn't hold it against her. With such a limited staff, who knew what errand Maggie was running?

Hannah's shipping trunk had been delivered to this room the night before, after she had told Mrs. Pocket she would be sleeping here for the foresee-able future. She grimaced, recalling the judgemental look on the woman's face. *It's none of their business,* she assured herself, splashing tepid water on her face from the washbasin.

Struggling to reach behind and tighten her corset laces, Hannah vowed to hire herself a personal maid as soon as she could. Back home, she had shared Teresa with her sister Lily. Much as Hannah would love a familiar face, she didn't want to uproot the young woman from America and drag her to this dreary country, far from her relatives and those who knew her. Teresa would be serving Hannah's younger sisters as they left their governess's protection and came of age, so the maid had no fear of being without employment in the coming years.

Attempting to fix her hair, Hannah found herself staring at her reflection in the dressing table mirror. Why had her new husband referred to her as pretty, twice now? Her skin was smooth, her eyes somewhat large, but beyond that, she offered little appeal to men who desired the small-mouthed, pert look currently in vogue.

Yet last evening, there had been a power ... a heat ... *something* between them. Something new and exciting. And she had made the supremely foolish mistake of moving into this dusty guest room as if she preferred it.

Did she? The thought of being physically intimate with Benjamin terrified her. Not because of the act itself, which she could scarcely visualize, but because of the strange power he seemed to wield over her. When he had touched her, she feared her own unprecedented desire to melt into him and lose herself. Perhaps her fatigue had caused her intense emotional reaction to him.

She longed to get to know him better, to understand her unusual feelings. Tucking a last pin in her hair, she perused her reflection, then left the room to find him.

Unfortunately, she found herself alone in a quiet, lifeless house. In the daylight, it appeared even more drab and run-down than it had the previous eve. Despite the size of the rooms, Hannah felt a sense of claustrophobia, of deep sadness and loss, which aggravated her own loneliness.

Valiantly, she fought down her melancholy and focused on getting through the day in a calm, orderly fashion. Since her stomach was growling, she headed for the small breakfast room off the formal dining room. In her parents' house at this time of day, her sisters would be filling the air with gossip and giggles. The maids would already be turning out their rooms. When each of her sisters appeared for breakfast, her father would greet them with a smile and discuss the busy day's events.

And the sideboard would be laden with platters of ham and eggs and rolls, until all members of the family had been served.

This sideboard was empty. Hannah wondered if it had already been cleared, or if Benjamin didn't take breakfast in his own home. She stepped toward the door which no doubt led to the kitchen, but froze when she heard Maggie's barely decipherable cockney.

"She talks funny."

Hannah found herself smiling at that comment. Dishes clattered, and she pictured the young maid washing them.

"She's certainly sleeping well past the cock's call, I'll say," the housekeeper, Mrs. Pocket, supplied. "Has no respect for the way a proper household is run. And she slept in the green room, all by 'erself! On her wedding night! Have you ever 'eard the like?''

"Lady G said girls from America don't got no manners, that's what she says, right enou'. There's so many good English girls about. Why'd the lord marry *her*?" Her jealous tone made Hannah wonder whether Maggie was smitten with Benjamin herself.

"Why, bless you, child, it's as clear as the nose on your face," Mrs. Pocket continued. "She's in the chinks. Richer than Midas! We can finally hire a cook, and I can get out of this blasted kitchen.''

Burning with indignation, Hannah stepped back from the door. She was tired of eavesdropping, tired of being shut out and being made to feel an outsider in what was supposed to be her own home. She thought of her mother, of how she would react to such disrespect from her servants. She would never put up with it. Hannah realized that respect—though it seemed to come with a title— still had to be earned.

"Mrs. Pocket!" she called sharply.

The clattering stopped. After a long moment, the door swung open, and Mrs. Pocket entered the breakfast room. "Ma'am?"

"I would like breakfast, please."

Mrs. Pocket's eyes darted to the sideboard, then the floor. "It's past breakfast time, ma'am."

Ma'am? Hannah knew even Lady Georgina was afforded her proper title. "Please address me as milady," she said coolly. "And it's obviously not past *my* breakfast time, or I wouldn't be standing here asking for it, now would I?"

Mrs. Pocket shrugged. "It's just that it was so late,

and the master already departed for Parliament, and—"

"I don't usually sleep quite so late, Mrs. Pocket. Yesterday, I rose early, was married, then traveled from France, arriving here well past nightfall. I assure you I will be establishing a reasonable schedule and sticking to it. Now, please get me a plate of breakfast." Without waiting for a response, she turned to the table, pulled out a chair, and sat down.

"Yes, ma'am—milady," Mrs. Pocket said. Hannah heard the kitchen door close behind her.

A few minutes later, the servant returned with a plate of eggs, ham, and toast and set it before her. Hannah felt the plate and knew the food was barely warm. "Mrs. Pocket, please serve me a *freshly cooked* breakfast. A beverage would also be greatly appreciated." She leaned back, indicating the woman should take the food away. With a put-upon sigh, the housekeeper retrieved the plate.

More than ten minutes passed this time before a proper plate of breakfast was placed in front of her, along with tea and milk. As Mrs. Pocket turned toward the kitchen door once more, Hannah called out, "One more thing, Mrs. Pocket."

The housekeeper turned to face her.

"My *chinks* can easily buy the best help in the city, both cooks and housekeepers. Please keep that in mind."

"Yes, milady," Mrs. Pocket said, this time with more deference and a curtsey.

"Thank you. That will be all."

After Mrs. Pocket left her alone, Hannah sat silent, amazed at herself. Back home, her family servants were almost like family. She would never have spoken so sharply to them or issued threats. But she knew her mother would have done the same in similar circumstances. She had had no choice if she was to be mistress of this house.

Perhaps she could win the servants' respect by demanding it. Unfortunately, there was another lady of the house, one who had been here her entire life, whom the servants deferred to above her. A woman who clearly resented her presence in the house, and probably in Benjamin's life.

After breakfast, Hannah was at a loss as to what to do with herself. The house was as silent as a tomb. The clock above the parlor mantel had already chimed one in the afternoon, and nothing had been said to her about lunch being served. She wasn't hungry, having eaten only a few hours previously. But she had nothing else to do. She had already moved her dresses from the trunk to the armoire in her chamber—or rather, the guest room that now served as hers. Maggie had disappeared again, so no servant had been available to help her.

At this time of day, her mother would already have completed her correspondence, even paid a few calls, and be sitting down to lunch with her daughters. Later in the day, she would be paying more calls. But Hannah knew no one in London to call on, and no one had come by.

The correspondence, however . . . That was something she could help with. Trouble was, she had no idea where it was.

But Georgina knew. Hannah wandered the huge house for several minutes, looking for her sister-in-law. Georgina's chamber door hung askew, and she wasn't in her bed. That relieved Hannah, knowing Georgina wasn't completely bed-bound.

In the morning room, Hannah noticed a woolen blanket tossed carelessly over a plush, plum-colored settee, as if someone had recently been reclining there. An uncapped bottle and spoon rested on a table nearby. Hannah lifted the bottle and took a sniff. It smelled suspiciously like laudanum. Was Georgina imbibing enough to become addicted to the potent painkiller? Deep in thought, Hannah replaced the bottle.

"Interested in my medicine?" Georgina stood in the archway, giving Hannah the coldest look she had ever received. She wore a wrap with a faded print even though it was midday and the servants might be about. Her dark blond hair, while put up, had not been styled carefully. Hannah also noticed that her impression of a weak woman from the night before had been a trick of the light, for Georgina, while thin, stood ramrod straight and appeared a force to be reckoned with.

Hannah squared her shoulders. "I've been looking for you," she said boldly.

"Me? Whatever for? My purpose is not to entertain you." She crossed to a roll-top desk in the corner of the room, and Hannah realized she was carrying a handful of what appeared to be correspondence and cards. She set them on the desk, atop a stack already there. Turning, she breezed past Hannah.

"Is that Benjamin's correspondence?" Hannah said quickly. "He asked me to help with that."

Georgina paused and gave her a cool appraisal. "Did he, now?"

"Do you usually handle it? That is, you must, I

know. Benjamin had no complaints, of course," she lied, trying hard to be conciliatory and knowing Georgina could see right through her. "He merely thought it would give me something to do."

Georgina's stare didn't warm one iota. Still, she scooped up a handful of cards and letters and held them out to Hannah—just far enough away to make Hannah come to her to retrieve them. Hannah bit down her pride, stepped forward, and grasped the letters. Georgina didn't let go. "You won't have the slightest clue what to do with the invitations, so why are you wasting both our time even looking at them?"

Hannah gave a gentle tug, and Georgina released the stack. Glancing through the cards, Hannah began to get a sinking feeling Georgina was right. She had no idea who these people were, whether they were Benjamin's friends or business acquaintances, whether Baron Heartscomb's invitation should be accepted or politely declined. She knew nothing of London society. Georgina reached for the letters again, but Hannah stepped back, pressing the cards to her chest. "Benjamin said it's important he attend a few functions, but from the dust on some of these cards, I can see they haven't been replied to one way or the other. Some of these invitations are six months old, the event long past."

"My brother has no interest in society. Are you so ignorant of your own husband's interests you don't realize that? Did you really believe you were marrying into high society? You, with your foolish notions of balls and parties and gaiety, when he couldn't care less about such things?"

Hannah burst out with a humorless laugh. "You

obviously have very fixed ideas about me, but I assure you—"

"Getting better acquainted?"

Benjamin's voice wiped the scowl from Georgina's face, replacing it with an indulgent smile. "Hello, Benjamin. Back from that dreary Parliament filled with pompous old men droning on and on?"

Benjamin chuckled. "Yes, and not soon enough. So much important work to do here." Benjamin leaned his cane against the chair and tossed his derby on a table. "Dreadfully dull discussion today, too, one to which I was able to contribute absolutely nothing."

"What was it, dear?" Georgina said, at the same time Hannah asked, "About what?" How awkward! As if he had two wives with whom to share his daily concerns.

Benjamin didn't seem to notice the uncomfortable situation. "Something to do with the tax rate brewers should be charged to sell their wares at public functions." He looked from Hannah to Georgina, a small smile on his face. His gaze returned to Hannah and settled there, his eyes brightening a notch. Hannah found herself staring back at him, entranced. Thoughts of their previous brush with intimacy made her skin tingle, and she imagined touching him again, having him touch her.

"Excuse me," he muttered, his gaze darting away to land anywhere but on her. "Unforgivably rude to stare. Not used to seeing you in my home, I suppose." He seemed bewildered.

"That's quite all right," Hannah said, her voice unnaturally breathless.

Georgina's voice cut into her thoughts, destroying the intimacy between them before it could even begin to flourish. "Your new bride seems to misunderstand her role."

Benjamin arched a brow. "Her role?"

"She is reluctant to admit her shortcomings when it comes to understanding London society and how to handle your social demands. She believes she will know how to answer your correspondence, when I am certain she doesn't know a single person's name on those cards." She nodded toward the pile of invitations Hannah held.

Hannah rapidly flipped through them again. "That's not exactly true. I have heard of most of these people, though, of course, I have never met them. Which reminds me, Benjamin. It's customary to send out a marriage announcement to your acquaintances, so that people realize you have taken a wife. With your permission . . ."

"Feel free. As long as you're willing to entertain the curious hoards when they come calling to inspect you."

That hardly sounded pleasant. Did he expect her to meet them without him there to introduce her? "Perhaps if you were by my side—"

"I'm behind schedule as it is. I cannot waste my time in hours of idle chitchat."

Hannah's spirits deflated at his complete lack of interest in introducing her to his acquaintances. "Maybe later, then," she said, feeling Georgina's triumph from across the room. "Still, these invitations can't be ignored."

"Georgina, you did show her the address book, didn't you?" Stepping to the desk, he retrieved the leather-bound book from its slot. He turned to his

sister. "I know you hate doing my correspondence.
I imagine you're quite thrilled by the prospect of
giving up the 'odious task' as you call it, now that
Hannah's here." He gave Hannah the book and
walked out of the room.

Georgina pursed her lips. Benjamin didn't see.
He was already gone. Hannah turned to follow
him, desperate to have just a moment alone with
this man she was only beginning to know. His long-
legged stride carried him quickly down a back corridor she hadn't yet explored.

Clutching her skirts and the letters, she hurried
after him. She caught up with him as he was
unlocking a narrow wooden door. "Benjamin."

He glanced up, but continued his well-practiced
movements, swinging open the door to reveal a
narrow staircase leading down. "Yes, Hannah?"

"I . . . I . . ."

He released the doorknob and crossed his arms.
"Yes?" He sounded slightly impatient.

Hannah glanced at the correspondence in her
hand, then back at him—and the staircase. Her
brow furrowed. "Where on earth are you going?"

"My laboratory." He said la*bor*atory, instead of
*lab*oratory, as Americans did. Hannah recalled the
Englishwoman Mary Shelley and her novel *Franken-
stein,* with its spine-chilling portrayal of scientific
experiments. What sort of experiments was Benjamin up to? What mysteries of the universe did he
strive to unlock? She longed to know. "May I see?"

"Perhaps another time." He began to turn away.

"But surely I could assist you. You know I'm
interested in your work."

He gazed down at her, and Hannah felt an echo
of the spell he had cast over her on their wedding

night. Too soon, he looked away and shook his head. "That is not a good idea."

"But I'll do whatever you need done. I'm capable, truly. I will do whatever you would like me to do, whatever you ask of me."

His lips quirked up at one corner in a remarkably charming way. "You're far too willing for your own good. You are hardly my servant, Hannah. You're the lady of this house, and you have your correspondence to tend to, among other household matters, I'm sure."

He looked overhead, toward a water-stained crack in the plaster ceiling. "Now that we have the funds, feel free to make improvements on this house. As you have no doubt noticed, it is in need of a few repairs." He chuckled. "Every morning when I wake, I'm amazed to find the roof hasn't caved in around me."

His wry humor caught her off guard. Yet she couldn't deny the truth of his words. Even if household management didn't intrigue her nearly as much as science, she would gain some satisfaction in upgrading the home's amenities. And, though she was confused, he seemed to believe the correspondence wasn't beyond her ken. Perhaps if she showed she had the household well in hand, he would allow her access to his laboratory. "Benjamin, about the correspondence—"

"What is it, Hannah?"

"Georgina is right. I don't know which invitations to accept, which ones to decline. Who you want to socialize with, and who you don't."

"I have every faith that a girl of your breeding will figure it out. Now, if you'll excuse me . . ." He slipped through the door and closed it behind him.

Hannah could hear him pounding down the steps as if anxious to get away from her.

"M'lady." Maggie's squeaky voice interrupted Hannah's reading. She had been poring over the newspaper and Benjamin's address book, gleaning clues about who was who, who mattered, who didn't, who might make good social connections for an up-and-coming scientist. She looked up from the morning room desk, a spot she had commandeered despite Georgina's protests. Since their confrontation several days ago, Georgina had stopped using the room to lounge in, and Hannah had rarely seen her. She had actually answered a few invitations, declining politely, saying that she and Benjamin would soon be making calls.

She hoped that was true. She hadn't seen Benjamin for days, not long enough to ask him. He had been either at Parliament, at his gentleman's club downtown, or in his basement lab with the door locked. Hannah was starting to grow quite irritated with the man. Did it not occur to him that she would want his company, at least for a few moments a day? Did it not occur to him that she had no friends, no family, no one? That his sister despised her? That the servants resented her? That he was *it*?

Whenever she thought of how he had unceremoniously dumped her in his home and ignored her, like a piece of furniture he had purchased, she flushed with anger. She deserved better, much better. She was intelligent, a good conversationalist, a well-bred lady. She was even starting to believe she could serve the functions of hostess, for she

was managing these invitations well enough—
"M'lady," Maggie repeated, finally capturing her
full attention.

"Yes, Maggie?"

"The master would like to see you, in his study,
m'lady. As soon as you can."

"He would?" He hadn't forgotten about her. He
wanted to see her, in private. Feeling a smile start
to pull at her lips, she forced herself to remain
outwardly stoic. She couldn't appear eager to see
her own husband, not in front of this girl. They
might suspect the truth—that she was that most
pitiable of objects, the neglected wife.

"Thank you, Maggie." Slowly, trying to appear
stately, she rose and smoothed the skirt of her light
blue day dress. She caught her hand on its way
up to pat her chignon. Maggie curtseyed before
leaving.

Alone, Hannah collapsed back against the desk,
grasping its edge for support. What did Benjamin
want? She had to prepare herself, not only for
whatever he might want to discuss, but for her
emotional reaction to him which, despite seeing
him so rarely, she knew had not diminished, but
grown in strength.

Straightening, she made certain her bustle was
aligned, her skirts smooth, her hair in place, her
emotions under tight rein. Then, with slow, regal
steps, she walked toward the study.

CHAPTER 9

"Did you want to see me?"

Despite having sent for her, at the sound of her voice, Benjamin froze. Carefully, he returned his fountain pen to its well and clasped his hands on his desk blotter. Only then did he lift his eyes to where she stood in the doorway of his study. "Yes, Hannah, I did."

Instead of disconcerting him with her gaze as he had feared, she wasn't even looking at him. She was studying his collection of ballooning memorabilia that he had collected over the years and displayed in this room.

She ran her delicate finger over a gold balloon-shaped clock on a shelf. "What a curious shape for a clock! How clever. Wherever did you find it?"

"Switzerland, actually. Hannah, thank you for coming." When she still didn't face him, irritation niggled at his patience. He never thought he would be jealous of his memorabilia.

"And this!" She lifted a crystal paperweight shaped like a balloon. "There's even writing on it."

"Yes, there is."

She read, "'In commemoration of the Montgolfier flight of June 5, 1767.' Hmm." She set the paperweight down and looked at a framed advertisement from the London Country Fair showing a lozenge-shaped balloon with wings and a long, narrow basket beneath. "It must be wonderful to devote your energies to a single pursuit. I could never figure out which field of study I loved the most, so my collections were rather eclectic. Of course, I know a man like you would consider them nothing more than girlhood passions."

A man like you . . . passions . . . She had no idea of his passions, or she would no doubt be running from the room in terror. "Hannah, please," he said, but his voice came out alarmingly choked. An almost overwhelming desire began to overtake him, to rise from his chair, cross the carpet, and enfold her in his arms, her own reticence be damned. *Seduce her, you idiot,* his carnal side demanded.

No. He was not ruled by his passions. He never would be. He was a thinker and intellect above all. Certainly he enjoyed the act, with women who made it their business to provide it. But to take a virginal maiden who clearly felt uncomfortable around him . . . He wouldn't stoop so low.

Instead, he suffered in silence.

She moved to a picture hanging on the wall of two dapper young men posing with an inflated and tethered balloon. The words "Suffolk 1884" were printed along the bottom. The photograph had been taken what seemed ages ago, in another, more carefree, lifetime. He and Peter, flush with anticipation over their first big adventure, had been two reckless young gentlemen about to make a high-altitude ascent, the highest two men had ever traveled. The photographer had perfectly captured their pride in their balloon and their project. And their lack of care for their own safety. Every time Benjamin looked at it, his heart ached, but he couldn't bring himself to take it down. Every time he came in here, it reminded him why he worked as hard as he did.

"This is a picture of you!" Hannah stared at it as if it held the secrets of the universe. "The balloon behind you—it's enormous! I've never seen one that size. The New York State Fair had much smaller ones. Who is this gentleman standing beside you?"

"Peter Faraday, a colleague." He had no intention of discussing Peter with her. As it was, he could barely manage his emotions when it came to Peter. But to actually give voice to them? He might never regain his composure, or his self-respect, if he allowed himself to break down, which he surely would do.

Thankfully, she concentrated on a less emotional question. "That isn't a hot-air balloon behind you, is it?"

"No, it was filled with hydrogen."

"Why do you fly that kind of balloon?" She turned to face him.

She actually found his work interesting. He tried to ignore the thrill this gave him. He explained,

"Hydrogen balloons achieve much better lift since the gas is lighter than air. And one needn't be burdened with the weight of combustible fuel."

"But how do you return to earth?"

Hannah asked better questions than the university students he had lectured. She most definitely had a sharp mind—and a lovely body. His gaze danced over her slender form. She was like a breath of fresh spring air in this stuffy room filled with dark memories.

"Benjamin?"

He struggled to remember her question. "Yes. Returning to earth. When you're ready to descend, you merely open a valve that releases the gas."

"That sounds simple enough."

"And pray you don't land in a farmer's pig sty." He smiled wryly, and she laughed. The sound sent a delicious tingle along his spine.

She moved from the photograph to a mobile, which hung from the ceiling. A half dozen painted wooden hot-air balloons bobbed among sterling-silver clouds. "This mobile is adorable."

"Georgina gave it to me for Christmas one year. Before . . ." *Before the accident.* Before she had made him remove all evidence of his high-altitude studies from the other rooms of the house.

"Oh." Hannah seemed to stiffen, then moved to a bookshelf and began perusing the titles. Benjamin watched her, intrigued by her interest in his books. Or was she merely avoiding him?

For the life of him, he could not figure her out. Who could understand the mind of an American woman? What was she truly feeling, about being here, being his wife? She told him nothing of her feelings, and he could not hazard a guess.

For certain, he enjoyed looking at her far too much. She was the worst distraction. Even now, simply standing there, he found his gaze sliding along her graceful form. Her back was slim, and no doubt her legs were long and shapely under that gown, beneath that bustle which hinted at her true feminine form in a tantalizingly seductive way. Wisps of hair curled at her nape below her tidy chignon. Today, only a few strands escaped, lending a softness to her angular face.

It had been so long since he had been in the company of a lady, a woman who truly cared about her appearance, about the finer things. A lady who understood society and could navigate her way through it, helping to guide him. Georgina had long ago stopped caring, stopped assisting him.

Even Hannah's earlobes, of all things, drew his eye. He could not recall noticing a woman's earlobes before, but these ... creamy soft, perfect, uncluttered by brassy rings such as the girls at Madame Hornbecker's wore. He imagined pressing his lips to them, running the tip of his tongue along their curved edges, nibbling gently, yet firmly enough to draw a sigh from her ....

A rash of heat shocked his system. He tore his gaze from Hannah. A proper gentleman wouldn't be thinking of a lady in such terms, but he was far too weak to stop himself.

While he had been daydreaming, she had turned around and was looking straight at him. Benjamin felt suddenly naked, his emotions, his *lust,* no doubt written on his face. He tried to wipe all evidence of his thoughts from his expression and ended up resorting to a frown.

Hannah frowned, too. "You're planning to break

the altitude barrier, aren't you? To fly higher than anyone before you?" Hannah asked.

He shifted uncomfortably in his leather chair. He hadn't told her as much, but she had figured out his plan. "The instruments are what matters, not the presence of a man on the flight."

"Poppycock! If Columbus felt that way, he would never have discovered the New World. I would love to help, Benjamin, if you'd let me. It's so exciting! When will you show me your laboratory?" She began to study his bookshelf.

"Later, Hannah. Perhaps it would be best to wait until . . ." He could hardly tell her what he was thinking, what he feared. For until she willingly invited him into her bed, the fire he felt for her could be a dangerous distraction in the close quarters of his basement laboratory. Afterward, however, when he could sweep her into his arms and take her to bed any time he chose, her nearness would no longer cause such a volcanic reaction within him. Simply put, once he had free access to her slim, lithe body, he would quit feeling this blasted uneasy longing and could think clearly. Then, why didn't he act now to resolve things?

Coward. The accusation stung him, but he believed its veracity as much as he believed he drew breath.

He cleared his throat, praying his voice wouldn't sound as unsteady as he felt. "Hannah, if you would give me your attention, I called you in here to do more than admire my ballooning memorabilia."

"Yes, I'm listening," she murmured, her voice husky. Would she sound as voluptuous beside him in bed? Damn, he had to get this interview over with, so he could again focus on his work.

"Very well, if I must speak to your back . . . I
would like you to arrange a small dinner party. Not
large, only ten guests."

"Me?" Slowly, she turned to face him, her
expression wide-eyed with what Benjamin could
only guess was anticipation.

"You are well suited to the task, of course. With
your skills and training, it will be a smashing success."

"Who—Who am I to invite to this party?"

"My colleagues from the London Society for Scientific Advancement. Here is a list." He held it
out to her. "It's time I introduce you to my colleagues, and it will give you a chance to contribute
your skills."

"Oh." Slowly, she stepped to his desk. Reaching
from as far away as possible, she took the list from
him. His heart clenched. Clearly she couldn't stand
to be near him. She avoided his gaze, looking
instead at the list. "When did you have in mind?
I suppose in a month or two, I—"

"Wednesday suits my schedule."

"Wednesday! That's only—"

"Three days from now, yes."

"That would hardly give your guests suitable
notice, Benjamin. It's so rushed!"

"An important vote is coming before the Society's board, and I want these particular colleagues
to realize I'm the man whose work they ought to
support."

"But—but you don't need their financial support, now that you've married me."

He nodded. "This is quite true." He loved that
blunt American way about her. She accepted why
he had married her and took no pains to paint

their relationship as anything other than a business arrangement. *Even though he had begun to long for more.* "While I admit I am excited about my new financial freedom, my next high-altitude ascent will be a waste if the Society's influential members don't accept my findings. Politically, I need them on my side."

"Politically. And you expect me to help you woo them, with my sterling social skills?"

She was smiling now, quite broadly. *You've given her a purpose, one she can pour her energies into.* Satisfied at his skillful management of his new wife, he smiled in response. "Quite right. Now, if you'll excuse me, I have work to do."

Hannah stood outside Benjamin's study and glared at the closed door, the guest list he had given her crumpled in her hand.

If Benjamin had seen how poorly she had managed her coming out the previous Season, he would be choking on his suggestion. He *ought* to be choking on his suggestion. He ought to be *choking*, period!

Damn the man! He treated her as if she were little more than hired help. Summoning her to his study, giving her an assignment as a headmaster would a schoolchild. Then sending her on her way with a pat on the head. Blast him!

The only saving grace was that he hadn't asked her to accompany him to a fancy ball. She dreaded such an event, but knew that day would come eventually. She prayed not for a long while.

In the meantime, she had to draw on her untried hostessing skills and arrange a dinner party for a

group of complete strangers—and stuffy English lords and ladies, to boot!

There was no help for it. She would have to arrange this dinner party and do her best at it, too. She couldn't conceive of doing less.

CHAPTER 10

The night of the dinner party, Benjamin stepped into the hall at the same time Hannah left her room at the far end. Her hair ribbons and the gold trim of her sapphire gown captured the light from the wall sconces, giving her an ethereal, otherworldly air.

His breath caught in his throat. She presented the perfect vision of a young countess. *His* countess. He watched her glide toward him, her sedate stroll, her high head perfectly befitting her station. He had never felt more proud of his choice of bride.

Tonight would be special, indeed. With her at his side, none of the old guard in the Scientific Society would fail to consider him socially prominent, a force to be reckoned with in their stuffy, politicized circle.

As she drew near, his gaze settled on her décolletage, more exposed skin than he had ever seen of this lovely stranger he had married. Her softly rounded shoulders begged to be cradled in his hands, her neck to be stroked. Her skin was as perfect as he had imagined, alone in his bed—creamy, glowing, no doubt exquisitely soft.

Indeed, the evening to come could be even more special. Perhaps afterward, flush with their success, his bride and he might finally begin their lives as a married couple. She seemed to anticipate this, too, for her face appeared slightly flushed, as she might after an evening of lovemaking ... He burned to share such intimacy. Tonight. It would happen tonight. He would make it happen. "Lovely, simply lovely," he murmured under his breath as she reached him.

She gazed up at him, her eyes huge and dark and innocent. "Excuse me?"

He lifted her downy-soft hands in his own. "You are quite a vision, Hannah," he said. Her hands seemed to be trembling, so he gave them a reassuring squeeze. "No need to worry. I'm certain everything will go splendidly. This is just the first of the social events we'll host. They'll stop referring to me as eccentric and unfriendly and start supporting my work. And it will be because of you."

"Benjamin, I did the best I could—"

"I know, dear, and I appreciate it, truly." He moved closer to her, slightly, but enough, he was certain, to signal his intent. "Perhaps, after such a significant night, we could take our young marriage in a new direction. If you're willing, of course," he murmured.

She opened her mouth to reply, but nothing came out. Benjamin found himself fascinated by her tender lips. To his shock, he realized he had never given her a proper kiss.

"Willing . . . That is how I want you, Hannah." Leaning over her, he breathed in the floral scent of her skin and hair, then gently, ever so gently, touched his lips to her cheek. A delicate gasp slipped from her lips. He slid his mouth along her cheek, whisper-soft, aiming to slowly drink of her lips with his. He had barely grazed them when something banged on the floor below, and she jerked away.

Annoyed, Benjamin looked toward the source of the sound and realized the insistent banging was at the front door. The first of their guests had arrived. He looked down the staircase toward the door, but saw no sign of his butler. "Where's Chauncy? Why isn't he answering that?"

"Benjamin, I—" Hannah began.

Benjamin hurried down the stairs and swung open the door. Lord and Lady Thornton, the Society president and his wife, waited on the stoop. Thornton tapped his cane impatiently as they stood in the light spring drizzle, their carriage on the street behind them with no one to show the driver where to park.

"Lord Thornton! So sorry to keep you waiting," Benjamin said, stepping back to give them access. "I don't have the faintest idea where my butler has got off to. Please, come in."

Thornton followed his wife across the threshold. "One must keep track of one's servants to present a good appearance to the world." He waved his cane in Benjamin's face to emphasize his point.

"I'll keep that in mind." Benjamin turned to the man's wife. "So nice to see you again, Lady

Thornton. You are looking well." The portly woman looked grayer than he remembered, but he could scarcely recall the last time he had seen her; he had been to so few events attended by gentlewomen in the past few years.

"When we received your invitation, I had to read it over several times before I believed it," Lady Thornton said. "I was beginning to think you quite a hopeless recluse."

Benjamin hated this part, where others passed judgement on the amount of time he spent in their company. "Yes, well, I've been busy."

"With those balloons, I've heard," she said dryly. "Then to learn you had married! A young gel from America, it's rumored."

"Aye, I have married. You will be meeting her soon. So good of you to come."

"Is there . . ." Thornton held up his cane and hat, and Benjamin jumped to take them. Where was Chauncy? This was his job.

"Let me . . ." Despite his hands being almost full, he found himself helping Lady Thornton remove her wrap. What in the blazes was he supposed to do with all these accoutrements? Conscious that he was keeping his guests waiting, he resorted to sliding the cane into the umbrella stand behind the door and setting the hat and wrap on the hall table. He reached for Thornton's heavy wool coat. "Allow me."

"Your butler is off tonight?"

"I—No, but he's . . . Here, I'll take it." Thornton shrugged out of his coat, and Benjamin took it, trying to hold the dripping fabric away from his pressed slacks. At a loss, he glanced around, then spotted the wooden pegs on the wall behind the door. He hung up Thornton's coat, but the six pegs couldn't hold many more coats. He would have to find someplace to put the guests' things. What did Chauncy usually do with them? Blast it all! Where was the man?

Trying to appear as relaxed as possible, he straightened his dinner jacket and gestured toward the staircase. "Please, follow me." He led the couple up the stairs to the drawing room on the first floor, where the guests would congregate until dinner began. "So good of you to come," he repeated, knowing he sounded as frazzled as he felt. This was not how he envisioned bringing the Society president into his home. He clasped his hands and smiled at the couple, who smiled back. Silence descended on the room, and Benjamin took a deep breath. "Good of you to come—"

"As you've said."

"Would you like a drink?"

"Certainly. A fine port, perhaps." Mr. Thornton looked about, and Benjamin realized no drinks had been set out, and no servant waited to offer them.

He held up his hand, praying Thornton would show more patience with his hospitality than he had with his experiments. "Please. Wait here. I shall return shortly."

Benjamin backed out of the room in as dignified a manner as he could manage, considering the panic that had begun to well up in his chest. The moment he had closed the door behind him, he turned and ran down the stairs. "Hannah?" There was no sign of her, not in the foyer or the front parlor. Nor did he spot any servants. "Hannah!"

Hannah hurried into the dining room through the opposite door. "What is it?"

"Where in God's name have you been? You're the hostess, and we have guests!" His gaze fell on her hands—wrapped in a kitchen towel. "What in the—You haven't been working in the kitchen, have you?"

Her face looked rather flushed, and while the heightened color was alarmingly attractive on her, he would much rather have a composed, tidy bride entertaining his guests upstairs.

"Drinks! We need drinks," he burst out. The door knocker sounded again, and Benjamin realized it had been sounding in the background for a full minute. "And where the hell is Chauncy?"

"Of course, drinks. I thought—Oh, damn."

"Did you just say 'damn'?" Now his gently bred wife was swearing like a sailor!

She didn't answer, but turned and disappeared toward the kitchen again. Benjamin ran back to the front door and let in more of his guests—two more couples. He awkwardly fumbled with their hats and canes and coats—he had never seen so many coats. Soon his arms were filled with them, soaking a spot through his jacket. He resorted to draping them over a chair in the darkened parlor. He began to lead his guests upstairs just as the door knocker sounded yet again.

"Blast it," he muttered under his breath, then practically tripped Mrs. Davenport on his way back down the stairs to the door. He barely heard Winthrop's greeting as he led his friend and his wife upstairs, his mind occupied with visions of him strangling Chauncy. After murdering Hannah, who was supposed to have everything under control.

She seemed to be concentrating on the actual dinner, so at least that part of the party should go well. Perhaps New Yorkers weren't used to starting their dinner parties in the drawing room with refreshments. He should have made his expectations clearer. It could be partly his fault, he supposed. But Chauncy certainly knew his duties. Where in the blazes was *he*?

By the time all the guests had arrived, and he had personally served them drinks in the drawing room, it was well past dinnertime. Georgina, looking healthier than usual in a black lace gown, entered at about eight and met his guests as a proper lady of the house should, chatting with them and generally keeping them entertained. He shot his sister a grateful look, and she smiled back at him.

His sister was doing Hannah's job, however, and Benjamin could barely sit still for worry over what his wife was up to downstairs. What would dinner be like? Why hadn't he checked earlier? He had assumed she could handle it, naturally. Only a fool would think a rich heiress couldn't manage a simple social event. Grabbing up his wineglass, he swallowed the entire contents and went to the sideboard for more.

At half past eight, Hannah herself finally joined them. "Hello!" she chirped, smiling all around. Benjamin fought down a groan. The well-put-together woman he had admired at the top of the stairs now looked blowsy and unkempt, as if she herself had been cooking dinner. Loose strands had escaped her once-neat chignon, which lay crooked on her head, and a gravy-colored stain marred her dress.

The men in the room rose, and Benjamin joined them. "Please, meet my bride, Hannah," he mumbled, wishing he could have introduced the *other* Hannah.

"Delighted, I'm sure," Mr. Thornton, the gentleman standing closest to her, tried to take her hand and bow over it, but she snatched it back in a terribly rude manner. Thornton looked as stunned as if she had slapped him.

"I—I need to wash my hands. Pardon me. I'm delighted to meet you all, truly, but we had a slight accident in the kitchen. Dinner will be . . . in a few more minutes. Not long, I assure you." She turned and fled the room.

For a long heartbeat, everyone in the room stared in silence at the door where she had disappeared. Then, to Benjamin's vast discomfort, his guests and Georgina turned their heads and fastened their gazes on him. *This is your fault,* their eyes seemed to say. *You married her.* He attempted a congenial smile, but knew it looked as false as it felt.

"I apologize, for dinner being delayed, and—and Hannah being—" Being what? Incompetent? Disrespectful? A silly chit of a girl he had married for her money? "Being tied up," he finally said, wishing he could tie her up and keep her out of trouble. "I promise dinner will be worth the wait." He prayed it would be true. Only an exquisite dinner could save this mess of a social party.

An hour later, Mrs. Thornton had begun to nod off, the port had run out, and a few of his guests were starting to make excuses about being expected at other social functions. Finally, Hannah reappeared and announced in a shaky voice that dinner was ready.

Thank God. Finally. He straightened up from where he had been leaning against the fireplace and began helping the ladies to their feet. How could Hannah have embarrassed him like this, in front of these important people? Did she not fathom why he had invited them? He would be the talk of the men's club tomorrow, a social disgrace.

Catching her eye, he gave her a scowl designed to communicate every ounce of the dissatisfaction he felt. She merely stared back, that odd, lost look on her face. At least she had taken a few moments to rectify her appearance. Though her dress was still stained, her hair no longer looked as if the slightest motion would send it flying.

Since Hannah—who still hadn't been properly introduced to their guests—appeared confused about the correct way to direct their guests to dinner, Benjamin slid his arm around her waist and pulled her along with him to the front of the procession. He tucked her hand in the crook of his arm. "Do you have any idea how late it is?" he muttered from the corner of his mouth. "Half the guests were on the verge of leaving!"

"Of course I know! I've been racing the clock for three days!" Her eyes shot fire at him.

He glowered down at her in turn. "What in the blazes were you doing in the kitchen?"

"What do you *think?*"

"That is hardly your place."

"Mrs. Pocket needed help. She's not used to cooking for more than two. She said she wasn't even the family cook until the real cook quit a few months ago, when you couldn't pay her, and—"

Conscious the social chatter of the guests behind

him had ceased, he whispered, "Shhh! We shall discuss it later."

"You brought it up." They stepped off the staircase into the foyer and crossed toward the dining room.

"Trouble in paradise?" Georgina asked from behind them. Benjamin ignored her.

If Benjamin had thought the evening could get no worse, he was badly mistaken. Never had he attended—much less hosted—such a travesty. The food, when it arrived, was either cold or burned. During dinner, Hannah kept jumping up from the table and rushing into the kitchen, as if she herself were a serving maid.

As for the servants, he finally learned where Chauncy had gone. Hannah had recruited him to serve as the lone footman. But Chauncy was at best a poor man's butler, having replaced the last butler. Hannah had apparently neglected to explain to Chauncy his new role, most importantly that footmen should be seen and not heard.

"Hear ya go, mate, another fill up to wet yer whistle," he said in his cockney bellow as he poured more wine into Lord Thornton's uplifted glass. "You'll drink us all under the table tonight," he added jovially, punctuating his audacious comment with a hearty slap on the shoulder. The impact caused the wine to slosh on Thornton's lap.

Thornton stared at the man in disbelief, then turned his hawkeyed glare to Benjamin. In turn, Benjamin sought Hannah's gaze. He gave her a pointed look to communicate his seething frustration. She bit her lip in that audaciously adorable way she had—as if her innocent demeanor could excuse this mess!

Benjamin squeezed his eyes shut. *Please Lord, strike me down. Now.* He longed to disappear—to his lab, to the other side of the moon, into thin air. Anywhere but in his own house!

An ear-splitting shriek from Mrs. Davenport startled him, and he jerked upright. A portion of chicken—served up by an overenthusiastic Chauncy—had plummeted into her lap. Lovely. Just lovely. Hannah leaped to her feet to help repair the damage, but the gown was the latest victim of the evening.

Hannah scrambled to collect the wayward chicken and mop up the mess. "I'll get you a new plate. And a new gown, too," she said breathlessly. She scooped up the plate and dashed to the kitchen.

"Surely she didn't rush out to purchase a gown tonight," Thornton said dryly.

Winthrop began to chuckle, and all of them—except the flummoxed Mrs. Davenport—chimed in, filling the room with laughter. Benjamin remained still as stone, containing his mortification as best he could.

Beside him, Winthrop leaned in close and whispered, "I say, old chum. It's good you married the gel for her chinks, as there's not much else to recommend her, is there? Except, of course, for . . ." He supplied a raised eyebrow, as if Benjamin didn't already know he was referring to bed sport.

Benjamin forced himself to give Winthrop a smile, which no doubt looked as pained as he felt. *Bed sport* . . . . As if Hannah offered him such a delicious benefit. Certainly, he had Hannah's money. But nothing else. Nothing. The woman could have been born in a barn for all the social skills she exhibited. She could be as untouchable as a nun for all the pleasure he had shared with her.

Why had he married her? He had been doing fine, before, if a little in debt. Certainly his reputation had only suffered from tonight's disaster. He would be the laughingstock of London by the end of the day tomorrow.

"What exactly is the aim?" Thornton's booming voice cut through his pained thoughts.

"Excuse me?"

"Your flight in August. Why, exactly, do you plan to take another balloon up there? What are you attempting to prove *this* time?"

Benjamin tried to focus his thoughts on his work and not his wife. This was why he had wanted to host such a dinner, to speak to Thornton about his work in circumstances where the Society president might be more receptive. He cleared his throat and tried to reclaim his composure. "I'll be sending my instruments aloft, of course, to prove once and for all that the Earth's atmosphere is composed of layered gases. And that it's cold high above the Earth, not warm as many of us assume."

"Of course it's warm!" Thornton said emphatically. "The closer you climb to the sun, the hotter it gets."

Benjamin shook his head. "The facts do not bear out that assumption, not when one passes forty thousand feet. I've sent dozens of balloons aloft, and they all tell me the same thing."

"Your instruments are unreliable, unless someone is there to keep an eye on them," Thornton said, a trace of challenge in his voice. "You keep sending up balloons and claiming the results you gather prove your outlandish theories. Yet, if no man is present, how do you know your instruments aren't registering the altitude or the temperatures in error?" He smirked. "And *no* man can fly that high and survive the flight. I'm sorry, Sheffield, but your research is a dead end."

Frustration surging through him, Benjamin slammed his fist on the table, rattling the silverware and making Lady Thornton jump. "It *can* be done, and my instruments will prove it."

"Easy, Benjy," Winthrop said. He smiled at Thornton. "Someone *will* be there. I've volunteered to man this next flight."

There. It was out in the open. The Society— eventually, the world—would know Benjamin was afraid of his own damned balloon. "That's right," Benjamin said, his voice tight. "Winthrop is kind enough to take my place. I trust you'll accept *his* findings." Even though he and Winthrop had made the arrangements and shaken hands on it, he still couldn't stand thinking about how his colleague—instead of himself—would explore the new frontier.

"Benjamin, you can't be serious." Hannah reclaimed her seat opposite his.

Benjamin hadn't noticed her returning from the kitchen. How much had she heard? "Our scientific research is always serious, Hannah," he said.

"But this experiment . . . It's so important. You'll be going almost eight miles into the sky, farther than anyone before you. How can you allow another man to take your place?"

Benjamin glared at her, hoping she would drop the subject. "Hannah, this doesn't concern you."

"But breaking the high-altitude barrier means *everything* to *you*. That's what you've been working toward for years, isn't it?" Silence met her question. Her gaze never wavered from his. "Isn't it?"

Winthrop smiled at her. "Benjy lost his taste for high-altitude flights. Hasn't been up in, what, five years or so?"

"Why?" In her intensity, Hannah leaned forward, providing a provocative view down her bodice. Winthrop obviously noticed, his gaze on the hint of cleavage nestled there. Benjamin wanted to strangle them both.

Winthrop grinned. "Because, sweet Hannah, Benjy got a tad chilly on his last high-altitude flight. Nearly froze to death, in fact. Lost consciousness, too. It's a miracle he survived."

Lady Thornton gasped and pressed a hand to her heaving bosom. "My word, how dreadful."

Her husband patted her beringed hand. "An exaggeration, my dear. It isn't that cold up there."

"Benjamin," Hannah said on a whisper. "Why didn't you say anything?"

Hannah looked shocked and, he realized, hurt. Why? Did she truly think he would share such a shameful truth with her? *Dear Miss Carrington: Will you be my bride? By the way, you're marrying a coward who isn't man enough to risk his own neck a second time, not even for science . . . .*

"We shall discuss this later, Hannah," he said, forcing a cold tone to his voice. It worked. Hannah sat back and looked away, ending the confrontation.

"Excuse me. Benjamin, I can't hear about this.

I simply can't." Georgina rose from the table, staggered slightly, then left the room. A fresh surge of guilt rocked Benjamin. The dinner had just surpassed disastrous. He had entered hell once more.

CHAPTER 11

Hannah collapsed in a dining room chair. The last of the evening's guests were finally departing. She could hear Benjamin in the foyer seeing them off. He sounded composed enough, considering.

The heavy oak front door closed, and Hannah heard his footsteps drawing near. She braced herself, but it did no good. He paused in the doorway and glared at her, his sculpted features revealing not a trace of empathy, his mouth tight, his eyes judging, condemning. His mussed hair fell over his forehead; color heightened his sculpted cheeks. He looked like an angry god.

Hannah tore her gaze from his and rose to her aching feet. How she longed to collapse in her bed; how she longed to be anywhere but here! She had been working nonstop to make this dinner party a success, but it had gotten her nowhere.

Needing an excuse to avoid his gaze, she began

gathering the used wineglasses and napkins which the servants had neglected to clean from the table, intending to take them to the kitchen.

A strong hand on her bare arm stopped her cold. "Put those down and come with me."

Hannah complied, knocking over two of the glasses in the process. She tried to right them; but the tug on her arm grew insistent, and she found herself propelled through the dining room door into the parlor, then down the hall toward Benjamin's study. He thrust her inside, then followed her in and closed the door. Hannah stepped well away from him before slowly turning to face him, bracing for his reproach.

It came immediately, without preamble, without pause. "You have made a mockery of me before my peers." He didn't raise his voice, but its chill cut her to the bone. "You have ruined what little social standing I possessed. That—that fiasco of a dinner party you perpetrated is the most—the most—" He opened his mouth, his barely contained rage apparently making speech beyond him.

"Appalling?" she supplied, managing only to whisper the word.

"Quite. The most *appalling* social experience I have ever endured. I cannot fathom ever living this down. To think my own wife was behind such a disgrace. You, Miss Carrington—" He pointed a finger at her, at the same time disowning her as his wife. His harsh reprimand nearly brought her to tears. She had had no idea this man had the power to cut her so deeply. She wanted to die.

His eyes glinted like chips of ice, his cold fury chilling her to the bone. "You misrepresented yourself to me. I took you to be a lady of some ability, not a fancily dressed *sham*. Now I understand what is meant by new American money." His voice lowered even more, his jaw clenching tight. "Precious little respect for manners."

"Benjamin, let me explain—"

"To think I had such plans for this evening, plans for after . . ." His expression froze into an unreadable mask, even more frightening than his controlled anger. He strode stiffly to the window, effectively turning his back to her. The silent rebuke stung worse than his words. Hannah wished he would storm at her, exhibit some passion, some raw emotion, instead of throwing up a chill barrier that kept her firmly at a distance.

Hannah tried again to explain, to garner some sympathy, or at least understanding. "You gave me only three days to plan this party. I've only just begun to get used to my new role. Perhaps my efforts were a failure, but in my own defense, I've never worked harder in my life."

He spun to face her. "I saw scant evidence of your efforts. Using Chauncy as a footman? What insanity possessed you?"

Hannah threw out her hands. "You're employing him as a butler, when he's really a carriage driver! That makes little more sense."

His expression turned even grimmer. "A resourceful girl would have hired more servants, proper servants. I gave you leave."

"In three days' time? Do you know how impossible that task is?"

"You could have borrowed some for the evening, or—something." He glanced away, and Hannah saw a crack in his cold mask, for he seemed as confounded by the problem as she had been. Then his head snapped up, his eyes glowing with triumph. "Georgina. You should have requested her assistance. She knows people—"

"Georgina's help? Are you completely blind? Your sister will scarce give me the time of day!"

His eyes narrowed at her sally. He lacked an immediate rejoinder, and she forged ahead. "The servants are little better. They detest me almost as much, whether I treat them with a firm or gentle hand."

He shook his head, as if unwilling to acknowledge the truth of her words. "Surely you've had *servants* before. Dealt with them."

"My family has hundreds of servants," she shot back, exaggerating only a little. She enjoyed seeing him stiffen at the reminder of her wealth. "I know perfectly well how to deal with well-bred *American* servants. But *your* servants are completely under Georgina's sway. Gaining their cooperation is like pulling teeth."

He crossed his arms. "You most certainly could have sought *my* assistance. Your hardheaded, proud nature no doubt prevented you."

"That's not true! I wanted to ask you. I *longed* to ask you. But you were never around."

He scoffed, "A foolish argument. Of course I was around. I live here."

"You were either at your club, or Parliament, or hiding in your lab—"

"I do not *hide.*"

"—locking the door, keeping me away."

"I assumed you had the situation well in hand. Evidently I was mistaken in your abilities, which I assumed to be those of any properly bred young woman of society. It's a mistake I shall not make a second time." He spun around and swung open the door.

"Where are you going?"

"To my lab, where I can make sense of things." He stormed out of the room.

Hannah looked after him, fighting back tears. He didn't care a whit about her or about what she had gone through. He didn't even know her.

He had no idea whom he had married and valued her for who she truly was even less.

He had passed judgement on her, based on his own needs and wants, having no concept of hers.

And she did have needs.

Hannah's hurt began to transform into something much hotter, something that caused her feet to move, to take her toward his lab at first slowly, then more rapidly. By the time she reached the laboratory door, fury coursed through her. She yanked on the doorknob, and the door gave, swinging toward her. He had apparently been so upset with her, he had neglected to lock it after himself. She realized she had expected to find the door secured, a barrier to her intentions. Briefly she reconsidered, then just as quickly shoved her hesitance aside. She *would* have it out with him, this moment.

She hurried down the stairs into the shadowed stairwell, toward the light spilling from the room at the bottom.

Rounding the corner, she entered his hallowed laboratory, victorious that she had finally breached the walls of his private retreat. She had no time to absorb details of the low-ceilinged room, caught only quick impressions of an open work area with bolts of silk and ropes at the far end and benches with instruments at the near end. Then her gaze found its mark.

He sat with his back to her on a wooden bench at a worktable, his head bent over something in his hands. He had removed his jacket, making him appear slightly more approachable. A small burner at his elbow warmed air in a glass condenser.

"Benjamin."

He started, his back stiffening. After a quick glance over his shoulder, he shot to his feet, his gaze accusing. "What are you doing down here?"

Hannah forced herself to stand ramrod straight, not to flinch or back down no matter what. Upstairs, he had had the upper hand. Now it was her turn. "I know you ran down here to escape me, but you can't escape me, or the fact you married me."

Her tone sounded reasonable, at first, but the more she spoke, the more her righteous anger took hold, her courage growing stronger as she gave voice to her feelings.

"I am *not* Miss Carrington. I'm your wife, no matter how much you regret that. No matter what assumptions you made about me when we agreed to this arrangement. Those assumptions were in your own mind. Not once did I say I was good at domestic or social duties, not once! In fact, it should have been quite clear to you, considering the manner in which we met, that my interests lay elsewhere."

She glanced around the lab, a streak of jealousy coursing through her that this man could ignore the real world and hide out down here any time he chose, while she was left trying to make his house a home.

"That's right, how could I forget," he said dryly. "Your schoolgirl's stunt."

"I gathered at the time my work intrigued you," she said, hating being on the defensive.

He didn't directly address her remark, which gave her some satisfaction. "You have no clue about true scientific experimentation, the rigors, the discipline, the dedicated passion. Do you truly think you can make a contribution, where a man of my standing can scarce garner the Scientific Society's respect without a fight?"

She found her fists clenching and thrust them out of view in the skirts of her evening gown. "You're being unfair. I haven't had a chance. I've been too busy throwing parties," she said with heavy irony.

"True groundbreaking science isn't a rich girl's hobby. It comes at risk of life and limb, an area gently bred women have no business pursuing." He moved as if to turn back around, but her next words stopped him cold.

"Risk?" she scoffed. "And what risk are you willing to take? You've asked Winthrop to take your place on the most important flight of your career! And you speak of passion. You lack enough heart to even care that he's stealing your glory."

At her words, his demeanor instantly transformed. Shocked, she watched his shoulders slacken, his expression close, his rage submerge under deadly calm. For several minutes, silence reigned, the storm having passed—or moved to a much more destructive level. Finally he spoke, his words toneless. "Are you quite through?"

"Yes," she said stiffly. "I've spoken my piece."

"I suggest, then, that you leave immediately."
He took a step toward her, then another.

Hannah stayed rooted to the spot, fascinated and
terrified at this new predatory side to the man she
had married. She couldn't have moved if her life
depended on it.

"For I have a mind to show you exactly how
wrong you are." He advanced once more, closing
the distance between them to an arm's length.

Hannah couldn't read his intentions in his eyes,
only knew she witnessed heretofore unrevealed
emotions. She had released a dragon with her hec-
tic words, and it was far too late to call it back.

She took a step back, then another, until she
found herself pressed against the cold stone laboratory wall. Still, Benjamin advanced, until he was
practically pressed against her. She could scarcely
breathe at his nearness, at the unholy light in his
dark eyes. "You have no idea what passions brew
deep inside me," he murmured. "If you knew, you
would run like hell."

Oh, good Lord, he meant to murder her. She had to
get away. Sliding sideways, she slipped away from
him and ran toward the center of the lab, thinking
to run around him to reach the door.

She traveled only a few yards before he threw an
arm around her waist, stopping her as surely as if
she had run into a brick wall. The force of his hold
knocked the breath from her. She gasped and spun
around, right into his clutches. She backed away,
but came up against his workbench this time. He
grasped it, trapping her between his arms.

Even knowing she was in mortal danger didn't
stop a mortifyingly strong attraction from heating
her blood and stealing her sense. Her breath came

harsh and fast as his intense gaze snared her as surely as his arms.

"You are the worst possible bride for me in any number of ways," he said harshly. "There is, however, one way to redeem this mess."

"One—" She sucked in a breath, drawing his gaze to her chest, of all places, where his eyes lingered long enough to make her skin prickle. He raised his hands to her sleeves—merely scraps of silk decorating her shoulders—and tugged downward, lowering her bodice even more. Hannah had never felt so exposed, so vulnerable. His gaze had set her skin on fire, but his hands—Oh, Lord, now he was touching her, running his fingers along the edge of her bodice, tracing the curves of her shoulders, fondling the column of her neck. Hannah knew she trembled at his touch, but was incapable of containing her fear—no, exhilaration—at feelings she had never imagined she could experience. Her dress felt so tight, her skin so hot, she would incinerate if her shockingly strong desire wasn't assuaged.

He locked his fingers in her hair, his other hand clasping her neck. His gaze captured hers in silent warning just before he pulled her mouth against his.

"Mphfh." Hannah had been about to protest, to say something, anything, to distract him. She hadn't spoken fast enough and now realized it wouldn't have stopped him. And how glad she was.

Sinfully good. That was how it felt to be kissed by him, to kiss him back. Both rough and soft, his lips claimed hers, at moments gentle, at moments demanding. She had never experienced anything like it and found her hands sliding around his silk-clad shoulders, drawing him even closer.

Like a flower opening before the sun, her lips parted, and she drank deeply of him. He responded, touching her not only with his hands, but pressing the full length of his body hard and fast against hers. Clasping her waist, he lifted her onto his workbench. He pushed aside her heavy skirt and slid his hips between her legs. The heat of his body transferred through the silk of her gown to caress her inner thighs.

Unaccustomed desire weakened Hannah's every muscle, and a delicious languidity stole over her, her entire body melting into compliance. She clung to him for support. Gradually, he lowered her to the surface of the table. She felt open to him, raw and vulnerable, ready to allow him whatever liberties he wished to take.

His mouth left hers and began traveling down her neck, his heated breath branding her skin. "I had no idea . . . a gentlewoman . . . so responsive . . ."

"Yes," she breathed, scarcely comprehending his words.

"You drive me quite out of my mind."

"Yes," she repeated, a litany of acceptance.

"I no longer know myself." His fingers slid into the bodice of her dress, beneath her corset, and he touched her swollen nipple. The burst of pleasure stunned her, and she gasped sharply. "No longer care," he murmured.

"Yes!" She threw her arms over her head, ready to be ravished, ready for him to possess her and make her his own.

Her hand struck hot metal. Pain flared, and she jerked away. Responding to her sudden stiffness, Benjamin tore his mouth from her chest and looked up. His expression cleared of passion, his face starting to pale. "My God. Fire!"

CHAPTER 12

Benjamin leaped away from Hannah so fast, she felt bereft and confused, until his words penetrated her foggy mind.

Fire? She glanced around. In her mindless passion, she had knocked over his burner, igniting a tall stack of papers and log books on the workbench. Already the flames were two feet high and climbing.

Hannah scrambled off the table as Benjamin swept the papers and books to the stone floor. Most of them landed in a pile, but a handful of papers fluttered several feet away, tongues of flame engulfing them. Benjamin leaped on the largest pile and began stomping out the flames. Following suit, Hannah jumped on half a dozen papers. She managed to extinguish the flames and rushed over to a burning log book which had been knocked across the floor while Benjamin continued to battle the main pile.

"Almost have it," Benjamin panted. "I think we've averted disaster. I think—My God, Hannah!"

Without warning, Hannah was tackled to the floor, her new husband splayed atop her. Her elbow smacked into the unforgiving stone floor, and she cried out. Benjamin rolled her to her side, then back again, then completely over onto her stomach, knocking the air from her lungs.

Then he rolled her to her back and pulled her up to sit within the circle of his arms. "What—" she tried to say, but lacked breath.

"Your gown is ruined. You must have dragged it through the flames."

"Oh," she breathed, sucking in gulps of air. "I had no idea." She leaned back in his arms, relishing the feel of his embrace, the way he supported her so solicitously.

"Of course not, with all this fabric dragging behind you." He held up a fistful of her lovely sapphire gown, the cloth charred beyond repair. He flung the handful away in disgust. "Impractical wear for a laboratory."

He sounded so distant, as if he hadn't been making love to her moments before. "If I was working here, helping you, I wouldn't be wearing an evening gown," she said reasonably.

He didn't respond. He helped her to her feet and stepped back as if he couldn't release her fast enough. Crossing to the pile of books, he knelt and surveyed the damage. They had extinguished the flames, but papers continued to smolder. He lifted a half-burned log book. "A year's worth of work was in this book," he said, his voice distant. "A steep price to pay for a moment's pleasure."

"Excuse me?"

He rose to his feet. "Never mind. It's time you went to bed."

Hannah couldn't imagine sleeping. Her nerves still buzzed from the combined excitement of Benjamin's seduction and fighting the fire. Still, she turned and headed for the door, knowing that Benjamin would want to continue their tryst in the proper place, his bedroom. If he planned to continue. Surely he would want to finish what they had started. There was no reason not to, now that he knew how much she enjoyed his attentions. At the door, she turned back. "Are you coming?"

He continued looking through the damaged papers. "I'll be up shortly."

He was giving her time to prepare. "Very well." Hannah left him, her skin already tingling in anticipation of more kissing, more touching. And all the wonderful mysteries that would follow . . . .

Benjamin hadn't fully expressed to Hannah his dismay over his destroyed work. With careful control, he had clamped down on his emotions. Becoming upset, dwelling on the loss, would do no good. Over the years he had become an expert at controlling his feelings—until he took Hannah in his arms and nearly ruined his life's work.

He would have to piece together his findings from old notes, if he could. He had memorized a good deal of it, the results if not the data. It wasn't as if the Society was prepared to accept the results of his temperature and wind experiments regardless of the data he had gathered. He had sent more than forty balloons aloft, and still they demanded more proof of a layered atmosphere. He had decided to call it the stratosphere, that layer above the atmosphere. So far, no one quite believed it even existed, except for him.

And perhaps Hannah. Was she truly interested in his work or merely trying to flatter him? He had no idea. He acted such a fool around her! He had never been so utterly affected by a woman, smitten like a green schoolboy. For years, he had done what any gentleman would do to satisfy his needs without despoiling gentlewomen or servants—he had visited Madame Hornbecker's once a week, until his wedding, of course. He took his vows seriously, after all.

Having sex was rather like scratching a bothersome itch. After visiting a lady of the evening, he could return to work without another thought about what had transpired. Rarely did he lose his focus.

But now . . . .

He had never felt so desperate for satisfaction when visiting Madame Hornbecker's girls. He had never been with a gentlewoman, so perhaps that explained this unbelievably strong desire, this obsession with his own wife. Hannah's soft skin, her taste, her innocent willingness . . . Did all well-bred women inspire such madness in men? He doubted it. For him, only Hannah seemed to cause this mindless need to possess. She affected him like a chemical reaction, one so incredibly strong it obliterated all logic.

He had acted like an animal, accosting her on his worktable, for God's sake! As if she were a penny trollop in an East End alley. Shame filled him, and he fisted his hands, crumpling a charred record sheet. Certainly, she had seemed willing enough, but did she even understand where their actions were leading? How could she? She had no experience of men.

True, they were man and wife. But she had said from the first she would let him know when she was ready. And he had agreed to wait, not force himself on her, no matter how much he wanted her. She deserved at least that much.

Hannah smoothed her nightdress and studied her reflection in the oval looking glass. The ruffled ivory gown she now wore had lain untouched in her bottom drawer, waiting for this night. *Her true wedding night.*

Any moment, he would be coming. Butterflies danced in her stomach, and her heart pounded in anticipation of the hours to come. Her first night as a woman, a wife. *His* wife.

The oil lanterns about the room cast a mellow glow upon her bed. Would he want to remain here or take her to his own chamber? She shivered, imagining him holding her, caressing her, every part of her.

Such an attractive man, her husband. Tall, strong, with eyes that cast a magic spell upon her. She had never felt so *womanly* toward a man before. Until she had met Benjamin, until he had looked at her with those fathomless, intense eyes, she hadn't realized how strongly a lady could desire a man's touch. Truly, she had thought of little else but him since their wedding two weeks ago. He held sway over her, and she anticipated giving in to his heady masculine power. Tonight, he would be the victor, and she would succumb.

A thrill ran through her. His kisses had been so potent. How wonderful would it be to lie naked beside him? Her breasts tingled as she remembered his touch. Involuntarily, she gasped and pressed her hand to her chest. *Such wondrous feelings* . . . .

Her knees shook in remembrance, so she took a seat at her dressing table. She began brushing her hair to give herself something to do, though she had already combed out her waist-long locks. The thought that Benjamin would soon see her in such intimate circumstances was enough to make her cheeks flame.

A knock sounded on her door. Hannah froze in place, terrified and thrilled all at once. He had come, just as he had promised. Clutching the brush to her chest, she rose and sucked in a breath. "Come in."

The door opened slowly, and he was standing there, looking at her. She waited, her heart pounding so hard she was certain he could see it. His eyes slid up and down her body, then returned to meet hers. "Hannah."

The way he spoke her name, so thick with intimacy, with longing, filled her with pleasure. "Are you going to stand there all night?" she asked, proud of how steady her own voice sounded.

To her consternation, he took a step backward, into the shadowy hall. "Excuse me," he muttered. "I won't keep you long. What happened in the laboratory . . . I apologize, from the bottom of my heart."

Apologize? His words, his demeanor . . . Something was wrong.

"I know this is scant consolation," he continued, his voice awkward and stiff, unforgivably stiff. "I assure you, I have never behaved in such a way, certainly not with a woman of your breeding. Please trust me, there will never be a repeat of tonight."

Never? He was never going to kiss her again? Never going to breathe heated, passionate words into her ear? Never touch her? He didn't plan on continuing their lovemaking, not tonight. Not anytime soon. Hannah suddenly wanted to cry.

"Considering our present difficulties, I believe it would be best for us to maintain our distance."

"Our distance," she said flatly, fighting to keep her voice steady. She refused to let him see her crushing disappointment. She tightened her hand on her hairbrush, desperate for an anchor as a wave of hurt engulfed her.

"I will await your consent before engaging in any such . . . *intimacies,* as I originally agreed." Intimacies . . . He made the word sound almost tasteless.

"Furthermore, it is quite apparent that a young lady such as you has no place in the laboratory."

"Why?"

He actually seemed surprised by her question. "That should be obvious, after what transpired." His lips bent in a humorless smile. "The house nearly burned to the ground!"

"And you blame me for that." Of course he did. She could never do anything right.

"Certainly not. I blame only myself. Me, and my base nature, which I had heretofore believed well under control. Considering my weakness, clearly it would be best if you refrained from visiting my laboratory from now on. Good night." He nodded and left, closing the door firmly behind him.

So that was that. She was a troublesome distraction. He would only consummate their marriage under proper, well-controlled circumstances. Apparently, he planned to wait until she welcomed him to her bed. How gentlemanly of him. How logical. How passionless! Very well. He could wait—until hell froze over. She had opened herself to him, her desire and passion, and he thought so little of her gift he would toss it aside as worthless! Her stomach spasmed in pain, and she realized she still longed for his touch, longed to feel again the ecstasy she had experienced in his laboratory.

But he would never know of her longings. She would never let him see she wanted him, never again. And he expected her to make the first move and invite him to her bed! What would possibly drive her to do so? Certainly not his deep love for her! He would no doubt prefer it if she had never moved into his house, as long as he could have her money.

Let him dream of possessing her body—he never would. He could come pleading to her on his knees, and she would turn him away. He could suffer alone in his dark basement laboratory, hour upon endless hour, dreaming of what he couldn't have for all she cared.

On top of all that, he actually forbade her entrance to his hallowed laboratory! Fury leaped to life within her. How dare he? She loved science; she would be an asset to his work, if he gave her half a chance! Damn the man!

She envisioned him standing in the doorway,

smug and superior and impervious to her feelings. In a fit of anger, she hurled her hairbrush. It struck the door he had so recently closed on her, then clattered to the floor.

CHAPTER 13

Hannah had just settled into one of the library's most comfortable chairs with Darwin's *Origin of Species* when a stranger walked in. The young man, dressed in a neat but unfashionable brown suit, didn't notice her, instead turning his attention to the ceiling-high shelves which lined the walls. A thatch of thick blond hair fell in his eyes, and he swiped it back as a child might.

"Good morning," she called out.

The young man spun around. When he saw her, his pale complexion began to pink. "Par-pardon me, miss. I didn't see you there." He stood rooted in place, staring as if he had never seen a woman before.

"You are . . . ?" she prompted.

"Oh, blast," he muttered, then grew even pinker when he realized he had cursed in the presence of a lady. "Excuse me, I didn't mean to—That is, my manners are usually much better. But you caught me off guard, you see." Pulling himself up straight, he gave a formal bow at the waist. "Hiram Spencer at your service. I'm Lord Sheffield's laboratory assistant. He sent me in here to retrieve a book, but I had no idea his personal library was so immense."

He glanced up at the shelves. "I don't really know where anything is, yet. As you may have guessed, I just started in his employ."

"Oh, really?" Hannah said dryly. "How interesting." Benjamin had hired a new assistant. Instead of making use of her skills, instead of tapping into her eagerness, he had found someone else. A young *man*.

Spencer smiled. "It's terribly fascinating. I can't believe how lucky I am, working with *the* Lord Sheffield. He's a hero, you know. Ever since I saw him lecture at university, I've longed to follow in his footsteps. Now I'm going to ascend in a balloon, along with Lord Winthrop. I'll be famous."

"How delightful for you," she said dryly, feeling years older than this boy, who looked as though he had just stepped from the schoolroom. And such hero worship! If he knew the earl for the stubborn, opinionated, flawed fellow she knew, he would certainly change his tune.

Spencer seemed oblivious to her sarcasm, his eyes dancing over her. "And whom might I have the pleasure of addressing? I had heard the lord has a sister, but I didn't imagine her to take the form of a—a *goddess*." He barely breathed the word.

Hannah lifted her eyebrows. The boy was actually flirting with her! "I'm his wife."

Color flooded Spencer's face. "Oh."

She snapped her book closed and rose to her feet to face her new adversary. "Tell me. What is your education, your training for laboratory work?"

"Well, I haven't had much, actually. I am, however, a university student, studying the natural sciences."

"How many years?" She took a step closer, and he stepped back.

His Adam's apple bobbed, and he swallowed reflexively, twisting his hands before him. "Excuse me?"

"How long have you been studying?"

"I'm in my first term."

"So, essentially you have no experience."

He opened his mouth to respond, but nothing came out.

Hannah continued, knowing she was making him uncomfortable and too angry to care. "Yet somehow you're qualified to assist my husband in his important work."

"Are you giving Spencer a difficult time, Hannah?" Benjamin was standing in the library doorway. Hannah watched as he strolled toward them, his demeanor reflecting his status as master of the house. She tried to ignore the stir of attraction she felt at his casual strength, his confidence, even more striking in contrast to Spencer's unease in her presence.

Benjamin glanced from her to Spencer, then crossed to the library shelves. After briefly scanning the titles, he yanked out a massive blue tome and tossed it to Spencer with one hand as if it weighed no more than a feather. Spencer scrambled not to drop the hefty reference work. "Take it back to the lab."

Spencer nodded and rushed out, the book pressed to his chest.

Benjamin turned to Hannah. "I think you terrified the boy."

"A boy you had no need to hire."

"Of course I did. I've needed an assistant for some time. Now that I can afford one—"

Her money again. That was all she was to him, a pocketbook. "*I* can be your assistant. That boy has no valid qualifications. He's not specially trained—"

"I'll train him."

"He has no experience—"

"That will come with time."

"Then, why not train *me*? I'm perfectly capable of helping you, taking notes, organizing your office, assisting with experiments—"

He arched a brow. "Including a dangerous high-altitude balloon flight?"

"Well, why not?"

His only response to that remark was a maddening look of amusement. "And while you're down in the laboratory, hour upon hour, who would be managing this household?"

She had no answer. Of course the household was her primary task. She had been bred for a domestic role, as little as it might interest her. He believed taking care of hearth and home to be her end of their marriage bargain and expected her to fulfill it. Yet to do nothing else, for the rest of her life, but answer correspondence and plan dinners . . . Such a prospect felt like a jail sentence. "I can do more, Benjamin. You have to believe that. I was at the top of my class in school. I learn quickly. I'm interested in everything—"

"Hannah . . ." His voice had taken on a strange, intimate timbre. She couldn't read everything in his fathomless eyes, but suddenly understood he was remembering their heated encounter following the dinner party.

She fought down a blush as she responded. "If it's to do with my presence in the laboratory, I could work here, in the library."

He sighed. Picking up the book she had left on the chair, he glanced at the spine, then snapped it closed. "If you direct even a portion of the enthusiasm you show for book learning to other tasks . . ." He laid a hand on her shoulder, and she fought the tremor that danced through her at his touch. "It may be interesting to see what can be accomplished." His fingers left a gentle trail of fire as he dropped his hand from her arm.

She was reaching him! She could feel it. "Yes, Benjamin. You must trust that I am capable. Very capable."

He nodded, his acquiescence filling her with fresh hope. "Very well. Since you are determined to prove yourself, I hereby leave management of the household completely in your hands. Once it is running like a well-oiled machine, once things are . . . sufficiently settled, perhaps then you could assist me in small scientific matters."

Frustration filled her. Small matters? And not until the household was in order? That could be months—or even years! "But—but you know how bad I am at household matters. You can't possibly want to trust me with such a responsibility."

He smiled, his eyes sparkling. "I am always willing

to give an apprentice a second chance." He handed the book to her, then crossed to the door.

The moment the door closed, Hannah threw the book to the floor, wishing she could have aimed it at his head. He was starting to make a habit of making aggravating pronouncements, then leaving her. "Because he knows how I'll react and doesn't want to argue with me any longer than necessary," she muttered.

She crouched to retrieve the book. No longer wanting to take out her frustrations on a precious volume of knowledge, she gently slipped it back in its place on the bookshelf. Pressing her hands against the dusty volumes, she lowered her head. Without even looking, she knew that not a single book in his immense collection would answer her questions about household management. In his mind, women should be born with such knowledge and think of nothing else.

Worse, and perhaps most hurtful of all, he had called her his apprentice. His apprentice! After their passionate encounter in his laboratory, she had thought of little else but becoming his wife in the most intimate way. Apparently, he had put her in quite another category, without a single regret.

Sighing, she collapsed on the sofa, her mind spinning. He *had* offered her a ray of hope, that someday she could assist him in his work. Yet she found herself dwelling on quite another revelation, one that mystified yet gratified her despite herself.

Against all odds, Benjamin thought her capable of the daunting task he had set before her. He believed in her. How could he bring himself to trust the inexperienced American girl who had so humiliated him? And how could she keep from disappointing him yet again?

All her life she had longed for a purpose to her existence, a chance to prove her worth. Even though she had given scant attention to her mother's lectures about running a household, she *had* been trained for this role. And goodness knew, the house needed managing.

Yet now that the job was in her hands, fear hung like a heavy shawl about her shoulders. Georgina's coldness, the servants' disdain, her own lack of knowledge about English customs—all of it presented a near-insurmountable challenge.

"I know nothing about making an earl's house run like clockwork!" she said to the empty room. "And even less how to please a discriminating Englishman."

She would have to put aside her fears. She would have to try her very best. There was nothing else for her to do.

Benjamin left his club early, tired of feigning interest in conversation when all he could think about was his disastrous marriage and his ridiculous passion for his new wife. He wanted to retreat to his study, perhaps read a good book. As the time for his high-altitude aerial flight neared, he had grown increasingly worried that he had overlooked something vital, that Winthrop didn't fully understand the importance of collecting frequent air samples once aloft. That something would go wrong.

That he had been thinking too much about his new wife and not enough about his work.

Before Benjamin could open the front door, it swung inward. A man he had never seen before bowed a greeting. In his mid-fifties, he wore a neatly pressed butler's uniform. "Good evening, sir. Allow me."

He held out his hands for Benjamin's hat and coat. Benjamin didn't hand them over. Instead, he backed up several steps down the walk and double-checked that the house he had entered was his own. It was.

"And you are . . ."

"My name is Harcourt, my lord. I have been retained as your butler."

"Oh. Harcourt. Very well."

A butler. This must be Hannah's doing. Well, he had said she could hire servants to replace those he had been forced to let go. Still, the unexpected new face made him a little edgy.

After handing his hat and coat over to Harcourt, he headed down the hall toward his study. Noisy voices drew his attention to the front parlor, and he paused in the doorway. A pair of workmen were hanging tan-and-rose wallpaper on the plaster walls. The previous dark plum paper lay in a heap in the center of the floor, the carpet rolled back, the furniture covered. Another stranger, a woman, was measuring the window, while a second woman sat beside Hannah on the sofa, turning pages in a sample book.

"It's utter chaos!"

Benjamin turned to find Georgina, in her wrap as usual, glaring angrily toward the parlor. "She's changing everything. I told her I liked it just the way it was, but she completely discounted my feelings! And she's hiring servants right and left—"

His gaze remained on his bride. "Hannah," he said loud enough to gain her attention.

She looked up and smiled. Rising to her feet, she crossed toward him. "Hello, Benjamin. Did you meet Harcourt?"

"I couldn't very well miss him," he said wryly.

Hannah rushed on, as if anxious to assuage any concerns he might have. "Harcourt comes very highly recommended. His references are impeccable. He served Lord Linley before, and he was an earl, too. Before he died, I mean."

"Yes, well, dying would put an end to that," Benjamin said with a smile. Hannah looked remarkably lovely today, in a pert pink-and-white-striped day dress, her cheeks rosy, her eyes shining. The glow of satisfaction, perhaps? "What about Chauncy?"

"I asked him if he wanted to be the butler or the carriage driver. He said it would be a relief to return to his previous duties. I've also hired a cook, so Mrs. Pocket can concentrate on being the housekeeper and not be overburdened."

"That sounds reasonable. What are you doing to this room?"

"I'm updating it. It was terribly old-fashioned, not to mention shabby." She darted a glance toward Georgina, and his sister frowned. "Since it's the first room guests see when they enter this home, I wanted a lighter and brighter atmosphere."

"Yes, I can see the effect already." With the heavy brocade curtains removed, sunshine flooded the room, and the lighter-colored walls made it appear larger than before. "Your selections seem most becoming." He smiled at his young wife and was gratified when her eyes warmed and she smiled in return. Suddenly, he felt more optimistic about their future than he had in days. Hannah wasn't just taking up the burden of managing his household—she was throwing herself into it with unbridled enthusiasm. On top of that, her choices were well reasoned and wise. He couldn't ask for more.

Perhaps they had hosted the dinner party too soon. She had needed a little longer to settle into her wifely role. Ah, well, live and learn, he told himself. Together they would move beyond that disaster, now that Hannah was finally embracing her traditional role as an aristocratic wife and forgetting her nonsense about pursuing a career in science.

Satisfaction filled him. With a new bounce in his step, he headed down the hall to his study.

His sister dogged his steps. "You aren't listening, Benjamin. She removed the portrait of our great-grandfather that hung over the fireplace. She plans to replace it with a landscape!"

"Oh? You mean this one?" They passed the portrait in question on their way down the hall. "See? She's merely moved it. It looks quite well here, hanging with our other ancestors, don't you think?" He resumed walking.

Georgina continued following. "You have to keep a tighter rein on her. She's changing *everything*. We had quite a row about it. It was most embarrassing. You must talk to her."

Benjamin turned to face his sister, frustration building within him. Every day Georgina brought to him some slight, some mistake Hannah had made, from using the wrong china to forgetting to close a window. At first, expecting the complaints to have some logical validity, he was willing to listen. Now he knew an unreasonable dislike of Hannah fueled her words.

"I asked her to make changes she deemed necessary," he explained, his patience strained. "Lord knows this run-down mausoleum needs a breath of fresh air, which she seems to be providing, if the parlor is any indication."

His sister's eyes began to mist, and Benjamin dreaded the flood of tears that threatened. Nothing made his sister happy, and he was at a loss how to help her. Certainly, after what he had done to her, he could hardly dictate to her how to live a happy life. Nevertheless, her constant melancholy and unhappiness weighed daily on him. Since his marriage, her attacks on Hannah had begun to strain his temper to the breaking point.

She grasped his arms, her fingers digging into his suit coat. A queer desperation filled her eyes. "Why did you have to marry her, Benjamin? Why? We were doing fine on our own, just you and me, like it's been for years."

Benjamin glanced around, conscious the servants could probably hear every word of their argument. "Please. You're getting hysterical, Georgy. Try to pull yourself together."

"You haven't taken her to your bed yet, have you?" Georgy had never spoken so blatantly to him before, and her words caught him up short. "Have you?" she pressed.

His throat felt raw when he spoke. "That's none of your business."

Georgy read the truth in his eyes. "Then, it's not too late. You can have the marriage annulled, since it wasn't consummated. Tomorrow, you can go to court, and—"

His patience snapped like a taut string cut by a knife. "Stop it! I'll not hear another word out of you about my wife, Georgy. I'm fed up with your unhappiness, with how you feed off of me and my life. Make a life for yourself, damn it! You knew I'd marry someday; it's my duty as the male heir. For better or worse, I chose Hannah. She's the mistress of this house."

His words caused the dam to burst and the tears to flow. Georgy's face crumpled. She pressed her hands to her mouth, then turned and fled up the stairs. Benjamin stared after her, shaken from their encounter. As his temper ebbed, fresh guilt flowed through him.

He had never spoken to her so roughly before. Why had he lost his composure this time? The suggestion he dispose of Hannah . . . He couldn't fathom doing so. He couldn't imagine never seeing her bright smile again, closing off all hope they would one day come to an understanding, become true man and wife.

Now he realized he had been worried that Hannah herself might seek an annulment. Hearing the possibility put into words had been more than he could bear.

And Georgy had paid the price.

That night, Hannah hesitated outside the door to the countess's suite, which Georgina still occupied. After she had taken dinner alone in the dining room, Susan, one of the new chambermaids, had told her Georgina wished to speak with her. The two women had avoided each other as much as possible, ever since Hannah had tried to involve her sister-in-law in the household redecorating, only to be rebuffed. Since then, she saw Georgina only at dinner, and often not even then. Nor did she usually see Benjamin. He took his meals in his lab or at his club, leaving her utterly alone.

Though she tried to convince herself she preferred her own company, the contrast with the bustling household where she grew up, with four sisters, two parents, and a passel of friendly servants, was sometimes painfully hard to bear. She longed for home, for a friend, more than she had ever thought it possible to long for anything.

Except Benjamin's touch. She tried hard not to dwell on how he had made her feel, just by touching her, kissing her. She refused to give in to her desires. If she was merely a distraction to him, she would hardly encourage that thinking by chasing after him.

She stared at Georgina's closed door, the silence beyond giving no clue as to her sister-in-law's purpose. Firming her resolve, Hannah knocked lightly on the door.

"Enter."

The terse command was exactly what Hannah had expected. She did as bid and found Georgina in her housecoat, as usual. Less usual, her hair lay unbound and tangled down her back. She sat at a small writing desk under the window, which framed a view of London roofs shrouded in twilight fog. A lantern on the desk illuminated a ledger resting on its surface.

Picking up the book in her thin-fingered hands, she held it out to Hannah. "This is for you."

Hannah paged through the book, an almost encyclopedic account of the household expenses and income. She had started her own accounting, but had felt blinded by her lack of knowledge of English costs and salaries. She still didn't know if she was over or under paying the household help. This book would contain the answer. She studied Georgina carefully. Why was she giving it to her now? "I didn't even know this book existed."

"You'll need it if you're to make sense of this place."

"Thank you. So, you kept the books before?" she asked in a conversational gambit.

Georgina's pale lips turned up in a wry smile. "A painfully obvious question."

"I suppose so. Then, why now?" As far as she knew, their strained relationship hadn't changed. From the first, Georgina had resented her presence and her role in the household.

"I no longer care." Georgina seemed remarkably composed.

Hannah stood uncomfortably before her and considered Georgina's words. Was it the truth? Was this awkward interview over? Hannah didn't know whether to stay or leave. She gazed back at the implacable light brown eyes which unflinchingly took her measure.

"You have no idea how lucky you are, and you don't even realize it," Georgina finally said. "Not every woman can be so blessed as to marry the man she chooses."

The man she chose? Only under duress. Hannah considered correcting Georgina, but held her tongue.

"He's a wonderful man, Hannah. Our father—

he squandered our inheritance. Benjamin's efforts
are the only thing keeping us afloat. You probably
noticed how ill trained most of our staff was when
you arrived. Despite our dwindling finances, Benjamin insisted we make do with whoever remained
in our service rather than find more suitable help.
He couldn't stand to turn out a single one of them.
Instead, he helped many of the staff find positions
with other households. Do you know how rare that
is, for a gentleman to concern himself with his
servants' livelihoods?''

"I think so," she said softly, beginning to see
her husband in a new light.

Georgina sighed. "No one is harder on Benjamin
than himself. No doubt I haven't helped matters.
Perhaps someday he'll learn to believe in himself
again. Please give him a chance."

Hadn't she? From the first day, she had longed
to make their marriage work, had tried to communicate as much to him. But she and Benjamin could
have been speaking different languages for all he
understood her, and she him. No matter her good
intentions, she continued to disappoint him. His
rejection of her after the dinner party had merely
firmed her resolve not to risk her heart where he
was concerned.

"I must make a small confession," his sister now
said. "They say confession is good for the soul, do
they not?"

Hannah nodded. "I suppose so."

"Very well. I admit I don't care for the fact that
you've come here, but Benjamin clearly needs
someone. I've spoken to the staff—the old retain-
ers, not your new hires. From now on, they should
be a good deal more cooperative."

"So you did tell them to make things difficult for me," Hannah said bluntly.

"Of course. It was within my power, one of the few things that were. Even so, I knew it would gain me nothing. Not even Benjamin's attention, he is so blind to the subtle antagonisms occurring within his own household."

"That's certainly true." Benjamin had never seen or understood the difficulties she had faced from the staff, from this new culture, from Georgina.

"That, too, will change, no doubt."

Hannah gazed at her carefully, feeling at a loss. What did she mean? Why would things change now? Georgina was acting rather strangely, as if she had reached a decision which drove all her words and actions. Certainly, Hannah had never seen her more melancholy or more open with her feelings.

Her eyes burned with intensity. "Know this. It was never you, not personally. Any girl—English or American—would have cost me the same."

In a flash of understanding, Hannah realized how unneeded Georgina must feel. She had taken to her bed months ago, but instead of her absence causing Benjamin to realize his need for her, he had merely found a replacement for her. Naturally she had resented Hannah's arrival. Georgina saw her youth and health slipping away as she became an old maid of no use to anyone. Then Hannah arrived and usurped the only role that gave her life meaning.

Georgina had no idea how well Hannah understood her pain and loneliness. Benjamin had cast her aside in a different manner, but just as surely.

She asked softly, "Do you love your brother very much?"

"Yes, when I'm not despising him." She spoke the words with little emotion, as if they were of no account. "But I'm too tired to hate anymore. It has gained me nothing, as you can see." Opening her desk, she removed a small parcel bound in linen and twine and held it out to her. "Give this to Benjamin. I would find it too difficult to face him."

"But he may still be awake. Don't you think—"

She pressed the parcel into Hannah's free hand and curled her fingers around it. "Just do it. Now go. I'm tired."

Hannah nodded. Taking the ledger and parcel with her, she left the room for her own.

The huge house had grown silent, except for the usual creaks and groans caused by the wind outside. Hannah's newly hired personal maid had retired, along with the rest of the household.

Hannah lay in her bed in the dark, staring at the ceiling, recalling her strange interview with Georgina. Why today, of all days, had she finally capitulated? According to Susan, her maid, the other servants had overheard Benjamin and Georgina arguing in the hallway, but she didn't know what about.

It was none of her business, Hannah told herself. Still, she had a strong hunch it had been entirely about her.

The ledger and the packet intended for Benjamin lay unopened on her bureau. Odd that Georgina would entrust to her something intended for the man between them. Hannah would wait until morning to give it to him. She had no idea if he had gone to bed or even where he might be spending his evening.

Georgina had acted almost as if she herself wouldn't be available to pass the parcel on to her brother. Why would that be? Was she going on a trip? She had heard no mention of a trip. The servants hadn't packed her things or made arrangements as far as she knew.

I no longer care . . . I'm too tired to hate anymore . . . The cold promise in Georgina's words struck Hannah like an anvil. How could someone stop themselves from caring, from feeling? Only a final solution could truly resolve the cares of a heavy heart.

The laudanum. "Oh, no." Hannah threw back her covers and scrambled out of bed. Was it too late? Hours had passed since she had seen her sister-in-law. Hours in which anything could have happened in the room down the hall.

Her breath catching in her throat, Hannah raced to Georgina's chamber door. She lifted her hand to knock. What if she was wrong? Georgina would mock her for her folly. Still, she had to take the risk.

She knocked, but heard no response within, and knocked louder. Soon she was pounding the door as hard as she could. Still no answer. She tried the knob and, thank God, found the door unlocked.

She ran into the dark room, unable to see anything. Fumbling with the lantern, she finally managed to light it. The golden circle of illumination highlighted a frighteningly surreal scene. Georgina lay flat on her back in bed, her arms crossed over her chest as if in death. An empty bottle of laudanum rested on her nightstand. Was this her normal drugged sleep, or was Hannah too late?

Hannah leaned close to her, felt the soft whisper of breath, barely there. Lifting her wrist, she felt for her pulse and found it just as faint. Not too late, then, but soon . . . .

Hannah found a small photograph tucked in Georgina's palm of a young man who looked familiar. A broken heart, then? She had never thought of Georgina as being vulnerable in that way, but didn't have time to consider it fully. Tucking the photograph in the pocket of her nightdress, she grasped Georgina's shoulders and shook her.

"Georgina, wake up. Georgina!" Despite yelling in the woman's face, she received no response. She tried slapping at her hands, her face, shaking her even harder, but nothing roused her.

"Benjamin!" Hannah cried. She ran to the suite's connecting door and found it locked. She pounded on it, praying he was within and would respond. "Hurry, Benjamin! Wake up!"

He didn't answer. She ran into the hall to the suite's other door and pounded on that, as well, calling for him. When he finally opened the door, she nearly fell against him. He caught her and righted her. He wore only his drawers and a knee-length burgundy dressing gown that gaped open, revealing his lightly furred chest. His state of undress roused a curious longing within her, but she had no time to ponder her feelings.

"It's Georgina. I think she's taken too much laudanum."

His brow furrowed, his gaze skidding up and down her own form, clad only in a thin nightdress.

This was no time to be embarrassed, however. Hannah grasped his arm and began dragging him into the hall, toward the open door to Georgina's room.

"She was acting strangely earlier, and I started to think what her words might mean. I'm afraid she intended to kill herself."

They reached the door. He took one look at his deathly still sister haloed by the lantern light and leaped into action. "Ring the servants' bell. Send someone after Doc Chambers. He lives on Grosvenor Square. Without a doctor, she could very well die."

CHAPTER 14

Chauncy dashed off to fetch the doctor as bid. Benjamin watched him sprint out the front door on his wiry legs, not doubting for a moment that the carriage driver would race through the streets as fast as possible.

Would the doctor arrive too late? Every minute stretched into eternity. Any moment might swallow his sister forever, an eternal punishment for his crimes against her.

Hannah's presence was a godsend. He hadn't realized a gentlewoman could be so stalwart in the face of crisis. She kept her head, instead of dissolving into a distraught puddle as his mother no doubt would have.

Together, they did their best to stimulate Georgina's system, rubbing her hands, pouring cold water on her face, even slapping her cheeks. Finally, they resorted to walking the comatose woman about the room, as if she were aware, as if she were awake.

Nothing roused her, and Benjamin felt the life ebbing from her minute by minute. "This is all my fault," he muttered as they settled her back in her four-poster bed. "All my fault. I pushed her to this. If you hadn't found her . . ." He glanced at Hannah standing on the other side of the bed. In her ivory nightdress with her hair flowing down her back, Hannah looked like an angel of mercy. He had never been so grateful for the presence of a woman—no, another human being.

"Benjamin, you mustn't blame yourself," she said, her soft brown eyes filled with concern.

"Easier said than done, my dear." He stroked Georgina's pale face, her sallow complexion accenting small creases at the corners of her eyes. When had they appeared? "I was contentedly sleeping in my warm bed while she lay dying, her life slipping away moment by moment. How did you know?"

"What she said to me, earlier today. She stopped fighting me—and herself, I gather. I had no idea of her intentions, or I would have said different things, tried to talk to her. She must be just as lonely as . . ." She hesitated.

His eyes focused on Hannah, and his heart hitched. "As lonely as you? That, too, is my fault."

She lifted her gaze to his, and he knew he was right. He hadn't thought about Hannah's loneliness or her feelings at all. He had been too concentrated on his work, his own confused heart. "I've always excelled at being an insensitive bastard. Just ask Georgina," he said, his remark drawing a faint smile from his bride. "Come, let's try putting her in a cold bath."

He lifted Georgina in his arms. To his dismay, he could feel her bones through her nightdress. When had she become so thin? With Hannah following, he carried his sister toward the bathroom tucked between the suites. Kneeling by the tub, Hannah started filling it with cold water, while Benjamin gently settled Georgina into it.

The tub was half-full, with no response from Georgina, when the doctor finally arrived.

Taking Hannah's place by the tub, the doctor checked Georgina's thready pulse and shallow breathing and declared what they already knew, that she had suffered an overdose of medicine. His gray brows pulled together. "Put her back in the bed. We must pump her stomach immediately. There is no time to lose."

Benjamin soon found he couldn't bear to be in the room during the nauseating procedure and retreated to his own suite to await the outcome. Hannah, however, remained, joining Mrs. Pocket in helping the doctor feed the long tube down Georgina's throat.

Hannah's character—her strength—astounded Benjamin. Throughout the evening, she had maintained her courage and composure, kept her head and moved swiftly to help his sister. That she had divined Georgina's intention when he had not—when no one else had—filled him with admiration. When he had married her, he hadn't begun to comprehend the jewel he had found. But the longer he knew her, the more certain he was that he could scarcely have done better had he sought a wife among society's belles in the traditional manner.

This, despite her social ineptness which, to his surprise, he now found more than a little humorous. *In the years to come, we shall look back on that calamitous dinner party and laugh,* he decided. *All three of us.*

The weight of his potential loss bearing him down, he collapsed in a chair by the cold fireplace and lowered his head to his hands. "Poor Georgy. I'm so sorry, Georgy."

Memories flooded his mind and heart, tangling and untangling in an emotion-filled dance. His little sister, only five, tagging behind him and his friends and longing to play. The two of them fighting over candy given them by their father upon his return from one of his long trips. Georgy crying despondently at the loss of her playmate when he left home for Eton at age eight. The way he had teased her when she had had her first crush, on a schoolmate he had brought home for Christmas. Their mother's death ten years ago, which left them with no one to rely on but each other.

And as adults, when they had been part of a different group of three and foolishly believed nothing could ever come between them.

His eyes filled with unaccustomed moisture. Feeling terribly weary, he leaned back and closed his eyes. "Ah, Georgy. Things haven't turned out well for us, have they?"

He felt her nearness before he looked up. Hannah stood in the connecting doorway of his suite, silhouetted by light from Georgina's room. Pausing by a table near the door, she lit a lantern, pushing the darkness to the room's corners. Closing the door behind her, she said gently, "The worst is past, Benjamin, or so the doctor says."

"She'll be all right?"

"He thinks so. He thinks she's been abusing the laudanum for quite some time. She's resting now, and he's going to observe her until morning."

"Thank God for Doc Chambers." The crisis over, Benjamin found his attentions turning to Hannah. She appeared wrung out by the night's events, dark circles under her eyes giving her a worldly air that belied her youth. Gratefulness and protectiveness mingled in his chest and made his breath catch in his throat. Pulling himself from the chair, he crossed to her and clasped her arms. "If you hadn't been here . . ."

Touching her arms couldn't begin to express how he felt. In an emotional display that surprised even him, he wrapped his arms tightly around her and pulled her close.

At the feel of her soft body in his arms, he found a hint of the peace that always managed to elude him. He pressed her slim, soft curves even closer, wanting to meld her against him, and was gratified when she responded, her arms clasping his shoulders in return. They needn't be alone after all. "Thank you, Hannah," he murmured into her ear, a breath away. "Thank you so much."

Hannah pulled back and looked up at him, her eyes darkening, her lips trembling. "I'm sorry, Benjamin. I fear I'm the cause of her melancholy. If I hadn't come here—"

He traced her slim jaw. "Nonsense. She knew I had to marry someday."

She ducked her head and stepped out of his embrace, leaving him surprisingly bereft. "It hurt her that I was taking over her role in this household."

Confusion filled him. "But—she showed no interest . . . Every day she complained to me of the difficult job it presented to her."

"Women aren't that simple, Benjamin. She wasn't complaining about the work. She was longing for more attention from you." Her eyes glowed with a sadness Benjamin had never seen. Did Hannah, too, long for his attention? He had taken her for granted as well. How foolish he had been!

He dug his hands into his hair and sank into the chair. "I had no idea the depths of Georgy's pain, no idea she was addicted to laudanum. I paid no attention, not like you. I didn't even try to understand." His throat tightened, and he feared he would dissolve into tears, shaming himself before her. Yet he had to confess his sin. "I lost my temper, Hannah, and said the most horrible, cruel things to her."

Hannah neither condemned nor excused him, and he could see guilt weighing on her as well. Yet she had nothing to feel guilty for. He had demanded she take over the household. All the guilt lay at his door.

Hannah paced away, her brow furrowed in thought. "No, Benjamin, my presence was the final straw, and not just because I was managing the correspondence and redecorating. Georgina said something to me about how lucky I am to have a husband."

"That's debatable."

"When I found her, she was holding this picture." Extracting a small photo from her pocket, she gave it to him. "It's Peter Farraday, isn't it? Your friend?"

Benjamin didn't need to look at the picture. "Yes," he said stiffly, memory thick like treacle in his chest. "They were to be married."

Hannah nodded, then pulled up an ottoman and sat near him. "Go on."

He slouched his shoulders and clasped his hands between his knees, folding in on himself in defense against the guilt, the pain. Once he told her, how would she view him? Already she thought little of her husband. Knowing he had destroyed his sister's life, how low would he fall in Hannah's estimation?

Already, the peaceful feeling Benjamin had experienced in her tender embrace had faded, no doubt never to return. Once she learned what kind of man she had married, how could he ever expect her to accept him? To care for him? Still, she had a right to know.

He forced the words out, slowly, haltingly. "Georgina trusted me to take care of Peter. He was my partner. Together we were determined to shatter the record for high-altitude balloon flight. She trusted me, and I failed her utterly."

She laid a hand on his arm, her touch tender. "Peter. He—he died?" Even her gentle tone couldn't soften the terrible truth.

He corrected her sharply. "I killed him."

CHAPTER 15

Benjamin's stark admission made Hannah ache inside. She longed to soothe him, but knew he needed to make this awful confession, for the good of his soul.

"We spent months preparing," he said, his tone curiously flat, revealing no hint of the painful emotions she knew he suffered. She clasped her hands in her lap to keep herself from reaching out to him before he had finished.

"I well remember the day of the flight," he continued. "It was unusually bright, with that crystalline clarity only a few summer days truly have. The perfect day, in other words, for the grandest of scientific adventures. A curious thing about scientists, Hannah, is how blasted superstitious we can be. I took the good weather as a positive omen."

He sighed, his broad shoulders lifting and falling as if with a heavy weight.

"Georgina herself helped us cast off, along with others in the crowd who had gathered. We left the bounds of earth behind and ascended rapidly toward the heavens." His voice softened, and his eyes took on a faraway cast as he painted the picture for Hannah. "It's an amazing feeling, Hannah, flying high above the cares of the world. You can see for miles and miles."

Hannah smiled in response, feeling along with him the thrill of discovery, the excitement of seeing new vistas spreading below. On the Eiffel Tower, she had gotten a taste of what it felt like to view the world from on high and could only attempt to imagine what Benjamin had experienced riding his balloon above the earth.

His fist tightened on the chair's armrest. "I'd been up many times, but I felt this trip would be special. This wasn't a joy ride. I'd never felt more satisfied, more certain we were on the path to glorious success. Our names would go down in the history books, Hannah. We would prove man could survive in the upper reaches of the atmosphere. We would go higher than any men ever had.

"For the first time, we were using an oxygen-breathing apparatus. I'd tested it in a vacuum chamber, found that it could, indeed, supply us oxygen when the air thinned, which was around fourteen thousand feet. Equipped with our thoroughly tested containers, the thin air posed no problem. No problem at all." His eyes grew shadowed, his jaw tense. "I failed to realize there were other factors to consider."

Hannah longed to stroke his brow and smooth the lines that had gathered, but she didn't want to distract him from his tale. She had the strong sense that he had never shared this story with another soul, until now.

"The first signs of physical discomfort began to plague us at about twenty-three thousand feet. Peter, especially, began to feel ill, and terribly drowsy. Whenever he did, he took a bracing pull of oxygen, and that set him to rights. The temperature had fallen, as I knew it would, to around ten degrees below zero. We had prepared for that eventuality by bundling up in winter wear. We knew we could make thirty thousand feet proceeding thusly.

"Despite taking in the oxygen, I began to feel weaker and weaker, especially as we passed the twenty-five-thousand-foot mark. I felt light-headed and strangely euphoric, as if I were losing touch with reality. I decided I needed more oxygen, but I couldn't—I couldn't even lift my arm to put the mouthpiece to my face." His hand cupped, as if holding a phantom face mask. "I couldn't even *speak.*"

"Oh, no," Hannah said, taking his hand in hers and squeezing it. He didn't acknowledge her touch, but deep down she knew it helped him put the horror into words.

"I don't mean to dwell on what happened to me. After all, I survived. I awoke, only then realizing I'd fallen unconscious for almost forty minutes. The balloon had been driven down by strong winds. Peter, however, remained unconscious. He was lying on the floor of the gondola, his eyes closed. I shook him awake. He was groggy, but came to. That's when I made a critical mistake. Instead of ending the flight, instead of landing and calling it good, I refused to give up. I threw out more ballast—along with a piece of equipment

that weighed eighty pounds. I was heady with
excitement. I didn't care about the equipment. I
didn't care about our safety. I only cared about
succeeding.

"The sudden change in weight shot us upward
at an incredible rate. I believe we reached twenty-
eight thousand feet, which was, indeed, a new
record. I can't be sure, however, because—fool
that I was—I fainted again.

"An hour passed before I awoke. The balloon
was careening toward the earth at a frightening
speed. Peter was again lying unconscious on the
floor. I crawled to him on my knees, pulled on his
arm, called to him. But he never responded. He
lay there, motionless and silent, his eyes half open.
When I managed to lift him to a sitting position,
blood spilled from his mouth."

His voice sounded almost emotionless, but Hannah knew he spoke from deep pain. "He was dead
long before I brought the balloon in for a remarkably soft landing, considering I was half-dead
myself. I could barely feel my hands and feet,
despite my leather gloves and extra layers. My precautions had been amateurishly inadequate.
Clearly, oxygen must be used continuously at such
heights."

"But how were you to know that? No one had
ever traveled so high before," Hannah said reasonably.

He ignored her comment. "Poor Peter. He paid
the price for my foolishness. He trusted me with
his life. And Georgina trusted me, too, to her folly.
Telling her the news, that I'd killed her fiancé—it
was the worst experience I have endured, excepting
one."

Hannah longed to know what the one other experience was, but she knew Benjamin needed comfort more than reliving another painful memory. No doubt her own words would be inadequate to assuage his guilt and pain. More than words, he needed to understand she was here, was listening, her own heart suffering along with his. She reached out and touched his shoulder.

He didn't draw back, nor did he respond. With more boldness, she leaned forward and slid her arms around his shoulders. After a long moment, his hands slipped up to her waist to steady her, and he settled his forehead in the crook of her neck and shoulder.

Gently, naturally, he pulled her onto his lap, cradling her in his arms as she cradled him. Time stretched out, the only sounds in the room their breaths and their heartbeats. His choked whisper against her shoulder warmed her skin through her nightdress. "I feared you would be done with me if you knew how cavalierly I destroyed the lives of those closest to me. Yet here you are."

She stroked his thick black hair. "My heart aches for you, for both you and Georgina. I wish there was something I could do, but I know nothing can undo the past."

"Sweet Hannah. Being here with me is more than I ever hoped for." Lifting his face, he kissed her gently on her cheek, then pressed her head to his chest. She listened to his heartbeat, strong yet heavy, and vowed to relieve the burden of guilt he carried within him. Somehow.

Yet she knew there was more than guilt involved. He hadn't been aloft in a balloon since that disastrous flight. He had tried to accomplish his experi-

ments using only instruments and putting no man
at risk. Failing that, he was allowing two other men,
Winthrop and his assistant, to take his rightful
place. Out of fear?

Hannah knew of only one way he might find
peace with himself and make Peter's sacrifice have
meaning as well as restore his own confidence. But
now wasn't the time to broach the subject.

Cradling her head, he lifted her face to his and
settled his lips on hers, giving her a kiss so gentle
and sweet it brought tears to her eyes. She blinked,
and felt a hot tear roll down her cheek. He leaned
his forehead against hers and sucked in a breath.
Hannah knew he was fighting for control. She grew
aware of the stiff evidence of his arousal under her
bottom.

Swallowing, she firmed her own resolve. Cupping
his cheek in her palm, she drew his face down to
her breasts, praying the intimacy might comfort
him, comfort them both. She could scarcely
remember vowing never to give herself to him. She
had never imagined feeling this deep connection
to this man, her husband, or this overwhelming
need to assuage his hurt. If only she could.

Her thoughts fled as his lips closed around her
nipple through the cloth of her nightdress, moist-
ening it to a wet, hot bud of pleasure. His lips and
tongue teased her, drew a moan from deep in her
throat. She tightened her fingers in his thick hair
and settled deeper into his lap, leaning back against
the chair arm to allow him freer access. He lifted
his head, his lips returning to her mouth, this time
plundering it with a demanding passion that stole
her breath. His fingers began working the laces

at the throat of her gown, separating the strands
enough to allow him to slide his hand within and
cup her breast.

His thumb flicked over her nipple, drawing
another gasp from her. She tightened her arms
around his shoulders, longing to fold herself
against him, inside him, let him take her wherever
their lovemaking would lead.

After a moment, he ceased the heavenly movement of his fingers, merely supporting her breast
but no longer toying with her. He pulled his mouth
from hers and rested his lips against her forehead.
His breath came unsteady, his heartbeat pounding
under her palm. When he removed his hand from
inside her gown, Hannah felt bereft. He began to
tie her laces, speaking low. "This isn't the right
time, as well we both know."

Hannah understood, and admiration filled her
for his restraint, a restraint she hadn't possessed.
She would have willingly tumbled into his bed at
that moment, heedless of the doctor and his ill
sister in the next-door room. Nodding, she slid off
his lap.

Before she moved away, he took her hands and
looked up into her eyes. "Another night, if you
still want to, if this wasn't merely the product of
pity . . ."

Pity? Was he so blind to her fondness for him,
so incapable of believing she cared? Hannah sighed
and tightened her hands on his. "We have a lot
to learn about each other, don't we, Benjamin?
But tonight was a good start."

Gently, she extracted her hands from his and
crossed to the hall door, leaving him alone.

* * *

The bright summer day that followed—coupled with Georgina's neatly dressed appearance—succeeded in chasing away the shadows that lingered from the previous night's ordeal.

Doc Chambers had made arrangements with Benjamin to escort Georgina to a sanitarium at Bath, where she would be treated for opium dependency and her chronically melancholy spirit.

The household gathered on the street to see her off. Benjamin looked worn, his eyes darkly circled as if he hadn't slept all night. "Doc Chambers says this is the best facility of its kind in the country, Georgina. He'll see you're properly situated."

"I know I need to go. Not that I won't miss you, brother."

"It won't be the same without you." He reached out to clasp her gloved hand.

"Oh, bother. You can do better than that." Stepping forward, she gave him a quick hug, which he returned despite his usual reticence, especially in front of the servants.

Hannah was relieved to see that Georgina's spirits seemed to have revived. Despite her ordeal, she hadn't lost her ironic sense of humor. Casting both she and Benjamin a wry smile, she said, "No doubt I managed to make you both feel terribly guilty. I suppose that was my intention."

Hannah met Benjamin's gaze. Georgina never backed down from speaking plainly.

Her gaze moved to Hannah. "I hear you're the reason I didn't succeed. I'm still not certain whether to thank you, but the doctor assures me I'll be grateful for a second chance in the months ahead—after I go through hell trying to wean myself from that demon drug."

Hannah clasped her hand. "When you come back, I would greatly appreciate your help in organizing Benjamin's social calendar. I lack the expertise—"

"I'm aware of that. I attended your horrendous dinner party, remember?"

She smiled ruefully, and Hannah couldn't help but respond in kind. For the first time, she felt Georgina and she might become friends.

"However," Georgina continued, adjusting her hat veil over her face, "it's probably best if I stay away for a while, give you a chance to start your marriage on the right foot." Leaning close, she whispered in Hannah's ear. "The countess's suite—it's yours now. Make proper use of it."

Darting her a final smile, she turned to accept Benjamin's help boarding the carriage.

Hannah stood beside Benjamin and watched the carriage trundle to the end of the street and turn the corner. Benjamin turned to her. "What did she say to you?"

"None of your business." At his consternation, she smiled and turned back into the house.

CHAPTER 16

A fortnight after Georgina's departure, Hannah received a most welcome surprise. She could barely contain her excitement at the appearance of her mother and sister on the threshold of the house. They would be in town, staying at a hotel, for at least two months while Lily took part in the Season.

"Mother!" She threw her arms around Mrs. Carrington, threatening to spill her into the overgrown shrubs framing the stoop. "And Lily!" She extended an arm to encompass her younger sister. "I've missed you both so much."

After exchanging exuberant greetings and tight hugs, Hannah led them into the morning room. "I redecorated this room first. I'm just starting on the bedrooms."

Her usually critical mother looked around with a smile. "Quite nice, Hannah. A very pleasant space." Satisfaction and pride filled Hannah at her mother's approval of her home. *Her home.* She realized with a start that she was making it her own, that she was putting down roots. That she was starting to belong.

Soon they were happily settled on the newly upholstered sofas and chairs, discussing a plan of attack for Lily's introduction to London society. "The first thing we must do is secure Lily an invitation to the Duke of Marlborough's ball," her mother said. "It's the most important event of the Season, or so I'm told."

"Oh, it would be so wonderful," Lily gushed. "I hear it's held in an actual palace."

"The Duke of Marlborough?" The event sounded familiar. Hannah rose and retrieved the pile of correspondence from her desk and flipped through the cards. "Yes, we've received an invitation to that one."

"That's perfect!" her mother said. "Why, the earl could easily secure an invitation for the sister of the Countess of Sheffield."

Hannah frowned. "As I recall, it's an overnight affair, since the palace is some distance outside London. Because we're drawing near to Benjamin's flight, we weren't planning to accept."

"Not accept!" Lily gasped.

"How could you not?" her mother asked.

Seeing the words "annual ball" had been enough to dissuade Hannah. She detested balls, despised them with a white-hot passion. Since Benjamin had given her leave to decide which social events to accept, she had chosen only a handful of intimate dinner parties, none of which had yet occurred. Just the thought of facing a roomful of curious strangers made her feel queasy. "I didn't think it would be important to attend," she said simply.

Her mother and Lily exchanged stunned glances. "It's quite the most coveted invitation in society," Mrs. Carrington said. "You mustn't ignore it. It wouldn't be seemly. How does the earl feel about this?"

"He doesn't care," Hannah said with a smile. That much they shared in common. "He's been working so hard, he has little time for socializing."

"Surely for the duke he will make an exception."

Hannah considered this. "No." Lily looked devastated, so she rushed to add, "Not for the duke. But he'll make an exception for my sister."

Her words transformed Lily's face. She grinned and clapped her hands. "Oh, thank you, Hannah! I'm so excited. Traveling to the country and staying at a palace will be so romantic, even for an old married like you." She giggled.

Hannah prayed she hadn't spoken wrong and Benjamin would be willing to attend the affair for Lily's sake. She would have to waylay her preoccupied husband and ask him. With his balloon flight less than a month away, he was even more difficult to talk to than usual. She had thought after their intimate moment following Georgina's illness that they had grown closer, that he knew she would be willing to share his bed.

More than willing. Longing for such intimacy as they had shared that eve. After receiving Georgina's blessing, she had even moved into the countess's suite adjoining his. But the connecting door remained firmly closed.

Her husband seemed to be avoiding her more than ever. His distance did nothing to encourage her to act on her feelings, and lacking experience, she could not fathom the best way to ask for what she desired.

She sighed, despairing of ever understanding her mysterious husband, of ever truly touching his heart.

A gentle knock on his study door drew Benjamin's attention from his weather charts. "Come in."

Hannah entered and closed the door, pressing her back against it. Her lovely brow creased in concern, her eyes wide. "Benjamin."

"Yes?"

"I need to speak with you about something important."

His heart began to pound, and he rose slowly to his feet. She looked so intent. Was this the moment? Was she finally going to welcome him to her bed? Somehow, he hadn't pictured this moment occurring in the broad light of day—or in his study. But he would take it. Oh, yes, he would most definitely take it.

Ever since their encounter in his chamber, he had thought of little else, despite his looming experimental flight. He could hardly stand to be near her, he wanted her so badly. Every fiber of his being called out to hold her, possess her, make her his own. But he had vowed to leave it up to her, and he would not back away from his vow.

He came out from behind his desk and approached her slowly, wanting to make it as easy as possible for her. Surely, for a virginal young woman, even thinking of intimate acts must be difficult, much less speaking of them. "Anything, Hannah. Whatever you need to say—"

"Wonderful!" she sighed in relief. "I was hoping you'd feel that way, but since I have never actually requested anything of you, I wasn't certain of the reception I would receive."

He drew near and clasped her elbows, tugging her close. His blood thrummed along his nerve endings at her nearness, her readiness. "Oh, Hannah, surely you must have known."

"We've never actually discussed attending a ball—and a country one at that—so I had no idea how you felt."

"Ball?" He released her and stepped back, disappointment striking like a physical blow.

"The Duke of Marlborough's ball, more specifically. My sister has arrived in town, and she desperately wants an entrée into society. She would love to attend, and if you could secure her an invitation, we could accompany her as chaperones. Certainly I myself have no interest in attending, but for her sake . . ."

Benjamin could scarcely concentrate on her words, his frustration was so acute. Waving his hand dismissively in the air, he turned back toward his desk. "Yes, yes, of course. Whatever you decide is fine with me," he said brusquely. He sat back down and returned his attention to his paperwork. His heart still thudded with unsatisfied desire; his hands tingled from touching her, even so briefly. How long would he have to endure this torture?

When the door hinges squeaked, he resisted the urge to watch her leave.

* * *

The carriage pulled up before Brown's Hotel on Albemarle Street. Chauncy hopped off the driver's bench and swung open the carriage door. Benjamin stepped out.

A moment later, Lily—accompanied by the hotel doorman—left the foyer and walked quickly toward the carriage, a bright smile on her face. Hannah gazed at her sister in admiration. She had never looked lovelier, her excitement over embarking on this trip bringing out a delicate blush in her flawless complexion. Her peach traveling suit made her appear older and less girlish, making her seem even more beautiful in Hannah's eyes.

Studiously, Hannah watched Benjamin's reaction upon seeing the vision that was Lily. He didn't seem overtly affected by being in the presence of a goddess, merely took her hand and helped her inside the carriage, then took his place beside Hannah.

However, Hannah knew Benjamin often kept his feelings to himself. What did he truly think? If he had been patient, he could have married Lily instead of her. Did that thought occur to him? For it occurred to Hannah.

"Oh, Hannah, your traveling suit is so lovely! It took me all day to decide which outfits to pack," Lily exclaimed. "Except for my ball gown, of course. It's the gold and cream one, remember? Didn't Worth do a fabulous job creating our gowns? Mother assures me they'll be the talk of the evening."

Hannah returned Lily's hug. "I'm sure yours will, sweetie."

Lily's exuberant spirit filled the carriage. What man wouldn't prefer to be in the company of such a lively, beautiful girl? Of course, Lily would never flirt with Benjamin, her own sister's husband. But she didn't have to flirt to draw men's gazes.

Hannah looked carefully at her husband, but he seemed content to sit in the shadows, his expression mildly amused, his gaze on each of them in turn. What was he thinking? What did he think of *her?*

The carriage jolted and began the trip to the train station. Blenheim Palace, the Duke of Marlborough's palace and the only nonroyal palace in England, was two hours away by train and carriage, in Oxfordshire.

"Thank you so much for accepting the invitation to the duke's ball," Lily said, clasping her hands. "I've heard it's the best of the entire Season. To think I'm going to be there! It's so exciting. This event is going to be fabulous!"

"I hope so," Hannah said, trying not to feel nervous about facing a crowd of strangers. "I truly hope so."

The carriage bumped across a stone bridge that spanned a man-made lake. Ahead and behind, a dozen other carriages had followed the same route from the train station in Woodstock. Across the bridge, the baroque splendor of Blenheim Palace came into full view. Rays of afternoon light shone on its yellow stone, making it appear like something out of a young girl's dream.

Lily hung out the window, straining to see. She leaned so far forward on her seat, Hannah feared she would tumble off. True, the great golden palace in its parklike setting was like nothing they had seen in their limited experience.

"Lily, sit back," Hannah whispered, conscious of Lily displaying her inexperience.

"Everyone gawks at Blenheim," Benjamin said, looking at her instead of the view out the carriage window. "Seven acres of opulence to honor Queen Anne as much as the Marlboroughs," he commented wryly.

Hannah wished she had a fraction of his worldliness to be able to dismiss the palace so readily. The carriage pulled to a stop in an immense paved courtyard, contained on three sides by wings of the palace. As soon as the carriage rolled to a stop, two uniformed and bewigged footmen opened the doors and helped them down. One of the footmen led them up the broad steps to the entrance, while the other helped their servants in the second carriage tend to the luggage.

Inside the great hall, Hannah tried hard to contain her trepidation at the awe-inspiring sight. She had never been in such a formalized, elegant atmosphere thick with tradition and history—a history she knew little of. Beside her, Benjamin appeared completely unaffected by the elaborately carved ceiling, gilded walls, and rows of footmen flanking them.

He was born to this. You weren't. She determined not to embarrass him this time, no matter what. She would act the proper role of countess and do her best not to be intimidated by her surroundings or the English aristocracy.

"Hannah, look." Lily directed her attention upward. A richly colored painting of a military battle spanned the ceiling.

"Glorifying war," Benjamin said with heavy irony. Hannah smiled. Benjamin was ever the rebel. Like her, he would much prefer that peaceful pursuits be immortalized, such as scientific discovery.

As if the painting wasn't enough, intricately detailed tapestries depicted the military exploits of the first duke. Past these, family portraits lined the walls, and rare pieces of porcelain and Venetian glass rested on carved pedestals.

A butler approached them. "Welcome to Blenheim Palace, Lord Sheffield, Lady Sheffield, Miss Carrington."

Lily's eyes lit up when he addressed her along with Benjamin and Hannah. Hannah found herself impressed by the man's efficiency—a far cry from her own lousy efforts at hostessing.

"Allow me to escort you to your rooms," the butler continued. "Dancing commences in the ballroom at precisely eight."

As they traversed the long, vaulted corridor leading to the south wing, Benjamin chatted with the butler about the weather and the stock market. While he was thoroughly at ease in these opulent surroundings, Hannah and Lily peeked into every open door, then exchanged glances at the sight of the ornately decorated rooms. In Hannah's experience, even the richest Americans didn't flaunt their wealth so openly, perhaps because they lived in a true democracy, without kings and queens.

How did one ever grow used to such surroundings? Benjamin clearly had. Would she, too, someday take such conspicuous grandeur for granted?

Hannah hoped she never forgot what it meant to be an American, even if her independent spirit frustrated her very English husband.

The butler paused before the door to a small but comfortable bedroom and turned to Lily. "Miss. I hope you will find these accommodations suitable."

As if under a spell, Lily drifted into the rose-and-cream-colored room, the perfect setting for a young lady. She turned to the servant and said coolly, "I believe I shall be quite comfortable here, thank you."

Hannah met her eye. Both of them stifled smiles at Lily's sophisticated act. For that was all it was. Hannah knew as soon as she was left alone, Lily would be squealing with delight.

Two doors down, the servant stopped again and opened another door. "Milord, milady," he said, bowing his head to Benjamin and her.

Glancing inside, Hannah's gaze settled on the large four-poster bed in the center of the blue-and-gold suite. There was only one bed. Of course there was. They were a married couple! How foolish of her not to realize they would be sharing a room—and a bed. She should have considered this—she should have prepared herself. What would they do tonight? Would he expect.... Would she be ready?

As if the situation irritated him, Benjamin's lips tightened. He extended his arm in a formal gesture, and Hannah realized he was waiting for her to cross the threshold first.

Lifting her head, she forced her feet to move. The servant left, and she found herself alone with her husband. She wanted to say something, say that perhaps this was fate, say that she never stopped longing for more kissing, more caressing. Before she could formulate the right comment, a knock sounded on the door.

More relieved than she expected, Hannah swung it open to find Lily.

"I'm so excited I can hardly contain myself. There's a schedule on the desk—did you find yours?" Lily held up a piece of parchment. "It says this hour ladies should be resting, but I'm far too excited. Let's go exploring!" She grasped Hannah's arm and pulled her into the hallway.

Hannah looked back at Benjamin, wondering if he would object, wondering if he cared where she spent her time.

"Go on," he said, as if her presence made no difference to him. "I saw Winthrop's carriage behind us. We have a few details to work out before the flight." Nodding toward them both, he strode down the hall toward the public areas of the palace.

Benjamin feared he was lost. The well-manicured garden paths he had been following had given way to a country track lined with tall oaks. He stopped at a corner and realized he had already gone to the left. He must have followed a road in a wide circle. This time, he turned right.

He had been so occupied ruminating on Hannah, he had lost track of where he was in Blenheim Palace's vast, parklike grounds. He had gone for a walk to attempt to sort out his thoughts—or rather, plan how best to win over his young wife.

Their sleeping arrangements here at Blenheim certainly magnified the issue. Hannah continued to fear him, fear his attentions. He knew this with painful certainty. How could he not? When she had realized they had been given a single bed, the trepidation on her face had cut like a knife.

As a perfect gentleman, he would make no move on her, even if it meant sleeping on the floor or spending the entire night playing whist in the parlor. She had to want him in return.

How long would he be forced to wait? Would she ever come to trust him? He had to win her over, or he would start dying inside.

Win her over how? He had never seriously sought to court any woman before. How did one achieve success in such a nebulous endeavor?

He passed a cricket field, where several youths were playing a game. He certainly hadn't gone this way before. He finally admitted he was hopelessly lost.

A boy of about fourteen had come to the edge of the field near the road to rest for a moment, his face flushed with exertion. Picking up a towel, he wiped his face.

"H'llo!" he said, waving at Benjamin.

"Good afternoon." Benjamin stepped closer. "You wouldn't, by chance, know the shortest way back to the palace?"

The boy tossed his towel over his shoulder. "I'll show you. I was born there, after all."

"Oh, do you live there?"

"Oh, no. I wouldn't want to live there. I doubt even the duke likes living there. It's too big!"

"I should say so." Benjamin smiled. He liked the boy's forthright manner. Together, they started strolling back the way he had come.

"You're Lord Sheffield, the balloonist, aren't you?" the youth asked.

Benjamin was interested to discover that his reputation had preceded him. "That would be me, yes."

"I loved reading about your exploits, in class at Harrow." He spoke with a slight lisp. "My mother told me you married a girl from New York. My mother is from New York, too. Lady Jennie Churchill. They're here for my uncle's ball. I'm on a break from term."

"And you are . . ."

"Winston Churchill." He thrust out his hand, and Benjamin shook it.

"Good to know you, Winston."

Leaving the tree-lined lane, they entered the formal garden area of the immense park, and the palace rose into view beyond. "You realize Blenheim would probably be a ruin, or a university, or something of that nature, if it weren't for rich American ladies?" Winston said.

"I'm not surprised." Benjamin sighed. No longer did he envision his own American heiress as a means to an end. Somehow, thinking of her dowry seemed to denigrate all that Hannah had come to mean to him.

She had brought so much more to his life than money, with her companionship, her spirit, her compassion. Did she realize that? Perhaps that was what he needed to make her understand, tonight. Perhaps then they could finally start their married life.

They approached a large fountain, and Benjamin paused. "Thank you for helping me find my way back. Without your intervention, I'd have been wandering the grounds the rest of the day and into the night."

Winston chuckled.

Benjamin added, more to himself, "And that would really have ruined my plans."

"Plans?"

Benjamin hesitated asking a child for advice, but then, what did he have to lose? And the boy did know the layout of this place. "You wouldn't happen to know of a particularly . . . idyllic spot here in the garden, would you?"

Winston smiled. "You might try the Temple of Diana." He pointed toward a hillock, atop which a small stone Grecian-style monument had been erected. "It's over that way. It's rather romantic, if that's what you mean. I think when I decide to propose someday, I might take the lady there."

Benjamin smiled ruefully. The boy had certainly divined his intentions quickly enough. They reached the point where the path split, leading to each separate wing. "I'm in the East Wing," Winston said, gesturing in that direction.

Benjamin nodded. "Well, good meeting you, Winston. Thank you for your help."

"I've been given permission to join the shooting party tomorrow. Perhaps I'll see you there."

"I hope I'll be otherwise occupied." Indeed, assuming he was successful tonight, Benjamin had every intention of spending the rest of the weekend in his suite—with his wife.

After a last wave, Winston jogged off toward the East Wing.

Benjamin tapped lightly on the door to their room. He had given Hannah plenty of time to dress for the evening. He had dressed before her and spent the past hour at the whist tables in the parlor and sampling food from the generous buffet laid out in the dining room.

"Come in."

Benjamin entered, then paused as his gaze settled on his young wife. She appeared a vision from heaven. Her form-fitting burgundy bodice emphasized her slim, seductive waist and long neck. No, he decided. Her allure was much too potent to be of heaven. She tantalized all his senses with earthly, feminine allure, and his blood pounded anew with desire to possess her.

She began to look confused, and he realized he had been silent far longer than was proper. He explained, his words as halting as a schoolboy's, "I'm sorry. I don't mean to stare. But you're absolutely stunning."

A delicate blush stained Hannah's cheeks, and she looked down as if embarrassed. "I—thank you, Benjamin."

Such innocence! Benjamin found himself surprisingly charmed by his own wife. Did she so rarely receive compliments that his simple remark would confound her?

True, she looked resplendent in her fancy satin ball gown, rich with trimmings. Yet it was her sudden shyness that made him long to take her in his arms, to comfort and protect her—an entirely strange yet welcome emotion.

Every day Hannah lived in his house. Still, he felt at times he hardly knew her. More and more he longed to know her, to understand her mind— and her heart.

Hannah didn't meet his gaze, instead toying with her flower-painted fan. He had never seen her so nervous. Not even their rushed wedding, or their ignominious time in jail, had brought out this side of her. This was the same bold lady who had climbed the Eiffel Tower, who had agreed to an arranged wedding.

But that Hannah had vanished, replaced by a strained, uncomfortable young woman who seemed to want to be anywhere else than about to attend a ball. Why? His curiosity piqued, he walked closer to her. "It's probably the proper thing, us attending this function. Your sister was no doubt right to suggest it. We can introduce both of you to English society. Certainly your introduction is long overdue, for which I alone am at fault."

She continued to look away. "Lily needs the introduction, not I. I'm happy to provide her with this entrée into the right circles."

Reaching out, he lifted her chin with his finger. "You're not nervous about attending this ball, are you?"

She sighed, her shoulders dipping slightly. "Perhaps. Balls are not my favorite pastime."

He shrugged and stepped back. "There's nothing to a ball. I find them tedious, sometimes, but nothing to fret over. Merely make an appearance, dance once or twice, then retire to the smoking room to play a few hands of whist. Once you've lost a respectable number of pounds, you call for your carriage and return home."

"Young ladies don't have the luxury of retiring to the smoking room. Sometimes married women can play whist, but gambling can ruin their reputations."

"Yes, I'm aware of that. But how much more difficult can it be for a lady to remain in the ballroom and dance with eager young gentlemen?"

She didn't reply directly, but spoke as if she hadn't heard his question. Benjamin soon realized the answer was apparent.

"And while you retire to the smoking room, young women are left on the edges of the dance floor, waiting for a passing gentleman to pay them mind. When no suitable young man asks you to dance, you're asked by old men trying to do a good deed, which is worse than being ignored. Then, when the young men do ask you to dance, you realize they've done something positively dreadful, like pour ink down the back of your dress. Of course, it's a while before you realize it, though you do begin to wonder why a group of *gentlemen* on the side of the room keep snickering when your partner swings you past them."

A pithy answer deserted him. This was Hannah's experience with balls? How awful for her.

He cleared his throat. "I take it this happened to you?" he asked softly.

She shrugged. "It was of no consequence. It was only my coming out party."

Such barbaric behavior from well-bred young men seemed inconceivable to Benjamin. "But—why?"

"My mother and a woman named Mrs. Astor have been at odds socially for some time. The ring leader was a cousin of that family."

"And you paid the price."

"That's why Lily and I were coming here to try our luck, away from those New Yorkers."

And he had married her so fast, she had never known what it felt like to be the belle of the ball. She had never been courted by infatuated young men, received love notes and flowers, danced until dawn. It was truly a shame. When he had met her, he had assumed other men had seen the spark of intelligence and beauty that he had seen and rewarded her for it with their attentions. He had assumed she was truly ingrained in the aristocratic society she had been born into, experienced with all its social customs.

He had learned better the night of the dinner party. But he hadn't thought beyond what it had meant to him. Hadn't thought of what Hannah had given up in marrying him so soon out of the schoolroom. He and Hannah were much more alike than he had realized. Both of them were forced by circumstances of birth to play roles that didn't come naturally.

Yet Hannah was so young! She needed to feel special, deserved to feel special. Because she *was* special. He couldn't erase the past, but he could attempt to make things right this very night. Suddenly, the idea of courting this woman seemed easy, if he allowed his heart to lead him. He thought of the romantic temple in the garden and decided that there he would tell her how he felt before the evening was out.

Leaning toward her, he clasped her hands in his. "Hannah, look at me." He waited until she turned her gaze to his. "I promise tonight will be nothing like that past experience. Not with me."

"Thank you, Benjamin," she murmured. "I know it won't be."

"I won't leave your side."

She pulled her hands from his, her expression darkening once more before she looked toward her satin shoes. "I should never have made such a confession of my past. I don't want you to feel

beholden to me. Truly, don't ruin your evening
on my account. Do whatever you wish.''

He smiled down at her bent head. That was
exactly what he would do. Because tonight, he
wished to court his own wife.

CHAPTER 17

"The Earl and Countess of Sheffield," the footman called from the ballroom entrance. "Miss Lily Carrington."

With Lily following close behind, the earl and countess strolled into the lavish ballroom and toward the receiving line, where Benjamin would introduce the women to their hosts, the Duke and Duchess of Marlborough. While Lily glowed with excitement, Hannah felt stiff and ungainly, as if she didn't belong, that any moment someone would point a finger at her, call her an imposter, and demand the upstart American chit be tossed out. Countess? Not her.

Why had she confessed her past shame, earlier in their room? Mightn't Benjamin think less of her? Yet somehow, his caring attitude had made the words flow from her, when she had never spoken of that night since it happened. Strangely, despite their problems, every day she found herself opening up to him more. Somehow, she had sensed he would understand the feeling of not fitting in.

Hannah realized many of the hundreds of guests watched them enter, causing her stomach to clench in terror. Benjamin seemed to sense her fear, for he tucked her arm in his, pulling her tightly to his side in a gesture both protective and proprietary. Hannah glanced up to find him smiling indulgently at her. His confident gaze bolstered her flagging courage.

Indeed, just the sight of him took her breath away. True, he looked more dapper than usual in his formal black suit, offset by a white tie and shirt. But it was the penetrating power of his gaze and his masterful possession of her that threatened to steal her sense.

When their turn came to greet the duke, Benjamin smiled and bowed. "Your Grace, may I present my wife Hannah and her sister Lily."

My wife Hannah. Benjamin had placed his stamp of ownership on her before the British peerage. As the duke smiled at her, Hannah realized she truly did belong, because of Benjamin. His connection to her as a peer of the realm gave her presence a validity nothing else could.

"Sheffield!" The duke, an elderly, balding man, clasped Benjamin's hand in an enthusiastic grip. "It's been ages since you've shown your face in public. I was beginning to think you'd ridden one of your balloon contraptions all the way to the moon."

"Don't be daft, George. You see me at Parliament."

"Dozing in the back, usually," the duke quipped.

"I know where you concentrate your energies. I wish I had as much freedom to indulge my passion for science."

"Are you still conducting your own experiments?" Benjamin asked.

"Most definitely," the duke said. "My fascination with electricity hasn't wavered. I'm even having a laboratory installed on the lower level."

"You're putting a laboratory here in the palace?"

The duke lowered his voice confidentially, but Hannah could hear every word. "The wife's funds, you know. No boost to the bankroll comes quite as easily as the right marriage, as you well know." He winked at Benjamin—actually winked!—and shot Hannah a sideways glance. She wanted to glare at her host for his impolite reminder of her monetary value, but valiantly resisted. Benjamin, however, smiled broadly. So much for her fantasies that she meant anything more to the man. She might as well have come to the ball dressed in pounds and coins.

She turned away from the men and studied the duchess, who was still chatting with another guest. No more than thirty-five, she was radiant in a white gown that flattered her rose-gold coloring. A tiara four inches high rested atop her head.

When Benjamin introduced her and Lily to the duchess, she greeted them in a surprisingly familiar accent. "Hannah, what a pleasure to meet you at last. Where have you been hiding her, Benjamin?" She leaned toward Hannah and said softly, "We American women must stick together."

Hannah began to feel as if she had entered a dream world. "You're American, too?"

"Born and bred in New York. Trust me, if you

want tips on getting along in this society, I'm here
to help. I would love to talk with you more, perhaps
later.''

"Oh, yes," Hannah whispered.

"Call on me during my reception hours, Wednes-
days at three." The duchess turned to Lily. "I also
am named Lily," she said. Then, to Hannah and
her sister's surprise, she leaned closer and whispered, "Actually, I changed it to Lily. I was born
Lillian, but that rhymes with million—a rather
gauche reminder of my value to the duke."

Hannah and Lily smiled and nodded. As soon
as they moved away, Lily said, "How sad, to be wed
only for your money! Thank goodness you were
able to marry for love. I am determined to follow
your example."

Hannah had the sudden urge to confess the
truth, to tell her closest sister she had done no
better than the duchess. Then Benjamin slipped
his arm around her waist and smiled down at her.
"The orchestra's playing a quadrille. Are you in
the mood to dance?"

"Dance?" Hannah knew she looked stunned.
She had never danced with her husband. Nor had
she imagined doing so when she proposed
attending this event.

"Unless you'd prefer to eat first."

Her stomach was far too tense for food. "I'm
not feeling very hungry."

"Then, dancing it is. Come." Taking her hand,
Benjamin began leading her toward the dance
floor.

"But—Lily. We can't leave her alone."

"Look." Benjamin gestured behind her. Lily was
already encircled by young female acquaintances,

girls she apparently knew from her finishing school.

"Lily! It really is you!" The girls clasped each other's hands and squealed.

"Oh, Isabelle, I didn't know you'd come to England, too," Lily said. "How exciting! I just arrived myself."

"Mother and Father brought me."

"And me."

"And me." A young man behind Isabelle smiled at Lily. "You must introduce me to this lovely young woman."

"This is my brother Andre," Isabelle said.

Hannah could tell Andre was already smitten with her sister. He bowed to Lily and whisked her onto the dance floor.

"Well?" Benjamin asked Hannah, his eyebrows raised and a smile playing on his lips.

Hannah lifted her chin. "Very well. We shall dance."

The quadrille ended, and a waltz began. Benjamin slipped his arm around her and whirled her onto the dance floor. Hannah reveled in the feel of being in his arms, even under the rigid rules of the ballroom. Despite the fabric separating them, the heat of his hand burned at her waist and where he clasped her gloved hand in his. Even better, he gave her his full attention, his penetrating gaze locked on hers.

His steps were swift and sure, and he was in total command of the dance. Hannah, however, stumbled more than once. "I'm so sorry. I haven't danced much."

"We'll go slower," he said, modifying the pace.

"No doubt I've had many more years of experience than you at this particular activity."

"No doubt," she said, stepping on his foot.

Instead of frowning as she expected at her clumsiness, he smiled. "Relax, Hannah. You're far too tense." He stroked her back. "And don't forget to breathe."

Hannah pulled in a breath and willed her muscles to relax. Halfway through the waltz, she found the rhythm of their movements. Suddenly, she was floating on air. She closed her eyes and drifted away, imaging what it would feel like if Benjamin and she were truly a couple, in every way. Her body yearned for it, as did her heart, like it never had before. Perhaps tonight, she would suggest he share her bed. But how?

She had never invited a man to her bedroom before. She wouldn't know where to start, what words to use. How could she request something so intimate without sounding tawdry and needy? Worse, would he think less of her if she initiated such a thing? Then again, he had said he was waiting for her permission. If she never took the risk, she might never reap the rewards.

And she was now certain the rewards would be great, indeed.

She opened her eyes and found Benjamin gazing down at her. The intensity of his attention reflected her own feelings, as if he had been thinking along the same intimate lines as she. Her concentration on the dance deserted her. She tripped over his foot and began to fall.

Benjamin's strong arm snagged her around the waist as if she weighed nothing. Holding her feet just inches from the floor for appearances sake, he swung her out of the circle of dancers to the side of the hall, where she was able to regain her footing and her composure. His arm remained locked around her as she stood beside him, so close she could feel his warmth through the thin fabric of her bodice.

That indulgent smile had returned to his face, and Hannah realized she had completely captured his attention. He seemed oblivious to the crowd around them, the music, the lights. For the first time in her life, she felt a man was actually entranced by her. Could it be so? Did he value her for more than her money?

"I need a rest. I'm not used to dancing." Impulsively, she grasped his hand, then rose onto her toes and kissed his cheek. "Thank you for tonight. I've never enjoyed myself more."

His smile widened into a grin. "You're quite welcome. Believe me, it was no chore. Perhaps we should attend another ball sometime."

"Perhaps so."

His gaze shifted down, as if he were considering something. Then he opened his mouth to speak. "Perhaps, later tonight—"

Lily's excited voice cut him off. "Thank you so much for bringing me. I'm having such a wonderful time," she exclaimed as she appeared at Hannah's side. Hannah wished her sister had waited just a few more minutes. What had Benjamin been about to say?

"That's wonderful, Lily," Hannah said, forcing herself to make small talk when her thoughts were decidedly elsewhere. "Are you meeting a lot of nice people?"

"Oh, yes. This is nothing like New York, Hannah.

But then, I don't have to tell *you* that. You're so lucky to be living here!"

"London does have its benefits," Benjamin said.

"Definitely." Hannah caught Benjamin's eyes and smiled. All three of them fell silent. Hannah longed to escape somewhere with Benjamin, somewhere private. If they were alone together, perhaps he would finish what he had started to say. Perhaps she would find the nerve to express how she was now feeling toward him. She shifted her tired feet. "I think I should like to sit down."

"Sit down, now?" Lily's eyebrows lifted in amazement. "Oh, Hannah, you don't want to waste these lovely waltzes, do you?" As the orchestra began another song, Lily glanced from her sister to Benjamin. "Do you?"

Benjamin shifted his own feet, then smiled at Lily. "I don't suppose you're free for this dance?"

"Oh! Yes, it so happens I've been saving this one for my brother-in-law." Lily latched her arm in his, and together, they strolled to the dance floor. Hannah stared after them. She was still winded from the last dance. How did Lily manage to dance so much without pause? And Benjamin, too. He was certainly fit.

Fit . . . Her sister and Benjamin fit, too, as far as dancing partners went. She matched him step for step, not like Hannah's own clumsy efforts to recall her dancing instructions. Benjamin couldn't help but notice the contrast. Unlike her, Lily had paid avid attention to their dancing instructor. Indeed, she had been her star pupil.

She was so light on her feet, as graceful as a swan, her entire countenance lighting up the room. The gold-and-cream gown Worth had designed for her perfect figure was obviously creating a stir among the women and drawing every man's eye. She was being watched by men she had danced with and others who longed to partner with her. She drew the gazes of those along the sides of the room and even others on the dance floor. Benjamin couldn't help but realize the jewel he held in her sister.

He said something to Lily. She laughed in response, the ribbons in her hair trailing out as he circled the floor with her.

Hannah suddenly felt weak-kneed, her insecurities clawing at her insides like demons demanding their due. *No.* She wouldn't grow jealous, not of a single dance. Not of her husband and her favorite sister. *No.*

Memories of the previous ball she had attended stabbed at her. Standing by the wall hour upon hour, as the women beside her were swept onto the dance floor . . . Young men whispering in small groups, their mocking eyes on her . . . Worst of all, matrons publicly cutting her and her family, their snubs hurting worse than direct insults ever could.

Lily had recovered easily, her scars not nearly as deep. After all, the ball hadn't been arranged for her coming out, but Hannah's. Lily still loved balls and dancing with handsome men. Right now, the most handsome man in the room had chosen her as his partner.

Hannah could no longer watch Benjamin and Lily dance. Turning away, she wandered down a hallway leading off the ballroom. In one cardinal-and-gold-decorated parlor, a knot of people had gathered in animated conversation. "Your upcoming balloon flight is quite the topic of interest at my club," a slender man said.

Balloon flight? Someone other than Benjamin was planning a balloon flight? Curious, she drew near.

Another man chimed in, "I say, everyone in the city will be turning out to watch you ascend. It promises to be most thrilling."

Hannah stepped around the man, just as Winthrop replied, "Yes, I'll shatter the altitude barrier in my specially designed balloon. It's taken years to perfect it—and the instruments I'll be bringing aboard."

Righteous anger filled Hannah. Winthrop had no compunctions about taking credit for her husband's hard work. While he didn't actually lie, clearly his avid listeners believed he alone had designed the balloon and planned the flight. He made no mention of the fact he was merely filling in for Benjamin, the true genius behind the work.

"You'll go down in the history books, there's no doubt of that," a woman said, setting her hand on his arm.

He grinned at her. "Are you coming to see me off, Baroness? When it's fully inflated, my balloon will be a sight to see."

Hannah could no longer hold her tongue. "Don't you mean Lord Sheffield's balloon?"

Winthrop turned his pale gaze to her. His smile faded for only a moment, then broadened. "Ah, Countess. Good evening. How charming of you to defend your husband's honor."

"I'm only setting the record straight about the true mind behind the flight. You didn't seem inclined to mention that it has been planned and prepared solely by my husband."

Winthrop shrugged and said to the interested

gathering, "It is, indeed, a partnership. Sheffield does the laboratory work, and I make the dangerous ascent."

Hannah scowled. He made it sound as if her husband did nothing but putter around in the lab, preparing Winthrop's balloon!

The group nodded, completely taken in by events as Winthrop painted them.

"I won't stand by and allow you to take credit for my husband's years of work," Hannah said to Winthrop, ignoring the curious gazes of those nearby. "If you think—"

Winthrop grasped her forearm—uncomfortably hard, as if in warning. He steered her toward the edge of the group, which began to disperse, having lost its center. Winthrop lowered his voice. "Were I you, I would think twice about discussing our arrangement in such a public forum," he said, his eyes and voice filled with subtle threat.

Hannah arched her neck and glared at him. "Why, Winthrop, you seem positively panicked. You don't want people to remember the work is truly his, do you?"

His fingers tightened on her arm, just enough to make her flinch. "You seem to have forgotten how we met, my dear."

Hannah ripped her arm from his grasp. "I could never forget. I know Benjamin and I owe you for bailing us out. But we paid that debt, with interest."

"Then, how can you doubt I'm a true friend of Benjy's?" His charm returned, and he smiled down at her. "And by association, yours."

Winthrop, her friend? Never. Not while her gut told her not to trust him. Not while she doubted that he had Benjamin's best interests at heart.

His expression darkened, and he drew even closer, so close that Hannah could smell the scotch on his breath. "You are no better than me," he said. "We've both made deals with Benjamin. We've bought our way into his circle of glory. And each of us is reaping the rewards. *Countess,*" he added pointedly.

Hannah stepped back. "You needn't remind me of my value to Benjamin. Yet it's extremely crass of you to do so."

"Crass?" His lips twisted in humor. "Again, I remind you of how we met. Not in one of Paris's finer establishments, I daresay."

Winthrop was one of the few people who knew she had been jailed, knew exactly why she had married Benjamin. How dastardly of him to keep bringing up her shame! For the life of her, she couldn't prevent heat from sliding up her face.

"Hannah? There you are." At the sound of Benjamin's voice, Hannah nearly fainted with relief.

"Winthrop, good evening. If you'll excuse us." He nodded at Winthrop, then slipped his arm around her waist. Hannah leaned into him, longing to lose herself in the protective circle of his strong arms.

He led her out of the anteroom, along the wall toward the open terrace doors. Beyond, the garden glowed with lantern light. Together they walked onto the terrace. From out here, the ballroom looked like a painting, the dancers swirling by in a mosaic of color and muted sound. Benjamin led her from the circle of light spilling from the open doors to a more secluded corner of the terrace.

Hannah glanced behind her, but Winthrop was

nowhere to be seen. "I do not like that man. I don't trust him. He's using you."

To her surprise, Benjamin didn't deny it. "I'm well aware of that."

"But—why do you let him?"

Sighing, he leaned his elbow against the stone wall. "Winthrop has been there for me when I needed a hand, as you well know."

"Been there with money, so he could charge you interest."

"He's one of the few Society members who takes my work seriously." He looked down, his fingers running along the smooth stone wall. "Since Peter, I mean."

Hannah's heart squeezed with sympathy. She had never seen Benjamin as vulnerable before, but he was. So vulnerable. She laid her hand on his arm. "I know you miss Peter," she said gently. "But Winthrop is no replacement for your dear friend."

He smiled thinly. "Perhaps not. But what I'm more curious about is you."

"Me?"

"Or rather . . . Us."

Hannah couldn't fathom his meaning. He never discussed their relationship. What did he mean? "I don't understand."

He looked up, his gaze capturing hers. "Do you think that when I look at you, all I see is a bank account?"

His bluntness took her aback. He must have overheard a part of her and Winthrop's discussion. "Well, frankly, yes."

He continued to gaze at her, not denying it. Hannah felt like dying. Her gaze turned toward the dancers spinning in gaiety about the ballroom floor. She caught sight of her sister, paired with yet another partner, a British officer this time. She was laughing at something he had said, thoroughly in her element. The belle of the ball as Hannah could never be. "It must have occurred to you that if you had waited just a little longer, you could have struck a better bargain."

She hadn't known she would say the words, until she had uttered them. She lifted her eyes to meet his and found him frowning.

"What do you mean?"

"My sister. You could have had money and beauty both."

His lips lifted at one corner in a curious smile. Hannah longed to know what he was thinking.

"Surely you're no different from other men," she prompted, longing for him to deny it. For he was different. He valued the same things she did. "Men adore her, and rightfully so."

He didn't disappoint her. "She's comely enough, but she has a tendency to chatter about inconsequential things. I imagine that would get quite trying after a while, if one preferred to discuss matters of an intellectual nature."

Hannah stared at him, then smiled in relief. She adored her sister, but knowing Benjamin hadn't fallen under her charms along with every other man at the ball was such a relief! She hadn't realized until then how worried she had been that her sister might capture her own husband's heart, however inadvertently.

He continued, "It seems to me that you're completely underestimating your own charms."

"Me? Charming?"

"You should have seen the eyes of the other men following you. I found it quite disconcerting."

"Are you certain?" Hannah's gaze widened.

His smile faded. "Quite certain, Hannah. It was a new and not entirely comfortable feeling for me. I have never before felt such an odd mixture of pride and territoriality toward a woman. A strange phenomenon, indeed."

Strange, indeed! He had felt the same jealous possessiveness as had she, when he danced with Lily. She took a step back. "Perhaps we should return inside so that I may see this phenomenon for myself. I could take notes, record your reactions. It might make for an interesting study."

Reaching out, he grasped her wrist and tugged her toward him. She stumbled forward until she was almost pressed against him. "I think I make a poor laboratory rat. Come."

Tucking her arm in his, he led her down the shallow steps into the garden. They strolled down a crushed gravel path between low boxwood hedges outlining beds of lilac and roses. The shadows lengthened, and the music grew fainter the farther they walked along the path, the gravel crunching softly under their feet.

Walking up a shallow rise past tall yew trees, Hannah and Benjamin entered a small clearing. At its center rested a Grecian stone structure, the Temple of Diana. From this vantage point, Hannah could see across the moonlit lake and the expanse of lawn leading back to the palace. The orchestra music wafted on the evening breeze, a perfect accompaniment to the romantic setting.

Benjamin led her to sit on a bench in the shadows. Then he stepped away, his back to her. "Do you rather I had married Lily? Or some other woman?" he finally asked.

The thought made Hannah queasy and faint. Another woman in his house. *Her* house, which she had made her own. Another woman in his arms ... in his bed, which she had yet to make hers. Would another woman already have become his true wife in every way? Did he consider her a failure in that regard? Pulling in on herself, she murmured, "No."

At her confession, he drew near, taking her hands in his. Looking up into his compelling gaze, Hannah realized that she had revealed her true feelings for him. She thought she would feel more vulnerable, but instead, the confession had felt good.

Benjamin sat beside her, tightening the sense of intimacy about them both. Keeping hold of her hands, he said softly, "I would like to believe we have something more than a flagrant exchange of money for a title. I know that is how we began. But we needn't continue thus."

Hannah's heart swelled with hope. She didn't know if she could ever be happier. Until he spoke again.

"Even before I proposed in jail, I was struck by your beauty, your courage. You're quite the most surprising young woman I've ever met."

"I—I'm speechless," she said, shock and glory mingling in her chest.

"That, my dear, is a first." Releasing one of her hands, he began working the glove off her other hand, one finger at a time. Hannah found the touch of his fingers on her own surprisingly sensuous. He gave her other hand equal attention, then pocketed his own gloves and took her hands in his. Skin to skin, he entwined his fingers with hers and held them between them.

"Every day, I find I'm more happy than I've ever been, more grateful that you agreed to my outlandish proposal."

She opened her mouth to remind him of what her money had bought him, but he cut her off. "And not because of your bank account, though I'm most pleased with the changes you've wrought in our home. It means more to me that *you* are there."

Hannah felt she had fallen into a dream. Benjamin, her husband, a man she had grown to care for so much, was telling her she meant something to him. Something important and wonderful.

"You have managed to get under my skin," he continued, his voice thickening with emotion, "to thoroughly distract me from my work when nothing else could. After Peter died, I buried myself in my work, to escape. I can honestly say I cared about nothing else. Until you."

"I don't know what to say," Hannah said, her voice breathless and her heart thrumming in her chest. "Thank you. I—I mean, I—Blast, I'm so unused to hearing such things, I'm going to be clumsy and awkward about it, I warn you."

"Perhaps we've said enough." Cupping his hands around her face, he pulled her forward and claimed her mouth with his own.

His kiss was languorous and thorough. Meshing his lips completely with hers, he took his time teasing her lips and tongue with his own. Hannah felt as if he were touching her entire body, joining her soul to his, binding her heart with his for as long as he desired to hold her close.

He tightened his arms around her, dragging her against him as if he couldn't get close enough to her. She twined her arms around his neck and clung to him, her heart pounding, her thoughts in a jumble. Finally, he granted her a reprieve and released her.

"Oh, my," Hannah uttered breathlessly. Her head still spun from the potency of his kiss. She hadn't wanted it to end. And she wanted more . . .

This wondrous evening . . . What a perfect prelude to making love with him. *If* she had the courage to follow through and invite him to her bed.

"It's getting late," he said, his voice also sounding unsteady. "I think it wise if we retire."

Retire together? He must be thinking along the same lines as she. After all, tonight they would be forced to share a bed. But being so intimate with him, letting him undress her and take her to bed . . . If she disappointed him, would her memory of this magical night be forever ruined? A silly fear, perhaps, but she well knew she didn't have the lush figure of a true beauty. Her bodice barely gave her visible cleavage, her bosom was so small.

She protested weakly, "Lily. She's having such a good time."

He seemed unmoved by her protest. "I'm of the opinion she can handle herself for another hour of dancing." He slipped his arm around her waist and turned her toward the terrace. He added in a teasing tone, "Or two hours. Or even three."

Not daring to question him, she walked with him toward the palace and their private room.

* * *

Despite feeling so connected to him in the romantic setting of the garden, by the time Hannah and Benjamin walked the long way back to their room in the palace's south wing, a tense silence had descended between them.

Benjamin said nothing as he swung open the door. Within, a fire lit earlier by invisible servants turned the room golden, intimate, and romantic.

Benjamin closed and locked the door, then turned to face her.

Hannah found herself almost afraid to look at him and definitely afraid to ask for what she wanted. If she said the wrong thing, would she ruin an evening that until now had been the most wonderful of her life?

She paused near the hearth and turned halfway toward him. He stood in place, not moving, and she realized he was waiting for a sign from her. "I had a wonderful time," she said with a tentative smile, setting her fan and shawl on a nearby table.

"Ah, yes," he said, looking past her into the flames. "It was a lovely evening."

"Yes. Quite lovely." Again silence descended between them. Hannah felt unbearably tense with indecision, with confusion. What should she say, and how? "Well, it's rather late," she began.

"Are you . . . quite tired?" he asked, his gaze settling on hers.

"I am, yes," she said, belatedly realizing he probably hoped to hear she wasn't tired at all. "That is, I'm *somewhat* tired. All the dancing . . . I'm not used to it."

His shoulders stiffened, and he turned partly

away. "Very well. I find I'm not ready to retire. Perhaps I shall join the gentlemen in the parlor for a few rounds of baccy." He took a step away from her, toward the door.

In an instant, Hannah saw what was going to happen. The magic evening would end, and they would never act on their desires. He would never give in, she knew that. And she would always regret lacking the courage to ask for what she truly wanted.

He took a second step away from Hannah, igniting panic deep within her. "Benjamin, wait."

He paused with his hand on the knob, then slowly turned and looked at her. Hannah took heart from the hope in his gaze. Suddenly, it became easy to smile, to reach for him, this man she had grown to care so deeply for. Slowly, she stretched out her hand.

CHAPTER 18

To Hannah's delight, Benjamin didn't hesitate to close the distance between them and clasp her hand. His grip firm on hers, Hannah took one step backward toward the bed, then another, leading him with her.

"Blast this," Benjamin swore. He scooped her into his arms, pressing her close to his chest like a victor claiming his spoils. He tore back the comforter and blankets and deposited her on the bed.

Hannah watched as he stripped off his suit jacket and kicked off his shoes as if he couldn't be rid of them fast enough. A slow, burning desire filled her at this renewed evidence of how anxious he was to bed her.

Undoing his cuffs, he stood over her, his eyes glistening with an almost feral possessiveness. "Do you need help out of that thing?" he asked, his eyes raking over her gown.

"I—I usually don't get undressed by myself," Hannah acknowledged, a blush staining her face. Her maid was abed, and Hannah had no intention of waking her.

"No matter." He stripped off his vest and shirt, then tore his undershirt over his head. Hannah gazed in awe at the full expanse of his broad chest. He was far more muscular than she had realized, his chest tapering to a ridged stomach and trim waist. Firelight played over his skin as if the light itself enjoyed caressing him.

His hands moved to the waistband of his trousers. In mere moments he would be completely naked. Strangely, because of his determined, sure movements, his innate power seemed to increase. Hannah's pulse pounded in her ears. Her eyes wide, she began scooting back on the bed, seeking to delay the inevitable just a moment longer, to give herself a chance to catch her breath.

At her motion, he glanced up. His fingers froze on his trouser buttons. "What am I doing?" he muttered. "You're . . . Christ."

Raking his fingers through his hair, he turned toward the window. "Forgive me. I'm not accustomed to . . . That is, I've never bedded a bride before." Pushing aside the heavy drape, he stared out into the night. Moonlight played across his corded shoulders, and Hannah found herself longing to caress his bronze skin.

"What sort of women *have* you bedded?" she asked, her curiosity getting the better of her. Did she truly want to hear his answer?

"The kind that don't require wooing," he said gruffly.

Ah, *that* kind. Hannah couldn't find it in her to

be jealous of women in such lowered circumstances. Tentatively, she slipped from the bed. Crossing to her husband, she laid a hand on his shoulder, reveling in the hot hardness of his body.

She slipped between him and the window, drawing his gaze to her upturned face. "I'm not so gentle as all that," she said, sweeping her hands over his chest and down his arms. She relished the smoothness of his skin, the silkiness of the hair peppering his chest. "You can consider this a grand experiment. Both of us are setting sail in uncharted waters."

His lips quirked up in a half smile. "You are an amazing woman, Hannah."

His own uncertainty emboldened her. "Not so amazing that I don't need help undoing the buttons of my gown," she quipped. Turning around, she presented him with her back.

His fingertips swept along her shoulders, and along her nape, sending shivers through her. He began working on her buttons, one by one freeing them from their loops. "I'm ashamed to confess I had a desperate urge to toss up your skirt, Hannah. I've waited so bloody long for this. Damn—they're so tiny."

Hannah shivered at the wisps of his touch, longed for her dress to open and be done with this slow torture. "Tear it," she suddenly urged.

"Tear—"

"Tear the damned dress, Benjamin."

A moment later, the immensely satisfying sound of fabric ripping and buttons dancing on the floor met her ears. She closed her eyes and sighed as the chill room air danced across the exposed skin of her back. She stepped out of the gown and kicked it aside, but unfortunately, they were far from done with her clothing.

Benjamin had already begun working the laces of her corset. "I don't suppose you have a knife handy?"

Hannah laughed. "They say patience is a virtue."

Benjamin yanked hard, and the corset opened wide enough to fall to her hips. She wriggled out of it and kicked it aside, then turned to face him. She still wore her camisole and petticoats. "Blast all this fabric," he said, drawing her close. "Kiss me."

Without waiting for permission, he pressed her against him and claimed her mouth with his own. Her breasts, now free beneath her camisole, felt tight and hot against his bare chest. Benjamin grasped her breast and gave it a soft squeeze, making her gasp in surprise. "You're mine, Hannah. Every square inch of your body."

He pulled on her nipple, making a liquid fire pulse between her legs. "Every round inch, too," she murmured. Somehow, she wasn't sure how, her petticoat and slip fell from her body. He must have worked the ties while she was lost in a pool of desire, her body weak with longing. The next thing she knew, he was lifting her underwear-clad body again into his arms. He laid her on the bed and took his place beside her.

He shoved up her camisole, baring her breasts to his hungry eyes. Her dusky nipples protruded tightly from the attention he had already lavished on them. "Oh, God, you're perfect."

Perfect? "But I'm so small," she protested.

He chuckled. "You're perfect. Lithe and lovely." He hungrily licked and sucked first one breast, then the other, his mouth and hands nursing a shocking ecstasy from her willing body. Hannah had no idea her body could be so sensitive. Her hands settling in his thick hair, she arched her back and found herself murmuring nonsense words, words of aching, torturously beautiful desire.

Benjamin slipped the camisole over her head and tossed it aside; then his large, strong hands slipped around her waist and toyed apart the strings to her bloomers. He separated the fabric, then lifted her hips, and finally removed the last shred of her clothing.

Kneeling over her, he unbuttoned his trousers, then quickly shed them. The hard evidence of his desire jutted from his own undershorts, which soon followed her bloomers to the floor, leaving them both naked.

Hannah stared at him, stunned and excited at seeing a naked man for the first time. He was so beautiful, so perfect. "Just like David," she said on a dreamy breath.

Benjamin pulled back and frowned. "David? Who in the blazes is David?"

Hannah reached out her arms. "A statue, by Michelangelo."

"Ah." He smiled, then leaned over her, his body hot and hard on hers. "A damn sight warmer, I should hope," he muttered, moving his hips and legs rhythmically against hers.

His member, so long and thick, throbbed against her bare thigh. Soon, he would put it inside her, claiming her as his own. "Is this it?" she asked.

"What?"

"Is this it? The moment."

He smiled, his teeth glinting in the firelight. "Not quite, darling. There are a few things we've yet to do."

"Such as?"

His fingers found their way to the burning center of her, causing her to gasp in shock. "This." His finger dove inside, and she realized how moist she had grown down there. "And this." At the movement of his fingers, the world began to spin out of control. Hannah dug her fingers into his shoulders. She hung on as he pleasured her, taking her so high into the heavens, she thought she had died.

Then it came, the waves of pleasure, washing over and over her in an endless dream. She danced among the clouds, on the pinnacle of a tremendous release, for what seemed hours. Somehow, someway, she managed to find her way back home, back into his arms.

She opened her eyes and gazed up at him. "That had to be it."

He arched his brows and shook his head. "Hannah, you must stop thinking and puzzling so much. Relax, and everything will become clear."

"I shall try."

"Excellent. You may start by allowing me to part your thighs . . ."

His hands had slid between them, and Hannah realized she had clasped them together at some point. In the back of her mind she had heard the stories of the pain virgins felt on their wedding nights, and her body had moved to protect her. Benjamin dropped kisses on her face, her lips. "Sweet darling, trust me. I shall be gentle."

Of their own accord, her legs opened, allowing him to settle between them. Then, he was in her, shocking her despite his promise. He seemed to fill her, every corner of her being, with his hard, sure length. He shifted her knees up, allowing him better access, and pressed deep into her. The movement shocked a shiver of pleasure through her entire body. She arched her neck back and cried out.

He stopped moving. "Have I hurt you too badly?" he asked, his voice incredibly gentle, so tender it made a tear come to her eye. Fearing he would misinterpret her crying, she turned her head and wiped the moistness on the pillow. "Not too badly. I've never felt the like. I never imagined . . ." She sucked in a shaky breath and smiled up at him. They were finally one. A broad smile swept over her lips. "So, this is it, then."

"Hannah, darling, there's more."

"More?"

"Ah, yes." A grimace passed over his face, and Hannah wondered if he was the one in pain. "In fact, if I don't move soon, I'm going to combust."

"Combust? You mean, like a chemical reaction?"

"Most definitely."

"Then, by all means, move."

And he did. He slid in and out of her, his rhythmic thrusting sending waves of pleasure through her body. Hannah gripped him tightly, feeling again that straining, that building of urgency toward a need for release. *It's going to happen again, this time better than before.*

This time, with Benjamin.

The climax hit her at the same time he cried out, so potent a force, Hannah had never imagined such a thing existing. His grip on her tightened, as if he would pull her into himself and keep her there, forever a part of him. After an eternity of bliss, his thrusting slowed, then ceased. He dropped his sweat-sheened brow to her chest and sucked in a deep breath. Hannah wove her fingers into his hair, relishing the feel of his spent body on her own.

Deliriously happy, Hannah smiled to herself. They were finally man and wife.

Benjamin lifted his head and gazed at her. Joy danced in his eyes. "That, my dear, was it."

Hannah stretched languorously. *"Wonderful,* Benjamin. Can we please do it again?"

His eyes widened at her question; then a broad smile stole over his face, and he started to chuckle. "As often as you want, darling. Give me a moment to gather my strength first."

Rolling onto his back, he scooped her into his arms. Sighing with contentment, he stroked her back. He gathered wayward strands of her long hair, smoothing them into place. His tender attentions made Hannah feel that no other woman could possibly mean as much to him.

"So, you don't mind being my wife after all, I take it," he murmured, dropping a kiss on her head.

She smiled into the curls on his chest. "Not this part, that's for certain. I had no idea it would be so . . . satisfying."

He wound a lock of her hair around his wrist. "Satisfying. Yes, indeed. It's a satisfaction I'd begun to despair of ever experiencing."

He hadn't said the words, of course. Nor had she. But Hannah began to feel that with time, he would admit he cared deeply for her, perhaps even loved her. Thinking about what it would feel like to hear his confession of love made her heart squeeze tight. She tangled her fingers in his chest hair, toying with it, watching it curl around her fingers.

"Hannah," came his husky whisper.

"Mmm?" she asked.

He slipped his hand around the back of her head and pulled her mouth to meet his in a passionate kiss. His lips teased hers as he murmured, "It's time to do it again."

Morning found Benjamin in a blissful state. The sight that greeted him when he cracked open his eyes filled him with a possessiveness that startled and intrigued him.

His wife. His.

Hannah lay on her stomach, her long dark hair fanned across the pillow and across his chest, her long lashes dark against her creamy cheek. She couldn't understand. How could an innocent like Hannah possibly know the void she had filled in his heart?

He hadn't thought it possible, feeling this content. After Peter died, he had been unable to feel much at all, except guilt and pain. His spirit had been deadened by a terrible weight, one he had borne like Sisyphus trapped in endless toil with no reward. Even his upcoming balloon flight paled as a goal, because Peter wouldn't be participating.

He had believed himself unworthy of happiness, of living life to its fullest.

Until last night. Hannah had opened an entire world to him. For the first time in years, he looked forward to the future, to new experiences, to building a life for them both. Hannah herself had done so much to build their lives together. She had begun turning that mausoleum he had been bequeathed into a true home, filled with light and smiles.

Last night at the duke's ball, they had mastered the art of social appearances, banishing the taste of the failed dinner party and replacing it with the sweet bouquet of success. Now many men would envy his darling American bride. They would be sought after socially, and his reputation would be cemented as a true Renaissance man, an up-and-coming scientist on the edge of true achievement.

Best of all, she had held out her hand. She had invited him to bed and opened herself to him in the most delightful way. Instead of being put off by the intimate act as gentlewomen often were, she had reveled in her primal side, as had he.

He had never felt so close to a woman, or so fulfilled. His visits to East End trollops had merely assuaged a bodily hunger, and that only temporarily. But Hannah fed his soul.

"What are you thinking about?" she asked, and he realized she had been watching him for some time.

He smiled down at her. "Good morning."

"Good morning." Crossing her arms onto his chest, she propped her chin on her hands. "You haven't yet answered my question."

He stroked her arm. "Ah. I was simply thinking how wonderful things have worked out, despite our rough start."

"Oh, you think so, do you?" Grinning, she danced her fingers up his chest. Her playfulness heated his blood and caused his member to stir in response. He trapped her hand on his chest to stop her teasing. He longed to make love to her again, but there was time enough for that. They wouldn't be catching the train until three, and it was not yet nine.

Now he wanted to talk. An unusual desire filled him to try to put his feelings into words. Poor as he was at sharing his feelings, he wanted her to understand something of the way she had changed his life.

"I most definitely think things are going well," he said. "We certainly made a good impression at the duke's ball. I can't say there's a man or woman there who didn't notice your beauty and grace."

"Mine?" Her eyes widened in that unaffected way of hers. Why was it so hard for her to believe in her own attractions, in all she had to offer?

"Yes, yours, Hannah."

A secret smile crossed her face, and she laid her head back on his chest. He combed her silken hair with his fingers. He still wasn't saying it quite right. He tried again. "Hannah . . . I can't tell you . . . I can't express how pleased I am with you."

"What do you mean?" she asked softly.

"It should be obvious. In so many ways, you've settled into my home and made it a better place. I'm incredibly pleased with how enthusiastically you've embraced your new role."

She lifted her head from his chest and laid her chin on her arms. "Excuse me? You mean . . . being your wife?"

He tapped her nose with his finger. "Of course."

She chewed her lower lip, which only made Benjamin long to suckle it. "There are things that I enjoy about being your wife, I will admit," she said slowly. Her eyes flashed briefly over his naked form. "But you know I have other interests."

Shrugging, he rolled to his side and propped his head on his hand. "Everyone has interests, of course. But you've quit talking nonsense about being a scientist, which is the most important thing. Don't think I haven't noticed, Hannah. I can't tell you how grateful I am." Tenderness for her filled his heart. His words could scarcely communicate the depth of his feelings, but perhaps she was beginning to understand.

Hannah shoved up to her elbows and looked into his face. "Do you truly think I no longer care about making my own mark in the world?"

He smiled at her. Had she no concept of how utterly important she was to him? "You have made your mark. As my wife."

"And you think that's enough for me?"

"It should be enough." Foreboding nagged at his contentment. Why did she continue asking these pointless questions? The answers should be obvious.

"You're a fine one to talk," she retorted, all signs of her smiles vanished. "Is being an earl enough for you?"

Being an earl enough? Of course not. It never could be. That was why he pursued his true love, science. That was why social connections were such a trial and a chore. He had been born to this life, but he was far from born *for* it. He rolled to his back and stared at the bed canopy. "We weren't talking about me."

She sat up and pulled the bed sheet around her. "Imagine being told you could never practice science again, that you must do nothing but fulfill your role as a nobleman. Going to Parliament, attending the queen's court, that sort of thing. Would that make you happy?"

He scowled at her. Now she was completely muddling the subject with silly comparisons. "I would hardly compare the two examples. They are nothing alike."

She arched a slim brow. "Oh, aren't they? Why is your dream more important than mine?"

This was getting entirely out of hand. He sat up and faced her, locking his hands over his knees. "Blast it, Hannah, I never said my dreams were more important. What I am saying is that you are my *wife*. As a woman, you were born to marry. You know that as well as I."

"Just as you were born to be an earl—and nothing else," she retorted. She climbed off the bed, dragging the bed sheet with her and wrapping it around her like a toga. She headed toward the door.

Benjamin yanked up the coverlet to conceal his own nakedness. Their argument had left him feeling far too vulnerable for comfort. "Hannah, don't be daft. Only very odd women pursue men's careers. Women who cannot catch a husband. You have no need of a career. You're a countess. *My* Countess." Hoping a no-nonsense approach would return her to her senses, he spoke with sharp command. "Now come back here."

His command had the wrong result. She spun on him, fury shooting from her eyes. She looked like a vengeful goddess, and Benjamin found himself surprisingly aroused by her angry passion. "I may be supporting your work, Benjamin. But I never agreed to give up my own dreams. Even if *you've* given up on *your* dreams.''

"What the devil are you talking about?'' A prickle of dread shot down his spine. He didn't want to go where she intended to lead.

"You're giving up on your balloon flight! You're allowing Winthrop to steal your glory.''

"I'm not after glory.'' God, he didn't want to talk about this, not this morning. Or tomorrow.

She strode back across the room, the sheet trailing her like a robe. Fisting the fabric at her chest, she used her other hand to emphasize her points. "Achievement, then. Why are you giving up so easily?''

He shook his head adamantly. "*I'm* the scientist behind the flight. Everyone who matters will know the work is mine.''

"You trust Winthrop far too easily, Benjamin. You'll let that conniving man take your work and pretend it's his—''

"Winthrop is too much of a gentleman to take credit for my research.''

"—rather than have faith in yourself. You can do it this time, Benjamin. It's not too late to assume your rightful place, to carve out your place in history.''

She took a step closer, her eyes filled with hope. She was seeing a man that didn't exist, that could never exist again. Couldn't she realize that and be done with it?

She continued, "I've thought hard about it, thought about the dangers. I *will* worry about you taking such risks. But I have faith you've learned how to make the flight safely. You're a brilliant scientist.'' Her voice lowered a notch, threatened to shake his composure. "Benjamin, I understand you better than you realize. If you don't take this opportunity, you'll regret it for the rest of your life."

"And you'll regret marrying me," he bit out. "That's what this is about, isn't it, Hannah? You want a hero for a husband."

His cold accusation had the desired effect. Finally, mercifully, she stopped her tirade. Her lips trembled, her reply so faint he barely heard it. "Just when I thought we were starting to understand each other."

Since she didn't deny it, Benjamin drew the obvious conclusion. She thought him a coward. And she was right.

He hung his head, praying she would leave the room. All trace of the contentment he had felt in her arms had vanished. In an instant, the black hole of the past had reopened, threatening once again to swallow him.

Hannah couldn't understand his true fear, for Peter's death was only part of it. Something even uglier than guilt resided in his soul. The horrid image of Peter's face, frozen in its death mask, rose up to haunt him, and he knew he wouldn't sleep well that night.

Five years ago, high up in the clouds, he had confronted his own mortality. Death had brushed its frigid fingers across his soul and left no question just how weak he was.

In his mind, Benjamin knew his fear was irrational.

In his heart, he felt quite certain he would lose if he dared face death again. And, coward that he was, the prospect of dying terrified him, especially now that his life had become so much richer with Hannah in it.

Instead of leaving, Hannah approached the bed and laid a hand on his head. Her touch startled him, and he jerked back. Her hand fell to her side. Her movements tentative, she sat on the mattress beside his feet. "Benjamin, please listen to me. Winthrop can't be trusted. Last night at the ball, he was referring to the flight as his, and his alone. The only way to make sure there's no question the flight is yours is for *you* to make it." Again she reached for him, laying her hand on his arm. "I know you can. You've done it before."

Before . . . Oh, God, when would she stop torturing him like this? He shook off her hand. "The flight doesn't concern you." His words cut coldly into the air, causing her to stiffen.

She stood up. "Yes, Benjamin, it does," she replied, her tone equally cold. "You're my husband—in every sense of the word, after last night. I have every right to discuss your work, especially since my money is funding it."

Money. Must she always think of their blasted trade of title for money? He gritted his teeth and glared at her. "It's no longer your money. It's mine, and I'll spend it as I see fit."

A dangerous spark entered her eyes. Her hand fisted and rose a fraction. Benjamin wondered briefly if she intended to strike him. He didn't care. He knew he deserved her disdain. A desperate urge filled him to make certain she knew it, too. To push her so far away, her expectations could never hurt him again.

His words came out tight and hard. "Say nothing to me about how to conduct my business, Hannah. From now on, concentrate on domestic matters. They alone are your purview. My scientific pursuits are mine. *Alone.*"

Her face reflected her hurt. Despite himself, the vision stabbed at him. Her fist tightened so hard on the bed sheet, her fingers turned white. Her body trembled, either in rage or pain, he didn't dare guess.

Her features grew stiff, and she bit out, "Then, mine will be mine alone, as well."

"What nonsense are you talking?" Her words made so little sense to him, he had to think to comprehend their meaning. "Ah. I see. You're referring to your wooden birds? You'd put your silly dabbling ahead of being my wife?"

She lifted her chin and glared down at him. "I could be a great scientist if I had the proper education."

Now she truly was talking nonsense, nonsense he had thought she had grown out of. Crossing his arms, he scoffed, "And how do you propose to accomplish that? You're a countess, not a university student."

Once more she stalked away from him, this time yanking the cord by the door to summon her maid. "I'll go elsewhere," she shot over her shoulder. "Back to America, where they won't care that I have this blasted title."

Back to America? She would leave him? Her words blew through him like a chill December wind, leaving him breathless and struggling to keep his shock and pain in check. She couldn't be serious. She couldn't.

Reason prevailed. Of course she didn't mean it. She was bluffing. Well, he would call her bluff, make her admit she belonged here. With him. "America, is it? I see," he said, keeping his voice calm and reasonable. "I hadn't realized you'd made plans. I think you should realize if you make such a move, you won't be returning to my home."

She turned slowly and faced him. "What—What do you mean?"

He shrugged, as if her choice was of no import. "Simply that. Be the wife I need. Stay here in England and do as you've been bred to do. If you can't bear this life, then fine." He waved his hand dismissively. "Leave me, and pursue your silly dreams. You can't possibly put us both first."

She remained as immobile as a statue, his ultimatum echoing in the air around them. As he watched the emotions pass over her face—hurt, shock, determination?—Benjamin began to regret he had uttered such a challenge to her. Surely she wouldn't choose to leave him. She couldn't want to live without him, could she? Not after last night.

And could I live without her? He already knew the answer, and it terrified him. Nothing he had accomplished, or would ever accomplish, could mean as much to him as spending his life with this woman, whether or not she ever felt the same.

Finally, she answered. "Fine."

Fine? What did that mean? "Well?" he called out, demanding an answer, an end to the suspense. "What's it to be?"

A soft knock on the door interrupted her answer, and she opened it to admit her maid.

"Hannah," Benjamin said, furious at the interruption. He had to hear her response, *now*.

Glancing at him over her shoulder, she said coolly, "You'll be the first to know. Good morning, Susan." With her maid trailing, she entered the bathroom, the door closing firmly behind them.

CHAPTER 19

Her stomach in knots, Hannah tapped lightly on the door to Benjamin's study. She knew he was inside, as he had been every evening since they returned from the ball. Alone. Avoiding her and keeping her outside his world. Outside his heart.

At first, she willingly gave him—and herself— space to cool off, to collect their respective thoughts. She had found forcing herself to avoid him more painful than anything she had done in her life. But she also was far too proud to chase after his attention, when he was so loath to give it.

Over and over, his ultimatum rang in her ears, wounding her spirit. Did her happiness mean so little to him? Could they ever find a happy medium, or would she be forced to make good on her threat and leave him? Now, when she had finally begun to feel at home here in this foggy land, when she had finally found a new intimacy with the man she had married, being shut out of his life cut like a knife.

She lifted her hand to repeat her knock, then reconsidered. He would never respond. Instead, she grasped the knob and twisted, surprised to find the door unlocked. She entered to find the room dark except for a low fire in the hearth. Benjamin slumped in a chair by the hearth, a whiskey glass in his hand. A nearly empty decanter rested on a nearby table.

"About time you showed up, Harcourt. Bring me a fresh bottle."

My God, he was soused! Hannah stared, stunned at this new side to her husband. Benjamin prided himself on maintaining control. She had never seen him drink more than one or two glasses of wine at dinner and had never seen him inebriated. "It's me," she said softly.

Despite the gentle tone of her voice, he reacted as if an enemy had breached the gates of his castle. He shot upright, shoulders tense, fingers grasping the armrest in a steely grip. His flinty eyes zeroed in on her. "What are you doing here?" he asked, his words a near croak.

His condition was so much worse than she had expected; she struggled to make sense of the image before her. He wore no jacket, only a shirt and vest. His shirt sleeves were rumpled, his tie askew. A lock of dusky hair fell across his forehead, and Hannah resisted the urge to push it back into place.

"Well?" he demanded as she continued to hesitate.

"I thought—I thought you were making arrangements. For your flight tomorrow."

A cold, humorless smile tightened his lips. "Why,

Hannah. Can't you see that I am? It's called liquid courage. Or rather, a coward's courage." He laughed, but the sound fell flat and raw on the evening air. Arching his tanned neck, he tossed back his glass, but found it empty. With a grimace of disgust, he flung the glass at the hearth. It shattered against the andirons, and Hannah jumped.

"Where in the devil has Harcourt got off to? I'm dry as a bone!"

Hannah pressed her hands to her thighs, determined to keep her calm despite his shockingly uncontrolled display. "He has the night off, Benjamin, to visit his sick mother in Haversham."

His eyebrows lowered as he stared at her. "Who—Who allowed that?" He looked so confused, it made her want to cry. She had mentioned it to him just this morning, at breakfast. Why was he doing this to himself? The most important flight of his career was fast approaching, and he was drowning himself in liquor! Memory of Georgina's foul moods and abuse of medicine came to Hannah's mind. God forbid her husband succumb to the same melancholy of the spirit. She wouldn't allow it.

He continued to peer at her. "No matter. You'll do as well. If you can bear to do anything for your husband, that is. Get me more whiskey." He grasped the bottle and upended it over his mouth to catch the last trickle. Most of it ran down his chin.

"I will not." Reaching over, she yanked the bottle from his grasp before it joined the glass in the fireplace. "You're disgustingly drunk, Benjamin," she said, planting herself before him so that he couldn't avoid looking at her.

His eyes burned above cheeks rimmed in shadow. "How nice of you to point out the obvious. With such astute powers of observation, you shall make a splendid scientist." His eyes burned with intensity, the fire at her back giving them an other-worldly spark. Hannah could scarcely breathe as his gaze slowly lowered to the swell of her breasts, demurely corseted and hidden in a modest evening gown. Nevertheless, his gaze alone caused her skin to prickle.

"So perfectly splendid," he murmured, no trace of irony remaining in his voice.

Hannah spoke quickly, to draw his attention back to her face. "Is this what you've been doing every evening when you disappear? Drinking yourself into a stupor? I thought you'd be making final arrangements for the flight."

"It's not your concern. No one should be concerned," he said, his voice miles away.

"From your lack of interest, if I didn't know it was tomorrow, I never would guess it was taking place at all! What arrangements have you made to publicize the flight?"

"The balloon is as ready as it will ever be. So are Spencer and Winthrop."

Winthrop. How she hated that name! Deep inside, Benjamin must know he was giving his best work to another man. Perhaps that was what was driving him to drink. "No, I mean, have you contacted the *Times*? Or the *Daily News*? Or the mayor's office?"

"Oh, my. How they will be fascinated to see Ramsey's second folly. God only hopes I don't kill too many more people before I make my mark." His words were infused with such bitterness, it drove her to the verge of tears. She blinked them back, hard. He needed her to be strong.

He thinks he's going to fail. He's lost his confidence! She was loath to see that happen. Guilt stung her. How much of this was her fault? Or did it have nothing to do with her? The man sitting before her, her husband, remained a mystery to her in so many ways.

Crouching beside him, she gently laid her hands on his arm. He started, but she kept her hands firmly on him, until he relaxed back into the chair. "Benjamin. You're not going to fail. You've been so careful in making preparations—until recently, I mean." She didn't think he had set foot in his laboratory in the past two weeks.

He didn't respond, so she forged ahead, trying desperately to find something to make him feel more confident, to show she was behind him, at least in this. "You need to let people know what you're doing, to publicize your plans so that when you succeed, everyone will acknowledge what you've accomplished."

"The Society members are well aware of Ramsey's Folly."

Hannah hated that term, which she knew some scientists had dubbed Benjamin's attempts at high-altitude flight. "Not them. I'm talking about the people—"

"I have never been an attention monger."

"This isn't about your pride!" He didn't respond, which worried her more than if they had had another argument. "Everyone is fascinated by balloons, by discovery and progress. If people learn about what you're trying to accomplish, your achievements will be properly recognized, your theories given weight. No one will be able to take that away from you." *Especially Winthrop,* she added silently. "Will you let me notify the right people, make arrangements?"

He sighed. "Do whatever you desire. It's of no import." Bracing his hands on the arms of the chair, he shoved unsteadily to his feet. "Now, I'm going to bed. And, as we know, you're going to yours. Good night." He took one step and nearly fell over.

"You can't make it upstairs alone." Hurrying to his side, Hannah slipped under his arm and walked with him sideways through the door into the hallway, then carefully and slowly up the stairs. Trying to keep the big man balanced while climbing the stairs winded Hannah long before they reached their suite.

Once in his room, he fell fully clothed upon the bed. Hannah removed each of his shoes, and his collar, so that he could breathe. He didn't protest, but made no move to help her. He must have already fallen asleep.

Leaning over him, Hannah began unbuttoning his shirt. Without warning, his arm snaked out and captured her waist, yanking her atop him.

CHAPTER 20

Hannah gasped, finding herself face-to-face with Benjamin, closer than they had been in weeks. Her entire body took fire from the predatory look in his eyes. Keeping her locked in his grasp, he rolled her to her back and pressed her into the mattress. He began rocking his hips hard against hers, his movements frantic—desperate even—to possess her.

And how she longed to be possessed by him!

"Do you like this, Hannah?" he asked roughly, his hand tight on her waist, his thumb scraping the crest of one breast, sending shocks of pleasure through her. "Do you enjoy being bedded by a coward?"

"I'm not—"

"How does it feel to be married to such a poor excuse for a man?" His fingers tightened around her wrists. Pinning them above her head, he pressed his lips to hers. His tongue invaded her mouth, seeking and finding, possessing her without giving quarter, taking without asking. His sudden passion swept Hannah away, and she found herself responding in kind.

Though she now slept in the countess's suite, she might as well have been on the other side of the moon for all the intimacy they shared. So many nights she had lain awake, just two closed doors from where he slept. So many nights she had longed for the courage to come to him, to experience again that potent connection they had shared the night of the ball. So many lonely nights she had hungered for his touch, for the comfort he alone could provide.

This time, his touch was anything but comforting. With every heated caress, every burning kiss, he demanded her acquiescence, taking her as his due. If allowing him such liberties helped assuage her own guilt, that was only a fraction of her compliance. In her heart burned a fierceness to give herself to him, to experience completely this primal, uncontrolled side of the man she had come to love.

In mere minutes, he had shoved up her skirts and plunged his fingers through the opening in her bloomers, exploring her moist essence with quick, masterful thrusts. Hannah gasped, her back arching in response, her entire body taking flame.

"This, I can do," he ground out, his voice throaty and harsh, pushing her closer and closer to the edge.

"Benjamin," she said on a sob, a tear rolling down her face. Frustration tangled with desire in her chest in a confusing mix. He sounded so distant, so pained, yet despite opening herself to him, she was failing to reach him. In desperation, she pulled at his shoulders, toward her, atop her. "Benjamin, be with me."

"Like this?" Propping himself on his arms, he slid between her legs. A heartbeat later, he thrust inside her, so deep and hard she cried out from the shock of it. He pounded into her, his face tight with tension, his eyes locked on hers. "You can live without this?"

"I won't—" Her words fell away as his thrusts increased in tempo, sending her to the brink of ecstasy.

"I *will.*" With one sharp thrust, he sent her into a spasm of pleasure so fierce, she feared she would be lost forever.

Somewhere in the heaven of sensation he had wrought, she knew he, too, had reached the pinnacle. He shook in her arms; then his body sagged atop hers. But only for the briefest, far-too-short moment. Then he rolled off of her and turned his back to her.

Hannah reached out a hand to touch his shoulder, still clad in his crumpled shirt. "Benjamin—"

"Leave me, if you must." A cold statement, without a hint of the intimacy they had just shared.

Hannah let her hand drop as a horrible sense of futility filled her. If giving herself to him couldn't reach him, what could?

Have you given yourself to him? The question nagged at her as guilt again threatened to swamp her. Despite her efforts, he had resisted her overtures. She knew full well the barrier that lay between them. But how could she give herself to him if it meant losing herself?

Sitting up, she attempted to right her gown, then crossed as quickly as possible through the connecting door into her own suite.

A team of horses pounded through his brain, over and over, each hoof beat sending a piercing agony through his head. Through the window of the carriage, he saw the silhouette of a lady. He knew her. He also knew where she was going. Away from him.

Nevertheless, the hoof beats never grew more distant. Instead, they grew louder, despite his certain knowledge that she was leaving. He watched as the woman finally noticed him. Turning her face toward him, she commanded, "Wake up."

The world began to shake. The movement shattered through his head like shards of glass, and he groaned. He cracked open his eyes and found himself gazing at an angel gripping his shoulder. Her oval face was framed by a halo of dark hair shot through with sunlight that pierced his eyes. He snapped his lids closed against the discomfort.

"No! Don't close your eyes again. You must get up. Your balloon is being launched today." Again that infernal shaking.

Not an angel precisely. His wife, Hannah. *Wife.*

His heart spasmed in fresh pain. Heaven had been within his grasp, but he had foolishly let it slip through his fingers. Until last night, when they— when he—

"Oh, God," he groaned, rolling away from her and clutching a pillow to his nauseous stomach. A hot river of shame filled him. Had he truly done what he now remembered doing to her? Thrown her down and forced her? Never in all his years had he thought himself capable of such animalistic behavior. He had wanted her, so he had taken her, feeling so desperate for her love that he had completely lost control.

Yet she remained here, in his house, instead of running from him as far as she could get. Why? Benjamin couldn't concentrate enough to bring the question into proper focus. His head throbbed with every pulse of his heart. Nothing made sense anymore, not his previously predictable life, not the comfort of his work. And surely not these unprecedented, devastating emotions.

Her hands pressing hard into his bare back, Hannah continued to prod him. "Benjamin, it's your own fault you're suffering from drink. But you must get up!"

"Leave me be," he ground out. Sometime during the night, he had thrown off the rest of his clothes and burrowed under the blankets. He wanted nothing more than to remain here, blocking out everything. If only his blasted nightmares would stop pursuing him.

Hannah continued to yank on his shoulder, her small hands surprisingly strong. Despite his guilt, her touch set his flesh afire. Instantly his body responded, sparking memories of the ecstasy he had found in her arms the evening before. God, she had felt so good, so right, here in his own bed. Perhaps, if he begged forgiveness for his dastardly behavior, she would once more allow him . . . .

Ramsey, don't be a blasted fool. She wants to leave you. With your despicable behavior, you've all but bought her a ticket back to New York.

"We need to be there by noon," she said. *"Please*

get dressed. Harcourt—" Her hands left him, and her voice sounded more distant. "Thank goodness you're here. I desperately need your help."

"I see that, milady."

"We have less than an hour," she said. "Put him in well-tailored business attire. He should look respectable, but not stuffy."

"Yes, milady. I know precisely the thing."

Benjamin heard the wardrobe doors squeak open. He tried to make sense of Hannah's commands. Why did she care what he wore? She never had before. Shouldn't she be packing her bags, running far away from the savage she had married? Why had she bothered to remain here?

God, Hannah, I'm so sorry. He thought the words, but he couldn't bring himself to say them, to bring into the light the awful events of the previous eve.

With her constant prodding, he finally gave up trying to retreat back into sleep. He rolled to his back and cracked open his eyes. Hannah and Harcourt stood before the open wardrobe, looking at his suits. She looked none the worse for wear, but he knew deep inside she must be devastated by how he had treated her. "Hannah? Why are you here?" he finally managed to say.

Hannah glanced at him. "You need to dress for your appearance before the press. Spencer left with the balloon hours ago."

"Left where?" Spencer left, but not Hannah? Nothing she said made any sense. He may have been drinking yesterday. But the press had nothing to do with his balloon flight. Did it?

"To Horner's field so that it can be inflated. Don't worry," she added in an ironic tone. "Winthrop is there, too, overseeing the process."

Benjamin pushed himself to a sitting position, struggling against the nausea roiling in his stomach. He burrowed his fingers into his mussed hair and shoved it out of his eyes. "The balloon is already being inflated? What time is it?"

"*Late,*" she said. "Inflating it early allows time for photographs before the flight. You may not look your best, but at least your balloon's presentable." Without further explanation, she turned to Harcourt. "Send him down as soon as he's dressed. Chauncy will have the carriage ready. We haven't a minute to spare."

"Yes, milady." Harcourt nodded. He looked at Benjamin and arched one slim brow, communicating clearly his expectations of his noble employer. "Milord?"

Benjamin sighed. What better indication that he was unnecessary to his own experimental flight? Winthrop was set to handle the flying, and Spencer had already begun inflating the balloon with gas, just as Benjamin had instructed him.

Benjamin longed to crawl back under the covers and sleep off his headache, forgetting for a brief moment that his balloon was going up today, without him. But Harcourt's expectant stare threatened to bore holes in his head. Foolish notion that it was, Hannah thought he needed to be there.

His head pounding in protest, he dragged himself out of bed. He might have been able to resist Hannah or Harcourt alone, but no way under heaven could he resist them both.

Too soon, Benjamin found himself alone in a carriage with his wife. Sitting on the opposite bench, she looked as sunny as a new day in her yellow gabardine dress.

Apparently, she had decided to stay with him long enough to witness the balloon flight. Her scientific curiosity couldn't allow her to pass up this opportunity. But afterward, nothing would prevent her from leaving. This might be his only chance to make amends.

"Hannah . . . ," he began, hot shame threatening to choke off his words. Would she be upset he had even brought it up? It was hardly a proper subject for the light of day.

"Yes, Benjamin?"

Just say it, man. "Hannah, last night . . ."

"You drank too much. I never imagined you could be so . . . out of control." She bit her lip.

Out of control. Those three words couldn't begin to describe his horrid behavior. He scoured his face with his palms. Sucking in a fortifying breath, he dropped his hands and faced her squarely. "I wasn't in my right mind. Not that I'm blaming the whiskey. I take full responsibility. I'm so sorry, Hannah. Truly. The last thing I ever wanted was to hurt you."

"Hurt me? You think—" Color highlighted her cheeks.

Regret swept through him. He should never have brought up this delicate subject. No doubt he was rubbing salt into her emotional wounds, wounds she had received at his hand. What a cad he was!

Then she laughed, the sound clear and bright like a bird's song. She slid from her seat and nestled beside him, lifting his hand into her lap. Benjamin relished the unexpected intimacy. How could she possibly be so forgiving?

"You didn't hurt me, darling. Quite the opposite." The color in her cheeks deepened further. She slid her fingers between his. "That's one area where we mesh quite well. I admit I relished seeing you lose control."

Benjamin stared at her, dumbfounded. With a few simple words, she had erased his guilt. Such power she had over him! Disconcerted, he still felt he had to explain. "I've never . . . that is, I'm not in the habit of . . . I didn't intend—"

"I'm a woman, but I have . . . feelings, too." She ducked her head, then lifted her gaze to his. Benjamin's heart lurched at the loving look in her eyes. "If I didn't want you to touch me, I'd not have allowed it. I'm capable of making up my own mind."

"I didn't mean to say you weren't. But husbands usually hold the upper hand." He exhaled, knowing he had probably said the wrong thing. He couldn't seem to manage to talk to this woman he had come to love.

Sure enough, she dropped his hand and slid away from him on the bench. "I'm well aware of that." She turned her attention to the view of London streets out the window. Just like that, their basic disagreement had reared its ugly head, separating them from each other.

The carriage turned from the country road onto a narrow lane bordered by elms, toward Farmer Horner's property. Months ago, the farmer had agreed to let Benjamin launch his balloon from his high meadow. The field, on the edge of London, contained no trees or windmills, obstacles that might snag a balloon before it reached a safe altitude. Yet it was close enough to the city gas lines that a hose could reach.

Ahead, two more carriages kicked up chunks of sod, turning the dirt track into a muddy mire. Benjamin frowned. "It's as busy as Fleet Street. Where is everybody going?"

"They're coming to see you, Benjamin."

Benjamin shot Hannah a stern glare. What had she been up to? When she had mentioned arranging an interview with the press, he had assumed there would be a simple, straightforward meeting with one or two fellows, not a parade!

Above the trees, the top of the balloon came into view, and despite himself, his heart skipped a beat.

Their carriage rounded a stand of elms and entered the broad, grassy field. Before them, dozens of carriages were already parked. A crowd of several hundred people stood around what looked like a stage. A stage? Again Benjamin scowled at Hannah, but she simply smiled and looked away.

Swaths of yellow and green bunting draped the front of the wooden stage, so sturdy it appeared to be a permanent structure. Yet it hadn't been there a month ago, when Spencer and he had scouted out the launch site for the final time. Hannah must have paid for its construction. So often he had imagined this day, but never had he pictured the celebration before him. "This must have cost a pretty penny to arrange."

"Some, especially for the stage, which was built overnight. But I consider it a worthy investment."

Following Hannah's directions, Chauncy drove the carriage around the edge of the field to the back of the stage, next to the equipment cart that had transported the balloon.

Benjamin stepped from the carriage behind his wife. As soon as they came around the side of the stage, a festive tune began filling the air. He spun around, looking for its source. On the stage's left, a five-man band played with gusto.

Behind all this commotion, Benjamin's pride and joy rose thirty feet into the afternoon sky, its golden fabric shining like a second sun. Unlike balloons filled with hot air, his hydrogen balloon was sealed, forming a perfect sphere. The balloon swayed gently above its rattan gondola, pulling the tether ropes taut. Inside, Spencer was checking the valve that contained the hydrogen in the envelope, while young boys guarded the anchors on the ground.

Benjamin turned around once, taking in the scene. "All this. Amazing!"

She smiled that elusive smile. "I had no trouble interesting the public or the press in your endeavor, though it was difficult explaining why you weren't making the flight yourself."

A ripple of anxiety ran up his spine. "What did you tell them?"

"Nothing." She ran her hand along his arm, as if she understood his discomfort over the ghosts of his past. "Only that you had arranged for a colleague to take your place."

As if on cue, Winthrop barreled through the crowd toward them, a broad smile lighting his ruddy face. "Benjamin! You're finally here. Now we can begin. Let's go." Grasping his arm, he led him toward the steps at the side of the stage.

Hesitantly, Benjamin approached the stage, his

attention pulled first by the exuberant crowd, now applauding for no good reason he could see, then by his glowing wife, who had never looked more fetching in her yellow gabardine, the color a close match to his balloon's. And she glowed even more.

She took her place beside him as he hesitated at the steps.

"I understand about the press," he said to her, his gaze on acquaintances from Parliament. "But it looks like half the city has shown up!"

His gaze passed a few faces he recognized near the front of the crowd. Esteemed members of the London Society for Scientific Advancement stood together like a flock of penguins in their black frock coats, frowning at him. No doubt they considered this show yet another indication of his eccentric nature.

As if reading his mind, Lord Thornton called to him, "A fine stunt you're planning, Sheffield! And a public one, to boot!"

"Never mind about him," Hannah said brightly, cocking her head confidently. "He's merely jealous of the attention you're receiving."

"I sincerely doubt that." He gestured toward the crowd. "Whatever got it into your head to arrange all this?"

She smiled up at him, her eyes sparkling. Despite his consternation over this surprise event, at the look in her eyes he felt as if the sun itself warmed him through. "I want everyone to know what you've accomplished. What you're *going* to accomplish."

If he failed, this stunt would become a public humiliation for her, a folly the likes London had rarely seen. She knew that as well as he. Still she persisted in her blind support of his work. "You have that much faith in me?"

"Yes." Her simple reply confounded yet uplifted him. *She believed in him.* Despite her longing to leave him, she believed in him.

Whenever he had considered marrying, he had never imagined a wife could exhibit such steadfast faith. He had thought of sharing finances, sharing a house, sharing—*God, yes*—a bed. Never once had he imagined a woman could make him feel like a more worthy man.

Yet she had. Somehow, since Hannah believed he deserved accolades, he was beginning to believe it, too.

He stared after her as she demurely picked up her skirts and ascended the six steps to the stage. At the top, she turned and, smiling brightly, extended her gloved hand to him.

He bounded up the stairs to meet her—and the expectant crowd—a matching smile breaking out on his face. Standing beside Hannah, he took her hand and gave it a squeeze. Confidence surged up from some mysterious place inside him, a place he had locked tight after Peter's death—until today.

This was, indeed, his day to shine. Today, whether or not his experiment failed, he could make people see why his work mattered and what he intended to accomplish for the progress of mankind.

He and Winthrop.

Winthrop. Had he been right to seek a pilot other than himself? It had seemed a logical decision at the time. In any case, it was too late now.

Standing on his other side, Winthrop waved both hands above his head, calling for silence. After a moment, the crowd's excited voices stilled. A half dozen newspaper reporters in the front row poised their pencils above their note papers, prepared to capture their words. A light flashed as a photographer captured the moment.

"On this field, this simple farmer's field," began Winthrop, his bombastic nature making him a natural speaker, "we are about to make history. I, Mr. Harold Winthrop, shall, with my young assistant, ascend in this glorious balloon farther into the heavens than any man has yet gone!"

He extended his arm toward Spencer inside the gondola, nearly hitting Benjamin. Reflexively, he stepped back, and Winthrop moved in front of him. The crowd cheered and clapped.

Winthrop continued, "This enterprise is not without great risk. Men before me have lost their lives and limbs in such an endeavor. But I am prepared." He extended his finger, and Benjamin prepared himself for his cue to explain the science behind the flight.

"With carefully crafted equipment, I will prevail," Winthrop explained. Benjamin scowled. Winthrop had yet to even mention Benjamin was involved, much less that he himself was merely the pilot of Benjamin's balloon.

A reporter raised his hand. "How far up are you going?"

"Forty thousand feet. More than seven miles, twice as high as any living man to date!"

The crowd murmured in awe.

The reporter persisted, "What makes you think you will succeed?"

"After a careful study of past failures"—Winthrop glanced toward Benjamin, as if reminding people how he had once failed—"I have come to the conclusion that oxygen holds the key. Breathing oxygen through a mask will enable me to thrive in a terribly dangerous environment, where the air is too thin to sustain life."

He had come to this conclusion? Hannah had warned him about Winthrop taking credit for his work. He hadn't wanted to believe it, but the evidence was right before him. He wasn't about to stand by and allow it to happen.

He glanced toward Hannah and saw by her gathering frown that Winthrop's claims had upset her, too. Their eyes met, and he could read her anger there, plain as day. And her question—*Have you had enough?*

He most certainly had. He stepped forward, interrupting Winthrop's colorful description of his own bravery against incredible odds. "Winthrop, pardon me. We need to talk."

"Not now, Benjy, I'm on a roll," Winthrop answered, then again addressed the crowd. "As I was saying, true grit and determination such as I will display rarely is seen—"

Benjamin's blood boiled at being dismissed by this man. *"Now,* Winthrop."

At the challenge in his voice, Winthrop faltered and glanced at him. "But, Benjy . . . Please." He turned away as if he intended to ignore him.

Benjamin realized if he waited for an opening, he would be standing there all day. Drawing breath—and courage—he called out, "There has been a change of plans." His voice boomed over Winthrop's and drew the eyes of everyone present.

Startled into silence, Winthrop looked at him balefully.

Benjamin grasped his colleague's hand and shook it. "Excuse me, Winthrop. I appreciate your efforts on my behalf, but—" His eyes caught Hannah's. Dropping Winthrop's limp hand, he reveled in Hannah's hopeful, excited gaze. He refused to disappoint her this time. Speaking loudly, so the audience could hear, he announced, "I will be piloting my own balloon after all."

CHAPTER 21

The crowd's reaction was immediate and dramatic, excited and confused discussions erupting everywhere.

"How dare you!" Winthrop confronted him, his face red with anger.

Benjamin pulled him to the back of the stage. "Sorry, old buddy, but I need to make this flight. I appreciate the effort you've put in on my behalf, but—"

"I should say so! How can you change your mind at this late hour? It's highly unprofessional."

"Unprofessional? What do you call stealing credit for another man's work?"

His charge took the wind from Winthrop's sails. "Benjy, I never intended—"

"Oh, didn't you?"

"Please, Benjy. I need this. I need to do something, or I'll be evicted from the Society. Don't you see? They practically worship the work you've done. But me, I'm nothing!"

Worship his work? The stuffy Society members whose support he had craved? "What nonsense are you talking?"

"Come on, Benjy," Winthrop pleaded. "Everyone knows you're a living hero, the only member of the Society to actually risk his life for his work. The rest of them—they're dilettantes, toying with experiments in their home laboratories." Winthrop's demeanor changed, became almost reverential. "But you—you've actually *been* there. And I need to be there, too. This flight is my chance. You owe this to me. I loaned you money—"

"Which I've paid back, with interest. I'm sorry, Winthrop. We can talk more later." He gave Winthrop's arm a reassuring pat. He wondered if his colleague would ever learn to make the effort needed to earn results on his own. "Right now, I have a balloon to fly."

With Winthrop's revelations ringing in his ears, he turned back to the crowd. A hero? The Society respected his work after all? Perhaps all this time he had been his own worst enemy, thinking himself unworthy when no one else believed it. Perhaps that was what Hannah had been trying so hard to tell him. She smiled at him again, and he filled with pride.

A reporter's shouted question interrupted his thoughts. "So whose balloon is it?"

"This balloon is mine. I designed and built it, as well as modifying the instruments and equipment to further my work."

A *London Times* reporter Benjamin recognized

called out, "Aren't you Benjamin Ramsey, the man who piloted that disastrous balloon flight in 1884?"

Another reporter chimed in. "You mean Ramsey's Folly? I covered that story."

The painful memory caused a pang in Benjamin's chest, but with Hannah gazing at him so encouragingly, he found he could easily maintain his composure. "Yes, I am the same Benjamin Ramsey. I have continued my investigations in atmospheric science."

"Wasn't a man killed on that flight?" the *Times* reporter persisted.

Pressing close, Hannah squeezed his arm. With her beside him, he found he could discuss the horrors of the past, even in this public forum. "My colleague, Peter Farraday, lost his life, yes. He died from the cold and lack of oxygen. I very nearly met the same fate. But, as Mr. Winthrop pointed out, *my* research since then"—he stressed his ownership—"makes me confident this flight will be a success."

His remarks had captured the crowd's attention. Their individual conversations had ceased, and they stood listening to his every word.

And, to his surprise, the words came. "My good friend Peter was a pioneer in the field of weather and atmospheric research. He understood that mankind's quest to enter the heavens should yield answers to our most basic questions about the world we live in. Together, we developed a theory about the atmosphere being composed of layers of various gases. I pray my balloon flight will honor Peter's memory as well as contribute to mankind's knowledge."

He swallowed past a lump in his throat, and continued. "You might wonder *why* I am willing to engage in such an endeavor, or"—he shot a look at Thornton—"what some consider a risky stunt. After all, why would any *sane* man risk life and limb in a flimsy, cloth balloon filled with nothing more substantial than gas?"

He caught Hannah's gaze and noticed she had grown a little pale at his talk of the risks involved.

"Permit me to answer my own question. If you wonder *why* I do such a dangerous thing, you need only ask yourself, What will the weather be like today? Will my crops fail? Will my ship be safe at sea?

"Answers about the winds, about the very atmosphere we breathe—these can help us understand the forces that affect each and every one of us, every day of our lives!" Filled with enthusiasm, he gestured toward the clear blue sky. The truth struck him. In all his efforts to gain the Society's support, he had never spoken with such conviction. He had never spoken from the heart. He had been terrified of putting his life on the line, and his own fears had kept others from believing in his dream.

"Whether you're a—a farmer, like Mr. Horner who owns this field we're standing in, trying to decide whether to harvest before the frost." He gestured to the farmer, near the front of the stage, and the man nodded. "Or a lady trying to decide whether to carry her parasol." He gestured to a woman with a ruffled pink parasol, and she smiled. "I hope my work will help us understand nature. To find answers which will enable us to one day travel safely to the heavens in aeroplanes, or even rocketships."

At his wild speculations, the crowd began to murmur. Sensing he wasn't helping his cause, Benjamin reined himself in. Perhaps they weren't quite ready for such leaps of the imagination. "I may be thinking too far ahead. But regardless of what the future holds, we won't get there without sacrifice." He slapped his palm with his fist for emphasis. "Mankind's quest for knowledge demands that we push for answers, that we push our limits. Peter was just such a brave pioneer. I pray, in my own small way, to make his memory live and his contribution be recognized." His gaze fell on the cluster of Society members. "By everyone."

He stopped speaking. A hush had fallen over the crowd. "Well, that's about it, then," he added, unsure what to say next. He had said all he could to convince them his work meant something.

A swell of sound began to fill the air, first in the front, then moving in a wave toward the back. Applause? They were clapping for him. Beside him, Hannah glowed with pride. Her approval filled him with more satisfaction than public accolades ever could. "Thank you," he said to the crowd, then once again, to the woman by his side. "Thank you, Hannah," he said for her ears alone. "For supporting my work."

"Like a proper wife should?" she asked dryly, and he realized with dismay that their battle hadn't concluded.

"Like a friend would," he said solemnly.

Her lips trembled with emotion, but she didn't say a word. He lowered his head, his lips mere inches from hers. "Thank you," he whispered again. Despite the crowd and his own reclusive nature, he couldn't resist placing a soft kiss on her sweet, tender mouth.

Color painted her cheeks, making her appear even more lovely and irresistible. He longed to spirit her back home and make his proper apologies for the previous evening, perhaps come to an agreement about their lives together. If she would only accept her place by his side. Surely no woman had complemented a man better.

A reporter shouted a question, and Benjamin turned to answer. No doubt the press was anxious to gather enough information to flesh out their stories before the flight—just in case he died.

A photographer asked permission to take his picture with his balloon. "Very well, if you include my wife." Hannah had already begun backing away, but he snagged her hand and pulled her to his side. Slipping his arm around her waist, he anchored her there, where she belonged. If only it were as easy to keep her there!

As soon as the photographer had finished, Hannah slipped from his grasp. Before he could ask where she was going, a reporter asked for more details about his experiments. He turned to answer. But without Hannah at his side, trepidation began to nag at him.

After a few more questions, the crowd began to grow restless, calling out for the flight to commence. Benjamin knew the time had come to climb into the balloon. He glanced at the huge sphere floating above the stage. All at once, horrific images filled his mind, of fabric ripping, of ropes snapping, of he and Spencer plummeting to their deaths. Was he mad? What had caused him to volunteer for this stunt?

Hannah . . . He needed her, needed to see her lovely smile, the light of faith in her eyes. He glanced around, desperate to find her.

But she had disappeared.

CHAPTER 22

Hannah hurried down the steps to the area behind the stage. Spencer stood next to the balloon, slipping on a heavy wool coat and scarf. He pulled a pair of goggles from a burlap bag on the back of the equipment cart. Despite the warm summer day, both he and Benjamin would need to bundle up before their flight. Once aloft, they would be entering extremely cold temperatures in under an hour.

Hannah came up behind him. "Spencer," she said softly.

Immediately the young man swung around, a smile wreathing his face. Hannah knew he had a slight crush on her, and she intended to use it to her advantage. "Lady Sheffield. Hello! I'm very impressed with everything you've arranged. And now Benjamin is piloting the flight himself. Not to say anything against Mr. Winthrop, but I much prefer to assist your husband.''

"Yes, it's wonderful, isn't it?'' Hannah glanced over her shoulder to be certain they were still alone. Benjamin was occupied with the press, his back turned. Still, Hannah lowered her voice. "Spencer, I need to ask a favor of you.'' She laid her hand gently on his arm to impress her urgency upon him.

His eyes widened at the unexpected intimacy. "Anything,'' he breathed.

"Come with me to the carriage.''

He nodded and followed behind as they crossed the uneven turf of the meadow. Hannah swung open the door of the unattended carriage, revealing its shadowed, empty interior. She turned and stepped back. "Please, climb in.''

Spencer looked thoroughly bewildered. "Now? But the flight—''

"Spencer . . .'' Hannah almost hated herself for using his weakness against him. Almost. But her future—and Benjamin's—was at stake. She slipped her fingers up the lapel of his tweed coat and gazed into his eyes. "You said you'd do anything for me. And I need you now.''

"Yes, but—'' He glanced nervously past her, back toward the balloon. "You need *me?* Truly?''

"Yes. Desperately. Oh, Spencer,'' she said, giving him her best pleading expression. "It can't wait. With the flight being so dangerous . . .''

His eyes glowed with the anticipation of an untried, yet randy young man, no doubt imagining all sorts of illicit acts, possibly his last chance to experience such intimacy with a woman. He climbed into the carriage and scooted along the seat to the far side, leaving her room to join him.

Hannah had no such intention. "Thank you, Spencer. Now, take off your clothes."

You can do this. You can do this!

Benjamin repeated the words over and over, hoping they were true. Saying he would pilot the flight while on the stage was one thing. Watching four men about to release the tether ropes and launch him into the heavens was quite another.

Spencer stood silently at his side in the gondola, wrapped head to toe in his cold-weather gear and goggles. He had been so late climbing aboard, Benjamin had feared the audience would grow bored and leave. They stood now with bated breath, silently watching, ready to witness this launch of a successful flight—or another humiliating failure.

He scanned the crowd, seeking a yellow dress. Where had Hannah gone? There was no sign of her. His heart thudded like a weight in his chest. He hated the idea of going aloft without saying goodbye to her, or even "I'm sorry." Two simple words he prayed might help mend the rift between them. *I'm sorry for what I said, for what I did. For failing you in so many ways.* Now, at the moment of his greatest risk, he longed to confess the depth of his feelings for her. But she was nowhere in sight.

Time weighed heavily on him, the golden balloon above seeming to press him down. He had no choice. He had completed all the necessary preparations. He had double- and triple-checked the array of instruments on the side of his gondola.

The oxygen bottles were full, the barometer and altimeter were working, and the sample bottles were ready with their cork seals.

Spencer waved to the crowd, and he followed suit. The crowd cheered. He had to do this, even without Hannah. He prayed she would look for him in the skies, would watch his ascent as long as possible. He prayed she would be thinking of him.

The four men at the tethers watched and waited for his signal. As if knowing he needed support, Spencer grasped his hand and gave it a squeeze. An unusual gesture between men, but somehow effective. "Hang on." With a single motion, Benjamin gave the signal. The four men released the tethers.

Immediately, the balloon shot into the air like a bullet from a gun. Spencer gave an unmanly squeal and gripped the edge of the gondola, his knees bending beneath him. "I warned you the ascent would be quick," Benjamin commented, hanging on to a guide rope above his head. "Be a man, Spencer."

Spencer gripped his stomach with one hand and landed on his bottom.

"Spencer," Benjamin sharply commanded, hoping to bring the boy around. "Hand me the first sample bottle. We're approaching one thousand feet."

Spencer didn't move to retrieve the bottle from its netting along the side of the gondola.

"Spencer!" Benjamin turned from checking the ropes to give him a sharp glance. "I need you, damn it. I can't do this alone."

Spencer struggled to his knees, and Benjamin pulled him by the arm to his feet. He needed to

see the boy's face to ascertain his health. Reaching
out, he yanked up his goggles and pulled down
the scarf concealing his face.

Hannah—her face appearing paler than he had
ever seen it—gave him a weak smile. "Hello, Benjamin."

Hannah could hardly breathe as she watched her
husband react. His shock gave way to that fierce
control she had come to recognize. His jaw tightened, his emotions retreating behind a stony mask.
"So, I see you've made your choice."

Hannah's body felt shaken by the rapid and
unexpected acceleration, by the shocking view of
London receding under her feet. But Benjamin's
reaction distressed her much more.

She said, "The choice is yours alone, Benjamin."

"Nonsense. You obviously prefer this role to
being my wife, or you wouldn't be here." Looking
away, he grabbed an empty bottle and cork and
thrust them at her. "Take an air sample, please."

Hannah wasn't quite sure of the procedure, but
it looked fairly obvious. She lifted the bottle into
the air beyond the gondola, then capped it to trap
the air inside for later analysis.

She must have done it right, since he merely
said, "Label it, and get another ready. We'll soon
be at five thousand feet." The chill in his voice
surpassed the cold wind now buffeting her face.
She readjusted her scarf and goggles, wondering
if she had made a horrible mistake joining him on
this flight.

She had been forced to do something. She had
to make him see she could contribute in so many

ways other than being a wife. But he looked positively grim, his mouth tight, his eyes distant. Despite their nearness in the small gondola, he wouldn't even look at her.

"We're going so fast," Hannah observed, hoping to get him to talk to her.

He spoke in a crisp monotone that revealed nothing of his emotions. "Hydrogen weighs a mere zero point nine grams per liter. That's seven times lighter than air, which explains our rapid ascent."

His explanation required too much thinking, especially since she felt a little light-headed. She pressed her fingers to her temples. "Perhaps you should tell me about it later. I'm barely able to keep my head as it is."

"I warned you science wasn't for dabblers—or women," he bit out. "Quite clearly you're not physically equipped to withstand the stresses."

"That's not true—"

"By your rash action, you've made this experiment immeasurably more difficult."

"It wasn't rash. I planned it out very carefully," she protested.

After they passed four thousand feet, she began to feel better. The view was fantastic, more all-encompassing than she had ever imagined it could be. Below her, the mighty Thames appeared like a silver hair ribbon, glistening in the sun. London looked like a toy city, each building only an inch high. The ocean—she could even see the ocean and the cliffs of Dover.

"No wonder you like to fly!" she cried in delight. "This is the most exciting thing I've ever experienced—except for one."

Her husband met her gaze, no doubt also imagining the incredible magic of their lovemaking. For just a brief moment, his façade cracked. "Hannah . . ."

Hannah grasped his arm. "Benjamin, please don't hate me. I didn't do this to upset you. I want you to realize what I'm capable of. That I can be more than your wife and still be your wife. If that makes any sense."

"Not much. Please take another sample."

"Yes, sir," she teased, then did as he said.

Just as she finished, a strong wind buffeted the gondola. She lost her balance and fell against him. He righted her, then continued to hold her, his gaze on hers. Pushing her away, he turned from her, but not before Hannah read the fear in his gaze.

He hid it well. "Wind shear," he explained coolly. "Common at this altitude. We're passing through a region of change between the two opposing wind flows. Once through, we'll be heading the opposite direction."

"I'm going to be fine, Benjamin. We're both going to be fine."

He continued to hide behind his science. "We're still in the layer of atmosphere where I hypothesize most of our weather stems—short-term changes in temperature, wind, pressure, and moisture. You might notice it's growing steadily colder. Don't remove your wrap. It could be dangerous to do so."

"I won't. Benjamin—"

Suddenly, he snapped, his expression furious. "Damn it, Hannah! If you die up here—" He struggled to regain his composure, then turned sharply away and studied his instruments. "We've reached five thousand feet. Take another air sample."

Hannah blinked back tears in her eyes as she set about filling and corking another bottle. She told herself the tears were from the bitingly cold wind, but didn't truly believe it.

She hadn't thought about how her stunt might hurt him, hadn't thought past the need to prove herself to the one man whose good opinion meant the world to her. In taking this flight, he had put his emotions, his soul, at risk. The last time he had tried this, he had suffered a tragic loss, nearly dying himself. And here she was, risking herself in the same way.

Silently, she completed his unfinished sentence. If she died up here, it would quite literally kill him.

I failed to protect her. Now she could die.

The balloon flew higher and higher, every second taking them closer to the limits of mankind's exploration. Benjamin's attention was torn between piloting the balloon and watching Hannah. She seemed to have found her air legs and was helping in her own small way to accomplish their mission.

He watched her carefully. No doubt her earlier light-headedness indicated a susceptibility to high altitudes. Women couldn't possibly breathe thin air as long as men could without fainting. She would pass out far sooner than the point where men required supplemental oxygen. Grasping one of the oxygen tanks, he pressed it against her. "Take this. Put on the mask. We're nearing six thousand feet."

"But you're not wearing yours yet."

"I don't know how well women withstand such altitudes," he said. He didn't tell her his biggest worry—that they lacked enough oxygen to keep them both safe. Despite his precautions, he hadn't counted on having a woman aboard. Yet he wouldn't risk Hannah's life, not for the world. Certainly not for his own life. He wanted her to start breathing the oxygen now, while he would only take intermittent pulls on his own tank—for the entire trip if necessary.

Peter had died from a lack of oxygen. But he refused to think of that.

With his help, Hannah slipped the mask over her head, then her goggles, then wrapped her scarf tightly around her head. Loose strands of her hair whipped about her face, though almost every inch of her was covered. She had fooled him completely, exchanging places with Spencer. Spencer wasn't much larger than his wife, and she had no trouble fitting into his clothes. She was bundled head to toe, wearing slacks and boots under her long coat. How had she convinced the boy to shed his clothes? Perhaps he shouldn't think of that now.

Discovering Hannah in Spencer's place had angered him, but only for a moment. What cut much deeper was realizing the truth. Despite his hopes for their future, Hannah had proven she wanted to pursue science. Indeed, other women had flown in balloons, and he himself understood the drive to be the first.

That, he could accept. Much harder to face was the cold truth that she had chosen science over him. She truly wanted a life of adventure and danger, rather than living in his house and being his

wife. After this flight—assuming they both survived—she would no doubt leave him, having
advanced her own notoriety enough to gain a foot-
hold in the scientific community both here and in
America. She could pursue her work wherever she
chose without his domestic demands holding her
back.

When they reached twenty thousand feet, Benjamin took a brief tug on his own oxygen bottle, the
air causing a rush of blood into his brain that made
him feel oddly alert. He glanced at the thermome-
ter. It read minus forty degrees Fahrenheit. He
studied Hannah to make certain she kept her cold-
weather gear in place. She stood mutely gazing
over the edge of the gondola, into space.

The balloon rose ever higher, through a swath
of cumulous clouds and into a layer of wispy stratus.
Icy winds buffeted the gondola, shaking it so hard
he grabbed the sides to keep from being tossed to
the floor. Or tossed overboard, into the wide blue
expanse beyond their tiny gondola. Far below,
nothing was recognizable except for the largest
physical features on the earth's surface—moun-
tains and oceans.

Benjamin shivered despite his wool coat. Now a
the extreme height of thirty thousand feet, they
were approaching the top of the known atmo
sphere. After that, Benjamin intended to prove
came a different layer of air altogether, one he
called the "stratosphere."

He fought to focus on the gauge on his oxyger
bottle, but the numbers swam before his eyes. He
felt slightly queasy, and so off balance he had to
sink to his knees. Hannah was there beside him
doing something with the bottle, shoving the mas

at him. Giving in, he took another pull of oxygen. His head cleared enough to enable him to read the gauges on both bottles. As he suspected, by insisting Hannah wear her mask so early, their total volume of oxygen had grown dangerously low. Hannah's was nearly empty, so he switched bottles with her, taking the near-empty one for himself. At this point in the flight, he had planned for both he and Spencer to be breathing pure oxygen. If he did so now, however, chances were neither of them would make it down alive.

Hannah attempted to slide the mask of his bottle over his head, but he shoved her away and shook his head.

He toyed with the rope leading to the release valve. If he pulled it, a small flap on the top of the balloon would open, releasing hydrogen and causing their balloon to descend. Not yet. He would pull it if he had to, but not yet. He wasn't ready to fail.

Cirrus clouds, he dimly noted. They were passing cirrus clouds. He would have to remember that such clouds formed at thirty-five thousand feet. He wanted to note the fact in his log, but his fingers were too frozen to hold a pencil.

He risked another breath of the precious oxygen and studied the other gauges. The ambient temperature had reached minus seventy degrees. Winds continued to slap the gondola, and it shuddered under the pressure from all sides.

Turning off the oxygen, he set the bottle aside, fighting to breathe through a crushing pain in his lungs. Something wet trickled onto his lip. He wiped at it, and his gloved finger came away bloody. Interesting observation. A nosebleed at . . . at . . .

How high were they now? How high? He couldn't focus on the gauge from where he sat. His vision had grown murky. Was it night? How could that be? They hadn't been aloft more than an hour or so. Or had it been days? Where was he? Why was he doing this? He could no longer remember. He longed to curl into a ball and go to sleep, nothing else but sleep.

Beside him, Hannah kept attempting to press the oxygen mask to his face. *Quit wasting it!* He felt himself screaming at her, but heard nothing through the winds scouring his eardrums. Her eyes sparked angrily above her mask, and he remembered how she had looked in their bedroom, when she had declared she would leave him. Like a vengeful goddess.

She is a goddess, strong and beautiful. A goddess who has no need of me.

The goddess tried to press the mask to his face. Like a bolt of white-hot lightning, fury exploded inside him, powered by frustration. He shoved her aside, vaguely aware that he had pushed her so hard that she had fallen on her back. She hated him; he knew that as clearly as he knew anything. She hated him, and she could never, ever stand to live with him. Yet he would rather die than live without her.

Grasping his oxygen bottle, he lifted it high above his head and hurled it over the gondola's side.

A high-pitched scream pierced the air . . . *Must be coming from the bottle,* he thought, incoherent as that concept seemed. *Perhaps it was alive . . . and I just killed it. What is alive, up here in heaven? Nothing, that's what. Nothing can live. Except it's not heaven. It's hell. You've returned to hell.*

He collapsed to his knees. His eyelids grew impossibly heavy, and he let them fall, as he dropped deeper into the misty, chill netherworld which closed in on him. *This is right. This is what was meant to happen before . . . Peter, I'm back.* That was his final thought before he sank into the void.

CHAPTER 23

Not until Benjamin threw his oxygen bottle overboard had Hannah been willing to accept the truth. He had lost his mind.

She fought to contain her panic, but it was difficult. She was trapped with a madman in the outer reaches of the atmosphere in a flimsy cloth balloon.

No. My darling isn't crazy, she reassured herself, warily keeping her eyes on him. What might he try next? He knelt on the floor of the gondola, not looking at her, or anything. His skin was so pale, it appeared translucent. His eyes closed, and he tumbled onto the gondola floor.

"Oh, my God. Benjamin!" Hannah scrambled over to his side and pressed her hand to his face. Even through her gloves, his skin felt horribly cold. She whispered into her mask, "You're not crazy, my darling. You're sick." Pulling off her own oxygen mask, she pressed it to his face.

Without her mask, the lack of breathable air struck her like a hammer blow. Her chest ached, and she feared she would pass out. *There's nothing to breathe up here,* she realized. *No wonder Benjamin passed out. What was he thinking, depriving himself of oxygen?*

Determined not to fail Benjamin or herself, she took another pull on their one remaining oxygen mask, taking only enough to clear her head. Their balloon continued to ascend, God knew where. They would die up here if they didn't return to earth.

The altimeter gauge clicked up to forty-five thousand feet, higher than anyone had ever traveled.

"You did it, Benjamin," Hannah said. In repose, his noble face looked like a marble statue's. Once again she secured the mask to his face, murmuring silently, "I won't let you die."

Glancing around, she looked for the release valve. She had no idea where it was, or what it might look like. She glanced over the ropes and nets, some attaching the gondola to the balloon, others securing equipment. Only one rope seemed to perform neither of these functions. Reaching for it, she pulled. Nothing happened, so she tugged harder.

The rope gave. The balloon dropped as suddenly as a rock, knocking Hannah to her knees. A wave of dizziness struck her, and she struggled to keep her senses about her. Borrowing the oxygen mask from Benjamin, she took another pull of air into her lungs, then stood up again. According to the altimeter, they had descended only a couple of hundred feet. She would have to keep her wits about her, juggling the oxygen for herself and Benjamin as well as operating this valve.

Reaching up, she pulled hard on the valve once more, bracing herself this time for the descent. The balloon dropped rapidly. Moving back and forth between the oxygen and the valve, Hannah brought them to fifteen thousand feet, then ten thousand. Her arms ached from pulling the release cord, her legs from repeatedly crouching by her husband's prone form. She didn't think about her own discomfort. How could she, when Benjamin's life hung in the balance?

Once again she pulled on the release valve rope. As the balloon shrunk, it grew smaller, wrinkling along its seams. Hannah prayed she was doing this correctly. She had no idea how to land a balloon safely.

"Hannah?"

Behind her, Benjamin's voice sounded weak and thready, yet it filled her with indescribable relief. Letting go of the rope, she hurried to his side. Carefully, she adjusted his position, propping his head against a sandbag. She smoothed the wind-blown hair off his forehead and stroked the strong planes of his face, unable to resist touching him in her relief. "I was so worried. You passed out. Do you remember?"

His lips were stiff as he replied. "Vaguely. I thought I saw a goddess, out in the sky . . . She looked like you."

She smiled. "Now, don't go giving me a big head."

"Demons, too."

Hannah shuddered at the haunted look in his eyes, as if he had seen something inhuman, something mortals weren't meant to witness. Desperate to anchor him back in reality, she kissed his lips, his cheeks, his forehead. "You're safe now, Benjamin. Everything's going to be fine, once we land."

Some of the confusion left his gaze, and he focused on her. "Where are we?"

"About four thousand feet and descending."

He pushed up on his elbows, a simple action that seemed to take a great deal of effort. "You— You manned the balloon by yourself?"

She smiled. "Maybe I *womanned* it?" Her heart ached with worry. "Are you going to be okay?"

Ever the scientist, he replied matter-of-factly, "I have no idea."

She traced his brow, then his cheek. His color had begun to return, but she could tell by his posture how weak he was. "Why did you do it? Give all the oxygen to me?"

"I don't—" As he gazed at her, his eyes shone with unaccustomed brightness. It took Hannah a moment to realize she was seeing tears. His voice came out rough with emotion as he confessed, "I didn't want to lose you. Even if I already have."

His expression was so painfully honest, her own throat tightened, and her vision grew misty. "I'm such a fool." She pressed her face to his chest. Shame filled her. She hadn't thought of the consequences of her actions. She had been selfish and impulsive, and had almost killed this man she had grown to love so much. All because she wanted to prove herself to him. How could he ever forgive her?

The gondola jerked hard, nearly throwing her off of Benjamin. She struggled to her feet against a wildly tilting floor. Gripping the side of the gon-

306 *Tracy Cozzens*

dola, she looked out and discovered they had struck the side of a cathedral. The wind began to drag them against it. "We're so low now we've hit a church," she called down to Benjamin.

A gust of wind sent them away from the cathedral and over a stand of forest. A tether rope caught on a branch and jerked the gondola, before their forward momentum dragged it free. "The tether ropes—they're starting to tangle in the trees!"

"Throw out some sandbags," he commanded. Hannah jumped to obey, tossing two of them over the side. Disposing of the ballast gave the balloon enough lift to clear the forest and send it out of the danger zone.

During the next few minutes, Hannah took instruction from Benjamin to locate a good place to land the balloon and bring it down safely. He struggled to sit, but his legs refused to support him, leaving the task up to her.

A half hour later, the gondola finally bounced against flat earth, coming to rest in a sheep meadow next to a country road. Only then did Hannah allow herself to breathe.

"We've landed." She knelt beside him and helped him to his knees. He swayed, pulling her close and letting her take his weight. Hannah knew if she wasn't supporting him, he would be unable to stay upright.

"We have to get you help." Worry tightened in her chest like a vise, threatening to squeeze the breath out of her. She had never seen her strong, vital husband so incapacitated, not even when he was drunk. That, too, had been her fault. She realized now how deeply he had feared losing her, despite his claim that he didn't care.

She looked across the meadow, desperate for help, from any source. In the distance, she spotted movement. "It's a farmer. He's coming with a cart. Thank the Lord!"

Pulling back, she studied her husband's face. He was still so pale, his eyes again unfocused. "Benjamin? Can you stand?"

"Of course." But when he attempted what should be a simple thing, he collapsed in her arms in a dead faint.

Clouds drifted by, propelled by strong winds. A golden sun rose high in the sky, a perfect sphere. All of a sudden, it began to plummet to earth, taking him with it. Falling ... ever falling ... He had never felt so out of control in his life.

Benjamin jerked awake, his heart thudding sickly in his chest. His entire body ached, his joints stiff, his chest burning. Yet none of his symptoms caused as much pain as his broken heart. He would never be the same. He loved her with all his heart. And he was losing her.

He didn't know precisely when he had fallen in love with Hannah, but he certainly knew why. She had brought magic to his ordered existence, shone a bright light on his life that made each day better than the one before. She had helped him rediscover his courage, defeat his self-doubts in the face of terrible risk.

She had even saved his life. He couldn't imagine loving her more. But he would have to learn to live without her.

He squeezed his eyes closed, desperate to shut out reality.

A strong male voice refused to let him sink back into the oblivion of sleep. "Ah, you're awake! Excellent. How do you feel?"

Benjamin cracked open his eyes. A burly, bald-headed man in a doctor's frock stood by his bed, checking his pulse and looking into his eyes. The man adjusted the oxygen mask that Benjamin now realized he was wearing.

Morning light spilled into the room from the window. It was morning? This had to be the day after the flight.

He pulled down the mask. "Where am I?" His voice sounded rough and unused. He cleared his throat and tried again. "Where—"

"In hospital, Cambridge Sacred Heart, to be exact. Your wife brought you here with the help of a local shepherd."

Benjamin closed his eyes. He would have to see Hannah at least once more, to thank her before she departed for America. Unless she already had. "My . . . my *wife*—" Knowing she would soon be leaving him, he could barely speak the word that had come to mean so much to him.

"She's resting as well," the doctor said. "Quite a stalwart woman you married. You two are the talk of London. Take a look." He handed him a newspaper. The story of their balloon flight was splashed over the front page. A photograph of them standing before the balloon accompanied the article. Hannah looked so lovely, his throat constricted. His lungs protested, and a coughing spasm overtook him as he fought for breath.

The doctor pressed the mask back to his face. "Don't rush things. It will take a few days for your lungs to recover, after the way you starved them."

Benjamin scanned the article. Shoving the mask aside, he said, "It says no woman has ever flown higher. No man, for that matter. Why—"

"Because you broke the altitude record." Hannah stood at the door to his private room. She crossed to his bedside, a gentle smile on her face. Despite knowing it was borrowed happiness, Benjamin's heart leaped at the sight of her. She was still here, at least for a little while. Even though she still wore Spencer's trousers and shirt, she looked like an angel. Captivated by the vision she presented, he was barely aware of the doctor murmuring something about seeing other patients and leaving the room.

She sat on the edge of his bed and pressed his hand between hers, her eyes shining with pride. "You reached forty-five thousand feet, Benjamin, higher than anyone has ever gone. Into the stratosphere, as you call it. Those stuffy men of the Society are raving about what you've accomplished. They keep reminding everyone you're a member of *their* organization, as if they had anything to do with your success. Universities want you to lecture. And the reporters—they can't wait for you to get better, so they can get the full story of how you saved my life."

He closed his eyes and absorbed the information. Considering he had finally achieved his goal, the thrill of victory was more muted than he had ever imagined it could be.

"This story is a little silly, though," she said, extracting the paper from his other hand and setting it aside. "It makes both of us out to be heroes, when we both know you're the real hero."

"Hannah, that's not true."

Ignoring his protest, she continued, "We put your balloon in Mr. Coleridge's barn—he's the farmer who rescued us—and Spencer is on his way to retrieve it."

"The samples . . . my instruments—"

"Everything's fine. Your instruments worked perfectly. And your samples are all intact. You'll be able to analyze them and show everyone how the atmosphere changes so high up, just as you dreamed."

His dream . . . That *had* been his dream. Now, he discovered, his dream was sitting here, beside him.

"Hannah, when—" His throat closed up, thick with unshed tears. He cleared his throat, fighting to suppress them. After another pull of oxygen from the mask, he tried again. He hated to hear it, but he needed to know, to better prepare. "When are you going?"

"Going?" Hannah looked confused, so he continued.

"Back home."

She shrugged, her posture communicating how little concern she felt over the question. "You're not ready yet, so I'm staying here."

Her lack of concern made him sick at heart. If he had done things differently, if he had treated her right, would she be willing to remain his wife? It was too late to wonder now. Far too late. Still, he owed her an apology. "Hannah, I was so wrong. You're as good an assistant as any scientist could hope for."

She smiled. "Why, thank you, Benjamin."

"But you shouldn't limit yourself to assisting anyone. I was wrong not to value your mind and scientific spirit. You have everything it takes to make a success of your chosen career, all the bravery and determination required. And you care about science . . . more than even I do." He lifted the paper. "With press like this, you'll be sought after by every major university. I suppose you're returning to New York—"

Her smile faded. "You think I should?"

"I want you to be happy, Hannah."

"Happy? You think going back to New York will make me happy?" Moisture glistened in her eyes, thoroughly confounding him.

"I thought—"

"Damn you, Benjamin." The tears slid over her lower lids and trickled down her cheeks. He had hurt her again, but he couldn't fathom how.

"Damn you." She furiously wiped at her tears. "If you weren't lying in that bed, I'd slap you."

Her anger completely mystified him. "I'm not sure . . ."

She clenched her fists in her lap. "If you think I'd be happy chasing after some dream without you by my side, if you think I care so little—" She choked, and buried her face in her hands.

He set his hand on her shoulder. "Hannah?"

Her shoulders shuddered; then she lowered her hands and looked at him. The raw emotion in her gaze rocked him to his core. Her lips quivered as she confessed, "I love you, Benjamin. I thought I loved you before, but kept clinging to a childish, selfish dream. I love you more than anything. I can't imagine being happy without you—even if you never want me to help you in your work again." She sucked in a shaky breath. "And I wouldn't blame you for that, after I nearly killed you."

"Hannah, no." He reached out and pulled her down into his arms, cradling her slim form as she shook with tears. This beautiful, brave woman loved him! His spirits soared, at the same time he ached to soothe away her pain. Stroking her back, he murmured, "You saved me. I should have realized how strong you were. If I hadn't underestimated you, I wouldn't have wasted so much oxygen early in the flight. You did nothing wrong."

"You cared enough about me to risk your life to protect mine," she murmured into his chest. "I didn't deserve it, not after the way I tricked you."

She sounded like a wounded child, but her inner strength astounded him. He vowed never to underestimate her again. "I needed tricking. I was block-headed not to accept your help." He slid his fingers into her silken hair, relishing her nearness, the hope in his chest flaming bright. "I can't imagine going on without you, Hannah, not as a scientist or a man."

Lifting her head, she gazed closely at him, her tear-streaked face making his heart squeeze tight. "Are you telling me . . ."

Suddenly, nothing seemed easier than speaking his heart. He smiled gently. "Yes. I love you, too, sweetheart. More than I've ever loved anything in my life. I wouldn't blame you one bit if you decided to leave me. But if you stay, I swear I'll do my best to make you happy."

"Oh, Benjamin. You have no idea how much I've longed to hear those words." She pressed her lush mouth to his, sending a surprisingly strong shock of desire through him. Having a wife who knew her mind definitely had its benefits.

"Can I—" She tugged at the oxygen mask resting near his chin.

Benjamin yanked it over his head and tossed it aside. Despite his close call, he felt more vital than he ever had in his life. He wrapped his arms tightly around Hannah, claiming her mouth with fierce possessiveness. She moaned and pressed even closer to him.

Despite his weakened condition, he longed to touch more of her, to express his feelings body and soul. His hand drifted to her breast, and he discovered to his delight that she wore no corset under her man's shirt. Sliding his hand between the buttons, he cupped her through her thin chemise, his thumb raking her nipple.

Heat shot through Hannah straight to her feminine center. Oh, how she wanted him! How she longed to feel Benjamin inside her, as close as physically possible, now that they had confessed their love. She knew it would be even better than before, that their future together would bring happiness she had never imagined. Sliding lower in the narrow hospital bed, she pressed her body full-length against his. He groaned deep in his throat, and she felt the undeniable evidence of his arousal through his thin bedgown and sheet.

"Interesting medicine the doctor ordered."

The teasing female voice startled Hannah. She sat up, only then realizing that Benjamin had unbuttoned her shirt clear to her waist. She yanked it closed.

"Georgina. You always did have excellent timing," Benjamin said wryly. He looked much less embarrassed than Hannah felt. He tucked one arm behind his head and looked at his sister, who was crossing toward them from the door.

Georgina had never looked healthier, or happier. She wore a light blue dress, gloves, and matching bonnet and carried a folded parasol. But it wasn't her sophisticated attire that put the sparkle in her eye and the color in her cheeks. Hannah sensed that she had regained her spirit along with her health. And perhaps more ... Curious, Hannah studied the dapper older gentleman who entered behind her. He smiled at Georgina in a proprietary way that Hannah recognized quite well.

"Goodness, Hannah, I recommended you seduce my brother, but I didn't think you'd be doing it in broad daylight in a public place."

Hannah fought for a reply. Benjamin came to her rescue. "I have no complaints."

Georgina laughed, and Hannah relaxed. Georgina wasn't passing judgement on her after all, not this time. "Benjy, Hannah. If you're through spooning, I'd like to introduce you to Dr. Gilham Anderson. He accompanied me from Bath."

Benjamin pulled himself to a sitting position and extended his hand. "Good to meet you."

"I'm sorry it's under such circumstances, here in hospital," the doctor said, accepting his handshake. "Georgy insisted we visit immediately and see the heroes for ourselves."

Georgina cocked her head toward her brother. "Well, Benjy, you did it. After all this time."

Benjamin nodded. "It appears so. I'm sorry it couldn't have been ..."

She waved her gloved hand. "Oh, stop it, Benjy. I think it's time you put that particular demon to rest. Peter would want it that way."

Benjamin looked honestly shocked. Hannah took his hand in hers and squeezed it reassuringly. Georgina forgave him. If she could set aside the past, so should he.

Georgina's breezy tone faded, and she grew more serious. "I'm proud of you, brother. And I appreciate that you dedicated your flight to Peter. I read about it in the paper."

Benjamin looked at her thoughtfully. "Strangely— or perhaps not so strangely—I felt Peter with me when we were high above the earth."

For a moment, a contemplative look entered her eyes. Then she chuckled. "Goodness, Benjamin. You're getting downright mystical in your old age. What happened to the practical scientist?"

He slid his arm around Hannah's waist and met her gaze. In his eyes, Hannah saw all the love he felt for her, the deep connection they had discovered by opening their hearts to each other. Smiling at her, he murmured, "Hannah knows." He leaned close, and Hannah arched her neck for his kiss, not caring that they weren't alone.

"Hannah? Benjamin? Are you two okay?" Hannah's mother appeared at the door, along with her sister Lily.

Hannah sighed. As much as she enjoyed her family's company, she longed to be alone with her husband. *Her lover.* The thought filled her with fresh desire. She had to force herself to keep her hands off of him and in her lap. As if reading her mind, Benjamin ran his fingers up her back, and she shivered at the tantalizingly brief touch.

"We came as soon as we heard," Lily said. "Oh, Hannah, you're famous, as I always knew you would be!" She rushed to her sister and gave her a hug.

Hannah reassured them, "I'm fine. Really. So is Benjamin. Georgina, Dr. Anderson, this is my mother and my sister."

Immediately after the introductions, Hannah's mother took her to task. "You've pulled many stunts over the years, trying to drive me to an early grave. But this one takes the cake! Risking your life in a balloon, of all things." She turned her ire on Benjamin. "You should darned well start watching out for her. That's a husband's first priority, young man."

He adopted a conciliatory tone, but a smile tugged at his lips. "Yes, Mrs. Carrington. I'll be sure to watch out for her, in whatever endeavor she chooses to undertake. Believe me, nothing in this world is more important to me." Leaning close, he whispered into Hannah's ear, "And I pray she'll be watching out for me."

Her heart brimming with happiness, Hannah whispered back, "Always."

If you liked FLIGHT OF FANCY, be sure to look for Tracy Cozzens' next charming release in the *American Heiresses* series, A DANGEROUS FANCY, available wherever books are sold in August 2002.

Lily Carrington's ambitious mother had set her sights on a Season. With three younger daughters yet unwed, high hopes for a titled marriage were pinned on Lily. As honorable as she was beautiful, Lily vowed not to disappoint her family—even as she became the pawn in a sordid plot of seduction by the Prince of Wales himself . . . and found herself falling in love with a most unlikely hero.

A known rogue, Alexander Drake was fully familiar with the intricacies of the seduction game. For that reason alone, he could not stand by and witness an innocent beauty like Lily being used as the Prince's plaything. So he set about making a match for her with someone of honorable character. And yet, Alexander hadn't anticipated his growing love for Lily or that she had embarked on her own matchmaking plot—to marry the object of *her* desire . . . him!

COMING IN JUNE 2002 FROM
ZEBRA BALLAD ROMANCES

__CHEEK TO CHEEK: The Golden Door
by Willa Hix   0-8217-7357-7 $5.99US/$7.99CAN
Leaving England for the United States and escaping an unwanted engagement was all well and good, until Olivia Marlowe learned her half-brother
had offered her services as a companion to a wealthy American matron—
with an incredibly handsome son. Adam Porterfield was a gentleman—
and far above Olivia's reach.

__SURRENDER THE STARS: The Vaudrys
by Linda Lea Castle   0-8217-7267-8 $5.99US/$7.99CAN
Desmond Vaudry du Lac is commanded by King Henry III to wed Aislinn,
the Poison Flower of Seven Oaks. He doesn't realize that the mysterious
and beautiful lady he encounters nightly in the garden is his bride-to-be,
or that she has fallen in love with him. While the passion he shares with
her is pure bliss, dark, secret forces swirl around them.

__CONQUEROR: The Vikings
by Kathryn Hockett   0-8217-7258-9 $5.99US/$7.99CAN
Gwyneth stands before the altar, thinking not of her betrothed, but of
Selig, the golden-haired Viking her father enslaved when she was a child.
The pendant she wears around her neck was a gift from Selig the night
she helped him escape. Suddenly, a raid halts the ceremony as Gwyneth
is abducted and tossed into a passionate adventure.

__DELPHINE: The Acadians
by Cherie Claire   0-8217-7256-2 $5.99US/$7.99CAN
Delphine Delaronde lost her heart to Philibert Bertrand when she was
just a girl. But when she finally confessed her love to the dashing smuggler,
he treated her like a child. When fate brought them together again,
Delphine had inherited a title. Now she seems beyond Philibert's reach
forever. But the countess will never give up her one true love . . .

DO YOU HAVE THE
HOHL COLLECTION?

__Another Spring	$6.99US/$8.99CAN
0-8217-7155-8	
__Compromises	$6.99US/$8.99CAN
0-8217-7154-X	
__Ever After	$6.99US/$8.99CAN
0-8217-7203-1	
__Something Special	$5.99US/$7.50CAN
0-8217-6725-9	
__Maybe Tomorrow	$6.99US/$7.99CAN
0-8217-7349-6	
__My Own	$6.99US/$8.99CAN
0-8217-6640-6	
__Never Say Never	$5.99US/$7.99CAN
0-8217-6379-2	
__Silver Thunder	$6.99US/$8.99CAN
0-8217-7201-5	

Call toll free **1-888-345-BOOK** to order by phone or use this coupon
to order by mail. ALL BOOKS AVAILABLE DECEMBER 1, 2000.
Name_____
Address_____
City_____ State _____ Zip _____
Please send me the books that I have checked above.
I am enclosing $_____
Plus postage and handling* $_____
Sales tax (in New York and Tennessee) $_____
Total amount enclosed $_____
Add $2.50 for the first book and $.50 for each additional book. Send check
or money order (no cash or CODs) to:
Kensington Publishing Corp., 850 Third Avenue, New York, NY 10022
Prices and numbers subject to change without notice. Valid only in the U.S.
All orders subject to availability. **NO ADVANCE ORDERS.**
Visit out our website at **www.kensingtonbooks.com.**

Romantic Suspense from

Lisa Jackson